THE BIG
FEAR

THE BIG FEAR

ANDREW CASE

THOMAS & MERCER

Published by Thomas & Mercer, Seattle

www.apub.com

Amazon, the Amazon logo, and Thomas & Mercer are trademarks of Amazon.com, Inc., or its affiliates.

ISBN-13: 9781503952225
ISBN-10: 1503952223

Cover design by Mark Ecob

Printed in the United States of America

*This book is dedicated to the memory of Jeremiah Minh Grünblatt,
the finest storyteller I've ever known.*

CHAPTER ONE

DURABLE GOODS

Ralph Mulino hated the sea. He was comfortable in the stairwells of housing projects and the stubble of vacant lots, but on the water he felt exposed. Knuckling the lip of the Harbor Patrol whaler, the Verrazano Bridge to his left and a blink of the Statue of Liberty deep in the dark to his right, he took in the kid steering. Sergeant Sparks, proud to have come up through the Seven-Seven in just three years. Proud to have stomped his patrol tour in Crown Heights, as though that meant anything anymore. Every precinct was soft now; even the once-rough ones were like summer camp. Mulino leaned over the edge of the boat, ready to heave, then caught himself and lurched back. A brush with humiliation spared. He stared hard at the sergeant. The kid stood smug; he had aced the exams and got his chevrons early, but he hit each wave heavy, the weight echoing through Mulino's joints, hips, and spine.

Mulino sucked in the hot night air and braced himself through the uneasy ride. His knee hurt; arthritis already. He had quit smoking and started with the chiropractor, the grapefruit, and the yogurt. You get old quick on the job, and at fifty-three, Ralph Mulino was an elderly cop. He had loved the thrill of the legwork once, but by the time he had made detective, he felt spent. There are only so many doors you want to be the first guy to kick down. After he had slowed down, shrill boredom set in: long hours, slick food, and surveilled apartments that no one ever seemed to come in or out of.

And on top of that had been what happened in the Ebbets Field Apartments. Nearly six months had been taken up with the investigation, the hearing, the trial. And afterward, though nobody on the force would ever come out and say it, he was stained. A tiny bit of the complete trust that officers must have in each other had been shaved away. Everyone on the force knew about it. The kid driving the boat probably knew about it, and he had only been in high school back then. Mulino had been wary after that: another reason he couldn't be the first one through the door. He couldn't be sure enough of the guys behind him.

Not to mention the busted lungs from eight months carting rubble and dust from Ground Zero to the Staten Island landfill. That had taken him on the water too. Nearly every cop who had made his twenty took the pension after that—three-quarters pay based on a year pregnant with overtime. But Mulino had only had eighteen years on then, so he kept slogging it out, year after year. Kept trying to prove that he was trustworthy to colleagues who would always look sideways at him. So that a decade afterward, he was still willing to jump out of bed at two in the morning on his regular day off. Ready to get his gun and his flashlight, slide the chain with his badge around his neck, and put on a jacket and tie too. That way the uniforms know you're a detective, and not the kind that runs around in a sweatshirt all day long either. All to ride shotgun to a sergeant whose crisp summer blouse couldn't hide his disdain. *The feeling's mutual, pal.*

A ship at anchor, waiting out the night to unload, had sent out an alarm. No news of what was wrong. *Come on out to Harbor Patrol, there's a sergeant waiting for you.* Usually when the captain calls you in the middle of the night someone is dead. This had sounded like a false alarm to Mulino. But the captain had pleaded: they couldn't reach the ship, there was no detective on the midnight tour at the Harbor Patrol, they needed someone who can be ready for the unexpected. The captain knew Mulino would go. He would always go. A couple of times a spot had opened up to run his own squad, and he'd put in his papers, and a couple of times word had come down that he was too good to promote. They needed him on the ground, maybe just so they could keep an eye on him, but even so. A legwork guy through and through, with legs that were already giving out on him.

The boat bumped along through the gunship-gray waves, its motor the only noise on the water. The Harbor Patrol's usual prey—drunks falling off the Circle Line or brawlers on gambling ships—had already come ashore. Sergeant Sparks pressed on without looking up from his GPS, hitting the waves hard. Mulino looked at the kid's knees buckling as the boat hit the surf. *That's going to catch up with you.*

"You think we could pick it up a bit? The call came in thirty minutes ago now."

The sergeant looked down at his bearings. "Twenty-two knots is regulation."

Mulino stared back out at the water. He knew Sparks's type—guys who had joined the police department because they liked to follow orders, and weren't about to kick the habit just to collar a criminal or save someone's life. Sparks was the kind of cop that had been thriving at the NYPD ever since the new administration decided that zealous cops were a bigger threat to public safety than zealous criminals.

Mulino had got his own badge the old way, by arresting people who had actually committed crimes. Once there were plenty of them too; you couldn't stumble through Highbridge without observing a hand-to-hand, you couldn't spend the day in East New York without someone brandishing a gun. And the more you locked them up, the more they kept coming.

It had all changed when crime started to go down. Suddenly the department was only judging you on how many stops you made, no matter if the guy was carrying a nine or a joint or a bag of groceries. Data-driven policing. It had seemed to Mulino that the stats had been in decline even before the push to do more UF-250s had come out. But no one cares what the foot soldiers think—crime was down and stops were up so everyone just figured there was a connection.

Mulino had made his numbers, hit detective, and landed at the Organized Crime Control Bureau. He had thought he would be free of the game there, listening to wiretaps and busting capos. But it had been the same routine as the beat: as soon as one mope hands a dime bag to another, that's a crime ring. The teenagers in One Police Plaza had issued their edicts, and so the word was out to OCCB: round up as many petty dealers as you can, and don't worry about which ones are in charge. Making detective had been like winning a pie-eating contest where the prize was more pie. And even now his phone would wake him from a deep sleep while guys who had joined the force just two years earlier were collecting his salary's worth of pension and living all summer at Aqueduct.

Farther from the shore, the water grew still, and against the dim lights on the horizon, he could see the outline of the massive ship, its bolts knitting shut the huge panes of steel. It was hard for Mulino to believe that anything so heavy could stay afloat at all. The cops' small boat bobbed in the water, but the waves could not disturb the cargo ship. It was weighed down by thousands of railcar containers, each painted a different dismal shade of orange, green, or yellow, a futile effort to bring cheer to the whole sagging enterprise. In the dim light— no moon, the only glow from the city maybe a mile behind them—the ship was a silent monster, already slain, waiting to be buried.

The kid cut the motor. Mulino stood, shook off the nausea from his ride, and looked up. He stretched his arms; his back was beginning to feel better. He slipped his finger inside his collar and loosened it a bit. The tie had already proven to the sergeant everything it was going to prove. He wanted to make sure his blood would flow, that he could breathe unrestricted. Because you never know.

Mulino smiled to himself, craning his neck at the ship above. Tired as he was now, he had always enjoyed the hunt. Police work had its misery and humiliation and discomforts, but hitting the ground and starting a chase brought his vigor back. He took a few breaths and felt young again. Looking up at the ship, the whaler now gently bumping against its massive steel hide, Mulino reminded himself that he would never be happier doing anything else in the world.

The sergeant was at the bow of their little boat, lassoing the lines onto an oversized cleat on the hull. He worked slowly, according to form, just like he had been doing everything. The boat was lashed on, a tiny fish stuck to the belly of a whale. They had made contact, but there was no one on the deck above for them to hail, only a rail-thin ladder bolted to the side. Mulino looked to the sergeant and spoke.

"Am I supposed to go up that thing?"

The ladder bore evidence of a week on the open ocean. It was wet and dark; fronds of seaweed dangled haphazardly. Maybe forty feet to climb to the deck, where there was no sound, no light, no evidence of what may have set the crew on edge.

"All I got told is I'm driving an OCCB detective out. I don't know what happens now." Exactly what he was told and not a lick more. "Maybe we should wait a little. Maybe we should call in, see if anything new has come over since the radio."

But Ralph Mulino wasn't the kind of cop who called up and asked what he was supposed to do every ten minutes. Maybe his fellow officers doubted him. But the captains had always picked him. He had been sent out, and he would do what needed to be done, whether or not the sergeant driving him was willing to help. He pulled his radio and his flashlight from the hull of the skiff and fastened them to his belt beside his gun. He'd resisted upgrading to the nine millimeter, had held onto his thirty-eight—not as many shots in a minute, but better control, better aim. You only need one bullet if you can put it in the right place. They had upgraded the guns, but the radios had never changed; they were still a foot long, brick-wide, and heavy. Maybe the brass wanted to make sure that the rookies still carried eighteen pounds on their gun belt, just like they'd had to.

Or maybe having quick access to a big heavy object that isn't technically a weapon still came in handy. On the streets of Highbridge, twenty years ago, Mulino had used the radio that way, bloodying gang-bangers with what they all called Motorola Shampoo. Try that now and the kid is going to find a lawyer who knows that the city would rather pay twenty grand in hush money than bother to defend a detective at trial. The new administration would likely throw you under the bus as well, even more so if you're middle-aged, white, and nearly ready to take your suddenly hefty pension.

They had done away with the numbers game, at least. All the speeches at roll call about how the neighboring precinct had logged six hundred stops last week and we had only managed five hundred and forty-eight were gone. And at first, Mulino hadn't been the only one to notice—none of the bad guys came back. There was no epidemic of car-jackings. No purses getting snatched from Times Square tourists. It had seemed at first that the whole decade had been a waste; a half a million kids had been tossed for nothing. Crime had gone down for a thousand reasons, and frisking teenagers hadn't been one of them.

At first. But soon it had started again. Mulino had noticed when the dog shit came back to the sidewalks. Prim corners of Brownstone Brooklyn dusted overnight with specks of it, then litter, and pretty soon worse. That spring had seen shootings rise, GTAs tick up, and two separate waves of muggings. The summer welcomed a parade of little disasters, each worse than the next. A water taxi had capsized as it ferried commuters back to Hoboken, drowning twelve. A crane had collapsed, then a chemical plant in Staten Island had sprung a leak, closing a school and sickening an entire block. A thousand rats had been found running wild through a four-star Manhattan restaurant, and a sparkling wine bar in one of the newly genteel corners of Brooklyn had simply exploded. There were ordinary answers for it all—a gas leak here, a faulty seal on the sewers there. But as the heat intensified and each day brought forth another small horror story, people had grown skittish. The latest news was that the sanitation workers weren't happy with their contract and were thinking of walking out. The last time that happened, trash piled like a snowdrift on the sidewalks. It was as though the 1970s were coming back from vacation. Another reason that a simple distress call from a stalled container ship merited more attention than usual. These days, anything could happen.

Mulino, always a cop, hauled himself onto the ladder and set out, the Harbor sergeant bobbing below him. It had been hot enough that even the iron was warm to the touch. The rungs dug ridges in his palms as he struggled upward. His back didn't hurt now, his knees felt fine, and he stared up at the edge of the ship as he huffed his way up, avoiding the slime of the seaweed, keeping his footing careful. The suit jacket cramped his shoulders as he climbed. He thought maybe he should have slipped into a sweatshirt after all; there was no need to impress anyone here. It was probably just a one-off after all. Maybe a seagull had landed on the wrong part of the deck and some panicky Canadian mate had put in a call to 911. But he still had to act as though it was serious. Like he always did. Just in case.

He heaved himself onto the deck. Everything on the ship was bigger than he would have imagined. The containers, each over twice his height, stacked four high and so deep he couldn't count. Hundreds of them, each bigger than a two-bedroom apartment. The deck was pristine. Not like the hull, with its slime and its rust and the decay that blossomed on the open sea. No sign of any person. No noise. No anxious crewmember standing on deck wringing his hands. The call had come in maybe an hour before; probably the poor sap was hiding out below, quivering in his bunk.

Mulino took out his radio and called in a 10-84—arrival on the scene, nothing to report. He leaned over the edge of the deck and waved down to the chipper sergeant. All clear for now. He hefted his regulation flashlight—almost two feet long, four solid pounds of steel—and turned it on. The waxed deck shone; the primly stacked containers left a path through which he could approach the bow. His feet fell softly as he sailed forward. He pulled his badge out from inside his shirt, the blue sunburst catching a tiny glint of starlight. The badge itself was one of the great perks of making the grade. Sergeants could crow all they wanted about their golden shields, but a detective's badge had the same hard royal blue as a captain or above—the same, for that matter, as a district attorney or a city commissioner. He could hear the waves below, but even the motor of the little boat had been cut, and the ship was at anchor, quiet. Just in case, he thought he would call out.

"Anyone there? This is the NYPD. We got a call. Is anyone on deck?"

Silence. He started down the corridor between the containers. It was maybe only three feet wide—the shippers encouraged efficiency and there wasn't much reason to make your way up and down the deck at sea. His thick shoes made no noise, but he wanted to be heard.

"NYPD. Anybody hear me?"

Down the aisle, about a hundred yards, his flashlight picked up something splayed across the deck. A couple bags of garbage maybe. Or a pile of clothes. It was too big to be a seagull. Mulino swept his flashlight. No movement. It didn't take him long to figure out that he was looking at a person. He picked up speed, checking the aisles as he did, always cautious, always keeping his head about him. He strode quick and careful, now glad for his silent shoes. He reached the figure on the deck and lit up the body with his flashlight.

He could tell the man was dead because of the way he lay perfectly still, even with the light shining at him. He could tell the man was dead because his chest was sunken and silent. But most of all, Mulino could tell the man was dead because of the hole where a third of his face should have been. A gunshot from close range had spread everything above and to the left of the nose like pepper spray across the otherwise spotless deck.

Mulino swiveled his flashlight up and down the aisle. No light. No sound. He knelt by the body. It was warm, but no warmer than the heat of the heavy summer night. The man wore a uniform, the unfamiliar name of the shipping company neatly stenciled on the left breast, boots polished and laced. Mulino looked up. Calling medical could wait. The alarm had come in about an hour before. If this man had tripped it and gone out on deck, he'd been killed since then. Mulino hadn't seen another boat on the way out. There was a good chance that whoever had shot him was still on board.

Mulino heard something across the deck. A high-pitched squeak. Shoes coming to a quick stop. He stood up and trained his flashlight down the narrower crosstown aisles. The light was harsh and bright and showed him nothing. Stillness. Container after container, in those decrepit fading pastels, held firm as the beam shone on them. No sign of motion.

"I see you down there." If you lie to them, trick them into thinking you know more than you do, then they might be afraid. And if they are afraid, you have the upper hand. "Come on out and come out quietly. I'm going to count to three."

He honed his flashlight toward the noise. Nothing. His heart slowly came to life—a new pulse, a new energy.

"One." He swung the flashlight back and forth. Maybe he had the wrong corner.

"Two." Someone out there, he realized, could hear him, and knew he was a cop, and wasn't showing himself. Someone who had maybe just killed a man. It was best to take some cover.

"Three." Nothing again. He ducked out from behind his corner; the aisle was clear. Then footsteps. They came from far up the ship and to the right. He took his gun out. He shut the flashlight off: until he knew where to shine it, it would only make him a target. Mulino crouched and scampered, damn the bad back now; he was filled with the scent and the thrill and the pulse of it all. Someone was running away, speeding through the thin aisle, and whoever it was knew Mulino was gaining ground. Just as he reached the edge of the narrow aisle, toward the starboard side of the boat, Mulino turned.

Dark. Quiet. Nothing. The faint glow of the faraway city kept the moonless night from pitch darkness. Mulino peered over the edge of the ship; steady waves slapped the hull. He looked along the deck. He couldn't see anything with his flashlight off. He wheezed deep to get his wind back. He couldn't run like he used to. His breath sounded so loud to himself. Loud enough that whoever was out there could probably hear it. Maybe could see him. He ducked by the railing of the ship to take some small measure of cover.

"Freeze. Police. Stay right there." Mulino wouldn't admit that he was afraid. He had been afraid, really afraid, only once before on the job, in the Ebbets Field Apartments, and that had almost ruined him. He squinted and caught his breath. He thought he saw something beyond the row of containers. He was out in the open now, the freight to one side and the railing to the other. Using his radio to call for help would mean putting down either his gun or his flashlight. He paced slowly along the aisle, clinging to the edge of the containers, gun drawn.

He raised the flashlight with his left hand and snapped it on. The row of containers lit up again, dull reds and cool blues, and behind one about thirty feet out, Mulino saw a small shudder, maybe a shoulder quickly vanishing behind the edge.

"Hold it. I have a gun on you. Come out slowly." Mulino held the gun cautiously. He pointed it steady where he had last seen the shoulder. But he had to be careful. Maybe the man hadn't heard. Maybe he didn't speak English. You have to think about these things, as a cop. You have to think of every possible innocent explanation before you take action. You have to imagine yourself in the trial room, being crossed by some kid who lives in the comfort of a perpetual game of Minesweeper. *Did you consider that the man on the boat might not have heard you identify yourself as a police officer? That he might be deaf? That he might have been out fishing for stingrays?* Mulino had been in the trial room before. You never come out of it the same.

But as careful as you have to be, you can't hesitate either. The plaques on the walls of every precinct in the city list the names of cops who stopped to consider. One or two seconds the other way and there would be a procession of uniformed cops at a cemetery in Queens instead of a trial. Better to be judged by twelve than carried by six.

As Detective Mulino spent those two seconds considering, the figure at the end of the aisle spun out again. He ducked low and crossed out of sight. Maybe Mulino should have shot him then. But he didn't see a gun. He didn't know this man had killed the sailor. Mulino noticed for the first time that his shirt was soaked through with sweat. He stepped forward and his once-silent shoes started to squish, like he was walking through puddles. He spread the light from left to right. Nothing moved at all.

Mulino was exposed and the other man had cover. If the man had a gun, he'd have a bead on Mulino, and Mulino wouldn't have a bead on him. The detective set down his flashlight, the beam askance across the row of containers, and gripped his gun with both hands. His heartbeat was beginning to pick up. His breathing too. He wasn't as calm as he liked. He shuffled the gun to one hand and reached for his radio.

"10-13. There's a body on the boat. And another unidentified male."

Which is about when the man ran, tight to the edge of the containers. Looking over the aisle toward the railing. Planning to jump the boat, maybe. The man was moving too fast for Mulino to see and had something in his left hand, something flashy and hard and dark. Mulino didn't hesitate this time. He whipped out his gun and gritted his teeth shut to overcome the fear. Through his clenched jaw, he called out "freeze," and the man pulled up his left hand with a glint that looked like a gun, and Mulino—for the first time in his twenty-four years as a police officer—fired his weapon at another human being. The guy crumpled backward to the deck, and the whole thing had taken only two seconds or so, and now the pumping of blood was noisy through Mulino's head and ears, and his knees suddenly, totally, started hurting again.

He stood up. He stretched. He breathed as deeply and as slowly as he could. He walked toward the man, patiently, precisely. Blood on the chest, the wispy breathing of someone about to die. He held the radio and called the sergeant. Called dispatch. Could they get a doctor out to the boat? Two men have been shot. One of them might live. He stared down at the twitching hand, next to it a gun. A nine. A real one. Mulino breathed relief. At least that. His flashlight on the man, Mulino saw too that he was black, and couldn't help but think of the shitstorm if that hadn't been a gun. The trial room would have been a party compared to it. His stomach started to give out on him; he had seen plenty of bodies but had never watched a man die in front of him before. He caught himself. He took a breath.

Mulino stepped forward and knelt by the dying man, smearing some blood on his knees. The man's eyes were nearly closed, rolled back. He was already gone. Mulino had always been a good shot; he had hit the heart and the man had died quickly. Mulino noticed a chain tucked under the man's shirt. He reached forward and slid his fingers beneath it, feeling something heavy at the end of it. He lifted it out. At the tail of the chain, a blue sunburst badge. Just like an ADA or a city commissioner. A detective's badge. Just like his own.

There was going to be a shitstorm after all.

CHAPTER TWO

THE GENERAL PUBLIC

The man smelled. Leonard Mitchell couldn't tell if it was the guy's body, hair, or clothes. Any one of them would have done the trick: the hands and neck were slicked with a dark alloy of sweat and dirt; the tangle above his head had coalesced into a single thick knot. But if Leonard had to guess, he would go with the clothes. Never mind that the air conditioning was busted at the Department to Investigate Misconduct and Corruption, or that it had been over ninety degrees for four out of five days running, the man wore three sweat-stained shirts, each one piled on top of the next. Probably the guy felt that if he left one behind it might get stolen. It was a heavy August morning in the shambling corners of a municipal office, and smelling this man—he signed in as Mr. Starr, but Lord knows what his real name was—was part of the job.

Leonard braced himself for the coming crowd. Not just Mr. Starr but the rest of them. The shoulders and collar of his discount suit rubbed him wrong; the shirt and tie were too tight for the heat. Whenever he put on this show, opening DIMAC to the general public, as required by the city charter, he felt like a petty bureaucrat. Alone in his offices drafting charges against a wayward cop or a bent building inspector gave him purpose and power. But the general public had a way of making him feel small.

The org chart might not say that Leonard Mitchell was precisely in charge of this little fiefdom, but he herded the general public when it trickled or poured in for the regular meeting. On the second Monday of every month, Leonard would smile and welcome the throng. They would wait on the dull plastic chairs under the harsh light in the lobby until he let them in, and then filter slowly into the even more miserable conference room. Dirty windows, smudged walls, and industrial blue plastic chairs that were said to be unbreakable but were certainly uncomfortable. The whole place looked like a cross between a neglected public school and an East German housing project.

At every meeting there would be a few earnest good government advocates, a few from the NYPD itself, and a few of the truly abused who came to file complaints, either because they didn't know or didn't care that they could call any time and make an appointment with an investigator. And there would be a few like Mr. Starr. Just about every city bureau held regular open meetings: all of these meetings were available to the general public, and all of them served breakfast. Leonard knew that every month Mr. Starr would come in and give another tirade about the police kicking him off his corner, the shelter administrator who told him his Old Spice smelled like he'd been drinking, or the woman at the disability office who was wearing a very nice pair of glasses and was therefore probably a thief. Mr. Starr raised no stink when he was given polite letters dismissing his complaints out of hand. He was only there to score a bagel off the people of New York.

Ordinarily Mr. Starr would be the first one in, but today there was a problem. Today it was mobbed. Cramming the lobby, keeping him from the meeting room, were about fifteen men, all wearing blazers and slacks that were very nearly the same shade of brown. Despite the heat, a few even sported loosely knotted neckties. Leonard would have known they were reporters by looks alone. The only other people who dressed like that were detectives, and detectives didn't step foot in DIMAC unless they were subpoenaed.

Leonard had been ready for them. After the call last night, how could he not be? Every major incident follows the same path: first the press, then the outraged public, then the meticulous investigation, slowed as if to ensure that no one would remember the original event by the time a report was finally issued. Leonard had been up since three, ever since the call from Tony Licata.

Tony had made his name twenty years ago by sneaking into crime scenes and pressuring detectives to offer details on unfinished cases. He had the stark accent of the true outer boroughs, the ones that had been getting squeezed ever closer to the perimeter for the last thirty years. He had spent those thirty years building trust from the PD, the DAs, and more than a few criminals. He almost always knew more than you did. If he called you after midnight, you had to take it.

"Youse guys got anything on the shooting?"

Leonard had been thick with sleep.

"Tony, I don't know what you're talking about."

"On the water. Confrontation situation. The shooter is from OCCB."

A confrontation situation. Two guys out in the dark with guns and neither one believes the other is a cop.

"I haven't gotten anything yet."

"Well, you will."

"And you want me to give it to you. Even though I'd be breaking about fifteen different laws."

"Don't be like that, Len. We're still friends."

"I'll get back to you."

Tony Licata was in the crowd now, along with a dozen others. Leonard knew most of them. Leonard had tried to prove DIMAC's value by getting ink on busts they'd made. His stories would get slipped in, four or five pages into the tabloids, maybe a spare graph in the back of the Metro section of the *Times*. The reporters would play grateful and promise they owed him one; he never knew when he might ask for something in return. Most of them usually ignored DIMAC. But they would show up when the agency caught a case with obvious press appeal. And other than savage murders of pretty white girls, nothing had more obvious press appeal than a cop shooting somebody or a somebody shooting a cop—and this one had both. So today Leonard was important; reporters who ordinarily ignored his hectoring all wanted to hear from him.

Or at least from his boss. Truth of the matter is that no matter how big he was supposed to feel by manning the door, he was really nothing more than the gatekeeper. Christine Davenport, the last city commissioner to hold over from the previous administration, would come out and give the official public statement. She'd done it before. It would sound impassioned, she would promise her full dedication, and she would call for unity. But afterward when you read all the words, you would realize that she pretty much hadn't said anything at all. Leonard checked his watch; six minutes until he opened the door, eight until she spoke. She was precise to the second, always.

Leonard hadn't been able to get back to sleep after the call from Licata. He was still foggy when he read the coverage before work. It had pushed the news of the pending sanitation strike deep into the papers. Subway strikes in winter; sanitation strikes in summer. You can't say they don't know where their leverage is. But that day, it was all about the shooting. According to the *Post*, the shooter, Detective Ralph Mulino, was a hero, gunning down a deranged cop who had busted onto the ship and probably killed a sailor. In the *Daily News*, Licata had written that Mulino was in plainclothes and might never have said he was a cop. He might have looked like he was up to no good himself, running around the ship with his gun out.

The kid who'd been shot—a detective named Brian Rowson, loved by his comrades—might have been responding to the same call, looking for the person who shot the crewmember. Detective Mulino might, after all, have murdered them both. As he surveyed the crowd of restless hacks, Mr. Starr lurching back and forth at the rear of the crowd, Leonard figured that each story had just enough truth in it to be dangerous.

And it wasn't only the papers that were here today. The activists had taken their places as well. The ACLU guy who showed up to every meeting and hinted that the commissioner may have filed false statistics was flanked by a pair of deputies, most likely college interns. The police unions had sent a rep, a glum little man in a gray suit who stood puzzled, unsure maybe if he was supporting the cop who got shot or the cop who shot him. And there was Roshni Saal from the August 15 Coalition.

The Coalition was an organization devoted to documenting every death at the hands of law enforcement in the world. Named for the date twenty years earlier when a man had choked on his own vomit in a holding cell after the arresting officers hadn't realized he was overdosing, the Coalition collected and published a phony "indictment" every time anyone died at the hands of the police. The circumstances didn't matter to the Coalition: a drug dealer gunned down while firing at the ESU team was the same as a twelve-year-old boy shot in the face while carrying an obvious squirt gun. They ran public service announcements pairing footage of Nazi guards beating concentration-camp victims with shots of the NYPD in Brownsville dragging teenagers into their cars. The head of the Coalition was Roshni Saal, a marathon runner in silk suits who showed up at DIMAC to present the Coalition's findings every month. She handed Leonard the paper; they had their routine down.

"Roshni, don't you guys see this as one more killer off the streets?"

She stared hard. She was sharp and straightforward and always serious. "It doesn't matter who the victim is, Mr. Mitchell. Murder is always murder."

"All right then."

Leonard saw a commotion at the rear of the crowd. Mr. Starr had grown impatient. He had decided to put his body odor to good use. He leaned toward the nearest reporter, who stepped away instinctively.

Suddenly the men in mismatched suits fell like dominoes, turning their backs to the smell and leaving a clear path to the doorway. Mr. Starr looked longingly past Leonard at the stack of bagels and Danishes inside the door. Leonard looked at Mr. Starr the way you do at the uncle who always gets drunk on Thanksgiving.

"Meeting starts in five, Mr. Starr."

"Leonard, I got twenty reporters out there. The cops kicked me off my corner last night. Let me in and out and I won't be any bother to you."

As second-in-command at a minor city agency, Leonard Mitchell wore a thousand hats: he was the policy wonk, secretary, or speechwriter, depending on the day. The Department to Investigate Misconduct and Corruption took the grievances of the general public and ground them into neatly presented statistics, every now and again actually catching the bad guys and kicking them out of city service. Sometimes even shipping them to jail. Leonard had mowed through feet of investigative case files and he had spoken at fiery community board meetings after teenagers were shot by skittish cops. His job was always to disappoint— every cop and firefighter and teacher being probed thinks he's wrongly accused, and every member of the general public thinks the cops and firefighters and teachers can get away with anything. Today it was his job to disappoint a homeless man who only wanted something to eat. But he didn't always have to do his job.

"Just grab something and get out of here." Leonard was the only one at DIMAC who could stand face-to-face with Mr. Starr without retching. He'd smelled worse. He eyed Mr. Starr as he slunk over to the table and pocketed a muffin, picked out something for lunch too, and scampered out the door. Leonard sighed to himself. It would probably be the most useful thing he did all day.

Having dispatched with Mr. Starr, Leonard checked his watch again. It was time. "Okay guys, have at it. Commissioner speaks in two." He opened the door to the stampede of curiosity, and the reporters swarmed the breakfast spread just as eagerly as had Mr. Starr.

CHAPTER THREE

OUT WITH THE NEW

Christine Davenport, rail-thin, not quite as tall as she seemed at first, but proud that she could look large when she needed to, was in her usual post. She angled back in the Aeron chair, feet up on her desk, Diet Coke in one hand and a pad of paper in the other. It was a big day. She'd busted out the designer goods—the notched suit from Barney's and the brogues from an obscure designer known only to the cognoscenti. It didn't matter that none of the people who would watch her perform today would know how stylish she was. It was enough that she would know herself. An angular collar peeked out above the suit, the final flair of class. To Christine Davenport, it was not enough to display power. She had to display taste as well. But taste costs money. And city government wasn't known for splurging.

She stopped to look out the broad semi-circular window and onto the West Side Highway. The window itself was covered in soot. The ledge was speckled with pigeon shit. Under the last mayor, city buildings had had exterior cleanings twice a year, and even that hadn't been enough. In her two years at DIMAC, no one had been by to clean the ledge once. Specks of garbage pitted themselves in the snow all winter and melted into a permanent slick come spring. The low-grade gray carpet that had been laid in the hallways sometime in the 1970s had sprung a series of runs that had never been fixed. Davenport suspected that some of her own employees hoped they'd trip on it so they could sue the city. She'd had Leonard go out and patch up two of the most severe tears with electrical tape. It looked even worse after that.

She hit the hallway with a fierce stare, ready to own the room. She could always own a room. As a prosecutor, before she caught the eye of the last mayor, she had led the Public Integrity Bureau at the Manhattan DA's office. There she had successfully jailed fifteen officers who had set up a crime ring within a precinct, taking payouts from drug dealers to plant evidence on their rivals and arrest them. One sergeant had cemented fifty thousand dollars inside his Suffolk County swimming pool. After she had imprisoned those once-powerful men who hid behind their shiny brass badges and their silly octagonal hats, she had never walked softly again. Not bad, she had thought to herself at the time, for a girl whose parents had run a tire store in Piscataway.

She slipped behind the podium and looked over the crowd. The reporters had already ravished the spread of bagels and muffins. As soon as they saw her, crumbs fell from lapels as they stopped chattering and sat to attention. Against the rear wall, Leonard Mitchell, her trusted deputy, met her eyes and nodded. But he stayed hunched and leaning against the wall. She looked him over and saw a man who looked as though he had been tough once, but had since been pressed and steamed into a compliant little bureaucrat. Someone who couldn't stand up straight even for a momentous occasion.

She flashed a powerful smile as the press snapped into place. She owned them. Even then, she thought for a moment, maybe she wouldn't go through with it. Maybe she would take one last ride, sink one last career, cut one more notch on her belt. She already felt the rush. But there was another, stronger rush pulling the other way. You can only be a hero for so long in this city. And if the shooting presented an opportunity to score one more victory, there was risk in it too. You play a death case wrong and you're not only fired, but your name is in all four papers. Good luck getting a cushy private sector gig after that. Better to quit on your own terms than to get clobbered again. Twelve years at DIMAC and she had been clobbered plenty. So just as they thought she was stepping up to take charge, she was actually saying goodbye.

It was going to be the end of the X-rays of fractured orbital bones, the medical records explaining how many times a man had to be hit in the back with a nightstick before his spleen ruptured, the autopsies. Stories of armor-piercing bullets and bribes from the Department of Buildings would all ease away into quiet paper investigations that would be plain and simple and would involve nothing more complicated than money. She took the podium proud and lulled in her willing audience.

"Ladies and gentlemen, I know you are eager to hear about the confrontation situation last night. I read your coverage this morning and can confirm that we have opened an investigation, but frankly I have nothing to add at this point."

This last bit was a tease. Tantalizing them, as though in the next moment or two she would have something to add. As though any of them didn't know that DIMAC, like every other authority, was required to wait forty-eight hours before interviewing an officer involved in a shooting. As though there wasn't a special provision in state law prohibiting the release of any information whatsoever about an investigation of a police officer. Of course the reporters would know this. They would know too that the press conference was a precise and meaningless burlesque. But they would also know that the real story would flow out over a phone call or a beer at a quiet nearby bar. And if you didn't show your face at the public presser, you wouldn't get invited to hear the real story later.

She could tell herself she was getting out because she didn't like the sight of blood or because she was afraid she'd be fired. But she knew it was really about the money. Her husband had tenure but was never going to get a real raise. The apartment had seemed spacious ten years ago, with a little nook that didn't quite count as a second bedroom where Adam had put the desk and worked on his tenure file. Soon the nook was a nursery and the office was in the middle of what used to be the living room. And now Henry was five and didn't really fit in a nursery any more.

They could have moved to New Jersey, they could have struggled through, or she could have taken a private sector job that would pay the astronomical salary you need to raise a family in New York. The last option didn't feel like selling out when you're walking away from twelve years of city service. Christine Davenport had served the general public plenty. Once the money came in, they could get a bigger apartment, a house in Brooklyn maybe. Adam would have a longer drive, but that would only mean more time to ponder the deeper meaning of *The Mill on the Floss* before giving a lecture to students who couldn't be bothered to leave New Jersey even for college.

Davenport went on. "I am not going to be able to speak about last night's shooting now. In fact, I am not going to be at liberty to speak about it ever. Because as of now, I am stepping down as the commissioner of this agency. I have spent the last two decades pursuing justice. For the Manhattan District Attorney, for the State of New York, and here at DIMAC. I have done everything I can to put the people first. And now it is time for me to move on to a new set of challenges. I leave you in the capable hands of Leonard Mitchell, whom I believe you all know. Leonard will serve as acting commissioner until further notice. And let me add that I think he would make a capable and qualified replacement for me when that decision is made."

Davenport smiled politic at Leonard as he finally stood up off the wall. This had at least gotten his attention. She hadn't told him beforehand; it only would have gone to his head. Or he would have called the press and leaked it himself, always trying to sound important. Now she could see him preening, finally ready to be the center of something. Davenport almost lost her place in her speech watching him. *Be careful what you wish for, kid.* That afternoon, she knew he would have a quick, horrid introduction to his new job.

After each monthly meeting, there was always a parade of discontents desperate to bring their complaints in person. People too invested to just call the agency on an ordinary day and have their case assigned to a line investigator. Sitting through the intake after the meeting could take all day, and often deep into the night. It was the glum duty of the commissioner, that one day a month, to sit and take it. If the commissioner is going to quit, it's best to do it on the morning of the monthly meeting. Spare yourself one wretched afternoon with the general public. Davenport felt a little sorry for Leonard. His dinner plans were shot, and the workday wasn't half an hour old. But not sorry enough to change her mind. If he wanted to be the boss, he would have to stomach it.

Leonard looked up as the crowd wheeled around to stare at him. A dozen sets of passive eyes. Tony Licata gave him a small mean wink. Davenport could see the pity behind the looks. Most probably figured that the promotion wouldn't last. She had been untouchable herself. She had come in with too many accomplishments for the new administration to simply abandon her. But with her out of the picture, her staff was fair game. Even the plug she'd given for Leonard at the end of the speech was likely to backfire. In a week or two he'd be out of a job. Maybe he'd show up at her firm, asking if he could be a paralegal or something. Maybe she'd even let him.

As the crowd turned back to her, she was already thinking of the next morning, when she would begin to read all of the dirty secrets of EHA Investments, a little player in a big market. For weeks the documents had been culled and processed, and they already were waiting for her on the desk of a Midtown tower. She wasn't leaving the corruption business. But finding corruption in the private sector was valuable;

people would pay you plenty for it. She didn't care whether she was looking for bad guys who hit kids over the head with sticks or whether she was looking for bad guys who had pried out information about the takeover of a Brazilian valve manufacturer. She had always been born to prosecute, and she had timed her move perfectly.

The reporters lapped up the coda of Davenport's farewell address. "I want to tell you all how grateful I am for your time, and for the patience of the people of New York. I have had a great time serving you. I won't be taking any questions."

As she left the podium, she felt like she was actually floating. Her hard shoulders were rolled back and her chin was high. She had spent twenty years grinding it out for the general public, and she was walking out on them while she still could, dodging a run in the miserable carpet on her way out the door and back toward her office.

———————

Leonard found himself leaning back against the wall as she finished, and pressed himself up again as the reporters turned toward him. Despite the crowd, once Davenport left the podium, the room felt empty and a little cold. Someone had to go talk to them about the business of the day. Whatever questions wouldn't get answered about his boss's sudden career change, there were still a thousand questions about the agency. The case closure rate had ticked down last month. The number of days to complete a full investigation was on the rise. And oh, yeah—there was a shooting last night.

Leonard could feel the thin suit pinch his shoulders again. The thing about working for the city is that you have to dress up just enough: You have to wear a suit so that when you walk into a bodega or a precinct or a taxi dispatch station the people inside recognize that you're important and feel they have to talk to you. But it has to be kind of a cheap suit, not just because you can't afford any better but because if you start walking around Highbridge in Paul Stuart people might suspect that their taxes are being wasted on you. Or worse, that you're on the take. But now, facing the wide crowd of reporters and activists, Leonard felt weak and underdressed. He realized why Davenport always broke out serious suits for these presentations. The air conditioning wasn't strong enough to keep him from starting to sweat.

He walked to the podium, swallowed, and prepared to be savaged by the crowd.

CHAPTER FOUR
THE BIG FEAR

Eventually Leonard had it figured out—the best line out of the subway was from the second door back in the third car. New York's antique infrastructure squeezed the rush hour throng through subway stairwells. If the bottleneck caught you, it could take twenty minutes to get out.

The Wall Street station on the Four train served two clienteles. The downtown platform spewed forth finance guys from the Upper Eighties who would prance past the shoeshine booths and up to the street of their dreams. Across Broadway, civil servants trekked from Brooklyn to the municipal offices down Rector Street. The crowds wheedled past each other, each crossing Broadway just after a pair of subway cars stopped simultaneously. They pretended that each other didn't exist.

Slower, sleepier, and in cheaper suits, the city guys mainly shined their own shoes. There was no urgency up the stairway on the uptown track, so if Leonard wanted to get out quickly he had to place himself at exactly the right set of doors. Which he did every single day.

He had been pondering the Mulino shooting the whole ride in. It had blown up the tabloids two days running. Each paper had an exclusive story with someone who claimed to be on the ship, the stories were completely at odds with each other, and Leonard knew they were each probably leaked by a cop on the force with some petty grievance to air. Still, there hadn't been any protests. No one was quite sure who they would protest for, exactly, with a cop as a victim and a cop as the shooter. There was going to be a full-dress funeral in four days, and the commissioner and the mayor had both issued simpering meaningless statements. For two days, Leonard's phone had been shut off; it was the only way to maintain even twenty minutes of silence.

And he needed silence to do his job. City law provides that a cop in a shooting can't be interviewed for forty-eight hours. A union rule, enough time so the officer can meet with his rep and put together a decent story. But the forty-eight hour rule gave Leonard time to prepare too.

He had spent the afternoon of the public meeting taking the complaints of the general public. He wouldn't have to investigate these cases, but the people who walked in on the day of a public meeting expected to talk to someone in charge, so Monday afternoon had been a parade of misfortune. The first was a seventeen-year-old who said a cop had whaled on his head with a nightstick four times before running scared when he saw how strong the kid was. A background check showed him to be a low-level drug dealer with a lawyer who made a living grinding out lawsuits that the city would routinely settle. The second person in brought X-rays of her husband, who actually had been hit in the head with a nightstick, just once. He had a broken orbital bone, a hairline skull fracture, and was expected to come out of the coma sometime in the next few weeks. It had gone on like that until well past eight, leaving Leonard only one day to prepare to interview Mulino.

Out of the subway, across Broadway, he trucked along Rector Street, the wrought iron fence of Trinity Church and its famous tombstones looming above him. There was a man curled in a ball by the low wall abutting the graveyard. Every day another desperate wraith on the sidewalk. Every day another reminder of the city's slow slide downward. Leonard stepped over him and looked up at the Bank of Bremen building. The last piece of the Trade Center puzzle, the sleek black tower had just been completed. The whole thing was over with, the obelisk seemed to be saying. After the horror on the day it happened, after the construction site that never seemed to end, after the armed men needlessly patrolling the subways and train stations, and after everything else, finally the whole place was just back to being a bunch of office buildings. Move along; nothing to see here.

Leonard had spent all Tuesday locked in his office reading the case file that had come through on the shooting. Even five years ago you had to wait weeks to get a single scrap of paper from the police department. But everything was digital now. Now, the day after a shooting, it was all waiting to be opened on Leonard's desktop. He could scroll through Mulino's personnel file, photos from the deck of the ship, preliminary ballistics. Maybe not a full report—not an autopsy, he noted—but Leonard was pretty sure he knew what had killed the other detective.

The dead man's name had been Brian Rowson. A twenty-six-year-old kid who had grown up in Cambria Heights, in the farthest reaches of Queens. Seventy years ago it had been a tight middle-class community, but then they built the airport and it found itself right under the flight path. Searing noise and slow decay followed. Most whites had predictably skipped out soon after, but the place had never crashed and burned like the worst of the boroughs. It was no Ocean Hill or Brownsville. Instead, it stayed mainly black and middling prosperous. A neighborhood of clapboard houses and churches and a very long commute if you wanted to come to the city. Rowson got his degree at York College in three years. He had joined the force and made detective by the time he was twenty-five. Not a superstar exactly, but well above average. One investigation by Internal Affairs; no disciplinary action taken. No indication of what he would have been doing out on a container ship in Buttermilk Channel on his regular day off. Too bad Leonard wouldn't get the chance to ask him.

Scrolling through Rowson's file, Leonard had thought about his own move, his relocation to the fringe. He was a funny sort of gentrifier; he'd lost a lease and realized he had nowhere to move but deeper into Brooklyn. It wasn't a housing project, he kept telling his friends, but the Ebbets Field Apartments sure looked like one.

The locals in Ebbets had been just as surprised as he was that he had joined them there. On the site of the old baseball stadium, it had been built to house the throngs moving to Brooklyn in 1960—twenty-six stories of thick yellow brick and tiny cement balconies. You had to walk up a flight of stairs from Bedford Avenue to get to the squat concrete plaza, a great wide space out of view of the street that had been Brooklyn's biggest open-air drug market for twenty years. Inside, the stairs were narrow, the elevators were broken, and there was a strange sweet smell in the hallways most mornings.

Most of the residents were middle-aged women or older—their husbands and sons locked up for long-ago minor transgressions—and the place was no longer dangerous. But it was still heavy, quiet, and old. It was nowhere you could bring a date. He could move to Nassau or Hoboken and live much better for the same price. He had been thinking it over between his bouts with the crime scene photos. If he didn't get fired in the next few weeks, he might leave the city altogether.

Leonard clicked back to the photos. Brian Rowson was just another corpse in a sweatshirt now, the blood from his chest indistinguishable, melting into the harsh shadow cast by an amateur flash. He was lying on his back, his left arm twisted behind him and his right arm stretched above his head. The blast had flung him backward onto the deck. There was nothing in the hand. Leonard scoured the cop's waistband. No sign of a holster either. It could have been behind his crumpled sweatshirt, but if it was you couldn't see it. Rowson had a beard too, which used to be against the regulations of the NYPD. Couldn't have put him on the best of terms with the real old-school guys, Leonard thought as he clicked to the next photo—black kid with a beard and a hoodie making detective. A sign of the times, and one that wasn't welcome to the Flynns and O'Briens of the department. Maybe Ralph Mulino thought that way too.

The next picture was from just to the dead cop's left, taken almost from ground level, showing his frozen eyes and the murky puddle erupting from his chest and engulfing his shoulders and face. The blood spattered in his beard could have come from the blast or it could have bubbled out after he was shot. Leonard had seen a good number of crime scene photos and autopsies: the tools of the paper investigator. He wasn't a doctor, but it didn't take one to see that Rowson had taken a single shot and been stopped in his tracks. From this angle, Leonard could see how close he was to the edge of the boat. His hand may even have hit the railing as he went back. They had removed his shield before taking the picture. Too inflammatory.

Finished with the photos, Leonard clicked open what had come through on the shooter. Less than he would have liked, if he was going to interview the guy the next day. Mulino had fired one shot from his thirty-eight. There were fewer than a dozen cops on the force who still used the revolver. Most of the ones who had fought off the upgrade to an automatic weapon changed their minds the first time they actually tried one out at the range, and the rest had almost all retired. Mulino had hung on to his old habit alone.

He had been stationed in OCCB for the past ten years. A catch-all assignment. One day he could be put on the security detail of a diplomat who wasn't in danger but wanted to feel important, and the next he could be catching a murder case. A funny unit, the Organized Crime Control Bureau, Leonard thought. It sure never seemed to have anything much to do with organized crime.

For someone who had been on the force so long, Ralph Mulino had a pretty clean history with DIMAC. Most guys who tough it out either get promoted to the upper echelons of One Police Plaza or start getting bitter and taking it out on the citizenry. There were a lot of cops waiting out their last few years of work behind a well-polished desk, serving as the Deputy Commissioner of Looking Like You're Doing Something Important.

There were also plenty of guys who hadn't retired yet because it would mean spending more time with a wife they didn't like. They would arrest people for petty crimes that they knew would get dismissed just for the rush of making the collar. Others would just set out and start busting heads. But Ralph Mulino hadn't been given so much as a Command Discipline in the past seventeen years. He had never fired his weapon on the job except at the range. This man had whiled away a quiet little career in the New York Police Department, only to shoot a colleague in the chest one late summer night.

Leonard always started with the questions he truly didn't know the answer to. Why was Rowson on the container ship on what the roll call showed was his day off? Why was Ralph Mulino called out to investigate when there were plenty of cops who regularly work a midnight tour? Who had killed the civilian officer of the shipping company? And where was Rowson's gun? He was a detective after all. He had been wearing his badge. The recovered evidence list wasn't in the packet that had come in Tuesday. Leonard would have to interview Mulino based just on the photographs. Maybe there had been a gun, but it was out of the frame of the pictures; maybe it flew off the boat when Rowson had been shot. Or maybe he was out on the ship unarmed. If Leonard could unravel it, maybe the administration would keep him on after all. With crime back on the rise, with the little disasters keeping the city skittish, the administration would want to show that it was still serious about weeding out bad cops. Middle-aged, white, carrying an old-school revolver, Detective Ralph Mulino would be a perfect trophy.

Clear of Trinity Church, Leonard was imagining himself at a press conference next to the mayor when he nearly stumbled into a teenager being grabbed by a police officer. The kid was very thin, maybe nine-teen, black, wearing loose jeans and a tank top. The cops were back to grabbing teenagers off the street—as soon as crime had started to tick up, there were more backs to the walls. The NYPD wanted to prove that they weren't stopping kids for no reason, not like they used to. So now they gave them summonses to prove they really thought they were up to something.

Leonard thought to intervene, but telling a cop you work for DIMAC is no way to get him to listen. Every cop on the force has a faded story about a brother or a friend who had been railroaded by DIMAC, had been forced off the street for doing his job and ended up sitting at a desk going mad while the hoodlums and the crazies took over the city. And even though the story took place twenty years ago, and even though whoever did this wrong had long since retired, and even though it probably wasn't even true to begin with, the cop will hear where you work and shrug you off. Ignoring you will be his little opportunity for justice, revenge, whichever.

No one was jumping to the kid's side either. People kept their noses out of it because they had all grown accustomed to a new city with low crime and fresh fruit on the corners, bright new apartment buildings and digital signs in the subways telling you when the next train was coming. They had become used to the warmth and the order, but had averted their eyes to how that order was maintained. When the order started to crack, and the old habits came back, people looked away. That was part of the deal.

Curmudgeons had complained, sure, that the grunge and the dirt had made New York special. They whined that there had been character in dirty bookstores on Ninth Avenue or junkies spread out across your stoop in the morning. But most people were glad for the swap, they were happy to give up the local color, or the mystique, or however you wanted to describe it, so long as they also were able to give up the fear.

Or, to be precise, to give up the Little Fear. People had become used to being free from any worry that someone would pull out a switchblade on the sidewalk and ask you for your wallet. That someone would climb through your window and take your television. Advertisements for fixing torn earlobes were long gone from the subway. The Little Fear had vanished.

But the Big Fear was always with you. The fear that the buildings would come crashing down, that the elevators would be filled with poison gas, that the subway stalling for a moment on the bridge means the bridge itself is about to collapse into the water—that was part of you. Maybe not like it had been just after, maybe tempered a little, and smoothed out by your New York attitude, but it was always there beneath, throbbing a little, reminding you, like an old scar that you can feel when you lounge back into an otherwise comfortable chair. You couldn't look away from the Big Fear.

As Leonard left the cop, who was dusting off the boy he had manhandled, he realized that even if he left the city, even if he moved out of the Ebbets Field Apartments into a bright condo in Hoboken, the Big Fear would stay with him too. He turned past the petty arrest and toward his office. He passed the fire-red sign for the John Street Bar and Grill pointing downstairs to cheap beer and sawdust hamburgers, the basement shoe stores hedging their boasts ("We are Probably the Lowest Priced in the City"), and the riot of egg sandwiches, weak coffee, and clutter. He was in a position of power now, but it came with risks. He could confront Detective Ralph Mulino, but the police department had its own way of bringing the Big Fear. If the shooting was dirty, there were ways that cops would go about taking it out on the messenger.

Leonard would have to be ready for them.

CHAPTER FIVE
COMPLIANCE

They were stacked four deep and three high and took up almost the entire desk. Two-inch-thick black binders, spreading a glum, dull welcome to Christine Davenport at the new job. Each one contained nearly three hundred tabs and each tab was set in perfect order. The labels on the covers and spines were precisely placed—EHA Investments, Internal Investigation, a date, a volume number. Most likely the paralegal had been scolded once after a label was found to be a half-inch off of perfect center. After that the kid had started using a ruler. In city government, when you want a binder of documents, what you get is a stack of loose paper and a level two admin who can show you that three hole punching and inserting tabs is nowhere to be found in her Tasks and Standards. And she has a copy handy if you'd like to look. In the public sector, everyone is her own assistant.

From the moment she had walked into the law firm, Davenport had learned that the paperwork, the binders, and the Post-its would always be precise and perfect. After all, there was an anonymous horde being well-paid to make sure. A few weeks ago, when she'd toured the place, when there was still some committee or other that was deciding her fate, they had shown her all of the various departments—office services, proofreading, three or four different kinds of "support" for tasks Davenport didn't know existed. All that had sunk in was that she wouldn't have to do anything that felt like work anymore. She would only be asked to do the thinking. She had met then with the team of junior attorneys, the people who would be sifting through the thirty thousand or so e-mails that were potentially relevant and come up with a few thousand that she was going to have to look at. The people who had gone through the four hundred and fifty thousand e-mails on EHA Investment's actual servers, and who had culled that down to thirty thousand for the law firm, were anonymous contract attorneys working in off-site basements. Davenport didn't even get introduced to them.

Davenport sat down and tugged at the first binder. This was her job now, to look through a few thousand carefully curated e-mails and see if she could find someone at a minor little investment house worth sending off to prison. But it was a quiet comfortable existence, and she smiled at the knowledge that she would never again be sweltering at DIMAC, making her own copies and taking lip from the general public. The office was a perfect sixty-eight degrees even though it was still broiling outside. She had a pristine view of the oversized marble woman rinsing her hair in MOMA's manicured sculpture garden forty stories below.

EHA Investments had come to the firm. Some broad worries. Some concerns about trading patterns. But not even enough to get them focused properly. Maybe that had been the holdup. Maybe it hadn't been the law firm at all. They had been waiting until they felt they had no choice but to submit to the investigation. They were very eager and wanted the help, but they were much less straightforward than most of these corporate clients as to what exactly they thought she would find. Usually what these places want is clear enough. They have already found some employee that would make a good sacrifice. Find out everything he did, and prove that no one else knew about it so we can wash our hands of him. But EHA Investments hadn't given her a target. They had only given her worry. And that set off red flags, because that meant the target could be anyone.

The firm had taken Davenport on but hadn't really included her. She had a reputation after her work at DIMAC, but she knew she wouldn't be fully welcome yet. She had done her prosecuting for the city government, which the white-shoe guys all thought of as a little dirty and a lot cheap. They themselves had all been prosecutors, but they had served their stints at one US Attorney's office or another. They got to give lip back to the federal prosecutor, if push ever came to shove.

Opened, the binders smelled like fourth grade. No amount of money could keep a black office binder from looking and feeling like a piece of cardboard with a thick plastic skin. Davenport licked her finger librarian-like and started in on the tabs.

The kids had done their best. There were some nasty exchanges between traders and their clients. People who thought they had been screwed. People who maybe expected their broker to be using non-public information to make them money. Who sounded pretty disappointed when they learned he hadn't. Traders who were carrying on affairs, who were cheating on their taxes, one series of e-mails showing that a guy wasn't paying his nanny's social security. Even the White Plains branch of the US Attorney's office, Davenport knew, wouldn't bother with that. Lots of e-mails from one guy talking about his suits. Davenport figured that one of the attorneys knew from the television that coke dealers used to talk about how many "suits" they were bringing in. Same with boxes of cereal, or pizzas, or anything that could stand in for drugs if you both knew what each other was talking about. But after reading an e-mail or two it was pretty clear that this guy was actually ordering his dry cleaning. Plus she hadn't heard anyone refer to drugs as suits in ten years. Not to mention that she was hoping for something bigger than a drug bust.

She was about two hundred e-mails in when she found something she had to read twice. It was the sender's address that struck her first. She turned to her computer to look it up and confirmed her suspicions. She reached for the neat packet of colored flags and marked the page. The smallest binder would be made up just of what she wanted them to see. Just what she would carry with her when she went to visit Eliot Holm-Anderson, the EHA of EHA Investments, in person. She read the e-mail again. It only made her more curious.

A few dozen e-mails later there was another one. The same curious suffix, the same worry. There would be more work to do. She would ask the junior lawyer to put together a list of the company's trades on the days just before and after this one. An outside vendor would run that e-mail address. Another green flag. Ten e-mails later there was another. Then more. Every few pages another one. The last one had been sent only a week ago. By the end of the day she had gone through three packets of the flags and had not noticed that the sun had set. If what she had found had only been about money, she would have been home hours ago. She had expected to find something to do with money. But what she had found had been enough to keep her there. She had missed dinner with her husband and son and she was the last person at work at a Midtown law firm. She turned the last page of the binder. It was about so much more than just money. She stared blearily down at the shuttered sculpture garden and smiled. She was on the hunt again.

CHAPTER SIX

COLOR OF THE DAY

The table was too big for the room. Ralph Mulino wasn't sure how they had even gotten it through the door, to be honest. It was close to eight feet long and four wide, the dull laminate nicked and stained from hundreds of terse interviews and cheap lunches. The walls were plain white paint over sheetrock. Barely any better than sitting in a cubicle. You listen closely enough, you can hear the guy in the next room giving his statement. The PD would never stoop to conducting confidential interviews in a room like this. There was a lot wrong with the job, but they had some standards. Mulino slouched in the flimsy folding chair and stared at the analog tape recorder. All they would need was a swinging light and the thing would be straight out of a '40s movie. Maybe that's why they did it; maybe these civilian investigators at DIMAC fancied themselves a troop of James Cagneys. Or maybe it was only that the agency's budget didn't provide for niceties like digital recorders or paint.

Mulino turned to his union rep as he heard footsteps in the hallway. He had every pin and button in place; he was trying to make a good impression. It had been bad enough to wear the suit and tie on the ship; here he had to submit to the uniform. He hated the ceremony of it all. Out on the ship, all the other cops who had come out had told him to stay strong, to keep it together. They all acted like they believed him, but they were just the first team out. They didn't have any say over anything. He hadn't slept all night, going over every moment on the ship, trying to think of when he could have found out that Rowson was a detective. He couldn't think of a thing. His wife had consoled him about the *Daily News*, that they had to make him look bad so they could say something different from the *Post*, but Mulino took it personal.

His collar brass was pinching his neck. The union rep was taking notes. They give you this one for free at the administrative interview. If there's an administrative charge you get a real lawyer, and if there's a criminal charge then you get to meet the guy in the two-thousand dollar suit who's the AA sponsor for half the judges on New York State Supreme. Getting the union rep means that the department doesn't think your problems are serious yet. Most were SUNY law school grads who had signed up with the police unions after getting turned down by the district attorney's office.

The footsteps stopped in front of the cheap door to Mulino's left. They put little windows in them so that anyone walking by could check in on who's subject to a confidential investigation that could cost him his job or worse. The window was reinforced with chicken wire in case some angry building inspector tried to break the glass and slit his wrists with the shards right there. Amateurs.

Mulino wasn't quite finished surveying the shoddy room when a lean man in a cheap suit opened the door and stepped in. This one looked patient, calm, not as jittery as most of the kids at DIMAC, who seemed to be play-acting at conducting an investigation. Mulino knew he was supposed to stand up, like he was in a court or visiting a priest. Ceremony again. He pressed himself up out of the plastic chair as gracefully as he could and held out his hand.

"Detective Mulino, I'm Leonard Mitchell." The investigator didn't shake Mulino's hand. Maybe they train them not to. "Let me get the tape recorder set up." The union rep nodded to Mulino, inviting him to sit back down.

Leonard took his seat and fired up the tape recorder. The big, heavy, old-fashioned kind where you can't press the button down all the way if you don't have a tape in. An extra bit of idiot-proofing. He breathed in and started with the boilerplate. The union rep nodded slowly to the patter. Maybe he knew it by heart. Maybe he wasn't paying attention.

"On the record at nine seventeen a.m. My name is Leonard Mitchell and the date is August 25. We are at the offices for the Department to Investigate Misconduct and Corruption, on the sixteenth floor of Forty Rector Street, New York, New York. For the record, could you state your name, rank, shield, and command?"

Mulino remembered what the rep had told him. What they always tell you. *Always answer direct. Say as little as you can. Don't volunteer.* This interview, the very first one, was already a dull routine. Like an appointment at the DMV except not as much fun. "Detective Ralph Mulino, shield 9284, Organized Crime Control Bureau."

The investigator went on. "And you have brought a representative with you today." Then he turned to the rep. "Could you state your name?"

"Bernie Andropovic, A-N-D-R-O-P-O-V-I-C." Mulino thought that the recitation sounded like more patter. He was here every day for some cop or other and probably spelled it every time.

"Detective, you are here pursuant to an investigation into whether you did use excessive force on or about August 23 at approximately two fifteen a.m." Mulino smiled to himself at the way the investigators would try to sound like cops. How many reports had he written where a perp "did conceal a glassine envelope" or "did display a knife with a retractable blade." They come after you, but they can't help but use your language. Lost in thought, he had almost missed the investigator asking his first question. "This investigation is being conducted pursuant to Interim Order 118-9. Are you familiar with IO-118-9?"

Mitchell looked up from the script. Mulino nodded. It's just a routine, he kept reminding himself. Be friendly. Agree. If you look like you're worried about something they'll pounce.

"I understand."

Mulino was asked to read his official account in the record. He did it slowly, spelling out the radio codes and the shorthand. A brief statement in a code they both understood.

"And can you tell me in your own words what happened?"

Mulino looked to Andropovic. The man nodded. Speaking carefully, he told the investigator about getting dragged out of bed, about climbing the wet ladder, the body on the boat. "It wasn't as though I had just dropped in when I saw Detective Rowson. By that point it was already a murder investigation."

Mitchell didn't look up from his notes. "Go on."

Mulino told him about the sounds. The squeaks. Asking over and over for the guy to come out. Saying over and over he was a cop. And then the running toward the railing, the flashing of the gun, the fear.

"Was that gun recovered? You can't see it in the photos."

"You'd have to check the log for that." Mulino noted that Mitchell didn't say anything about the log. Maybe it wasn't in yet. Maybe the gun was logged and the investigator was testing him. But if he doesn't say anything, don't volunteer. Mulino thought about the swarm of cops that had come in. They had crowded him out and taken pictures, then taken inventory. He'd been kept to the side the whole time, and had eventually been taken off the boat by helicopter after they gave him the now-standard breathalyzer. He had never even seen Sergeant Sparks.

"Regardless of the log. You see this gun get recovered?"

"I saw it on the deck. When I approached the body, the gun was in Detective Rowson's hand. Or just by his hand. A department-issued nine millimeter."

"I saw you still carry the revolver yourself."

Mulino was about to talk when Andropovic tapped his knee. A signal. They had worked it out beforehand. *If the guy says something and it isn't a question, you don't have to say anything. If he asks you a yes or no question, you can just say yes or no. Keep it short. You aren't at a bar with your friends.*

Mulino saw the investigator's eyes dart toward Andropovic's hand. He'd seen the tapping. That probably didn't make Mulino look so smart. Mitchell finished a note and spoke. "The log isn't in yet. If you want to wait I can bring you back down after it comes in."

"I saw the gun when I went up to him." Mulino only noticed after he had said it that Andropovic had been tapping him again. It hadn't been a question.

"Tell me when you first noticed anything that you thought resembled a gun."

"Well. I saw the guy. When I saw him first it was dark and I didn't see anything. He was out on the deck and he went behind some of the containers. Then when he came out, when he charged, he was running pretty fast and I saw it in his hand then. I was pretty sure of it. As he ran toward me screaming."

"You were pretty sure of it?"

"I was sure of it."

"And what did you do before you shot him?"

Mulino had practiced this part. "I considered whether it was safe to retreat and I determined it was not. I called out 'Freeze, Police' while holding my gun out. When he continued to charge I fired one shot." Mulino was never comfortable lying. He had thought about whether to admit he hadn't said "police," about whether to try to make Mitchell understand what it is like to have so many things going through your head at once. But it was easier just to say he had done it. He had said freeze, and he was a police officer, after all. He'd called out "police" a half-dozen times on the boat, just not right before he fired. And it wasn't as though Rowson was going to wake up and tell them otherwise. It just would have made things all the more complicated.

Mitchell turned back to his notes. He cocked his head and stared straight at Mulino.

"Detective, what was the color of the day Monday?"

"Excuse me?"

"When you were out on the ship, late night Sunday early morning Monday, what was the color of the day?"

Mulino thought to reach out for his memo book, but it wouldn't be there. That was his usual habit when asked the color of the day. At the start of every tour, roll call tells every cop in the city a color code. If you come across someone out of uniform, and he says he's a cop, he can only prove it if he knows the color of the day. The true undercovers—guys doing their best to look like criminals—will actually wear wristbands to prove it. The idea is that it will end the standoff when two cops are pointing guns at each other, each convinced that the other is an imposter. A pretty low-tech trick. They stick close to the familiar with the colors: white, green, blue, red, black. Detective Mulino would always write it down, but could never remember half an hour after he was told. He hoped that if he was ever face-to-face with another cop with their guns drawn, the guy would let him reach into his back pocket to look it up.

But it wasn't there now. When they had called him, they hadn't bothered with that. Sergeant Sparks hadn't told him on the little motorboat. Not the sergeant's fault, maybe. The lieutenant who called him maybe was the one that was supposed to tell him. Mulino wasn't even sure. When he'd gotten the call, the last thing he would have expected to find on the boat was another cop. Mulino shrugged.

"I don't have any idea."

"When you were called to go out with the harbor unit, did they give you a color of the day?"

"No."

"Did any one, at any point, tell you the color of the day that night?"

"It wouldn't have mattered. He never said he was a cop. I wouldn't have had the chance to ask him for it. And he didn't ask me for it either."

"But no one told you."

When he asks you a yes or no question, you have to answer. "No."

The investigator turned a leaf of his notes, and the sharp flap of it startled Mulino. "I want to talk about the detective. Brian Rowson."

The union guy pushed his glasses up on his nose. "I understand why you're curious about Detective Rowson, but your only jurisdiction is to investigate Detective Mulino. Who, I'm sure you're already aware, saved his own and possibly other people's lives by making a quick and correct decision."

Mulino knew that Andropovic didn't mean a word of it. He was there to protect Mulino so he'd say whatever he thought would work. If the shooting had gone the other way, the union rep would be boosting Rowson and skewering the dead Mulino. There was no comfort in the paid praise.

"Anyone ever figure out why Detective Rowson was on that boat?"

The rep was silent. Mulino figured it was safe to answer. "One of the techs that was on the crime scene unit knew him. Said he'd had money problems. Maybe he had sticky fingers."

"The ship was filled with refrigerators and washing machines. Could they even have gotten one appliance off of it?"

Mulino shrugged. "I don't even know myself. It's just what the guy on the deck told me." Mulino couldn't make sense of it either. "The guy was out of money. I got called out to the ship. Someone drew a gun at me and I took a shot. The other way around, then I'd be dead and you could ask him what he was doing out there."

"You think of any reason you in particular would get called out onto that boat?"

Mulino almost told the investigator the whole story. Almost spilled about how he was the reliable cop, the one that would always go on the call that others turned down. About how he had been kept from being promoted, how he had been on the job for ten years, watching people retire around him with healthier pensions than he would ever see. "No."

The man stared at Mulino, waiting maybe to see if he could coax a longer answer out of him by staying silent. Mulino knew to keep his mouth shut now without being prompted. The investigator took a quick jot of a note, turned another page. Mulino wondered if this guy had ever been in the field for anything. If he'd even taken a witness statement at a bodega, a dispatch stand, a hospital.

Mitchell went on. "Let's talk about what happened after the shooting." But even Mulino knew he was safe on this part. After the shooting, he had done everything as close to proper as it gets. He had called right away for the backup and the medic. He hadn't touched anything. He was supposed to have tried CPR, but it wouldn't have mattered. The helicopter took twelve minutes to get there and Rowson was probably dead within three.

Soon the interview was over and they were both standing. Mitchell reached out and shook Mulino's hand. Mulino wondered if that was a good sign, given that he'd turned him down before they started. Then Mitchell turned back to the cardboard hallway and was already gone. Andropovic stood up, already thinking of his next case, and patted Mulino on the back.

"You did great. It's probably all over."

Another lie. Mulino knew the guy was there to protect him, but it made him feel dirty just to have representation. Having a lawyer felt like an admission that he'd done something wrong.

Leonard Mitchell had done his job, Mulino supposed. He was supposed to ask. He had been told the color of the day a thousand times in his career and barely remembered it when he did. He did begin to wonder about the gun though. He saw it in the detective's hand. The thing was, though, there was no moment where the crime scene guy lifted it up and showed the whole crowd and put it in the bag. They do that on a street shooting because by that time there are reporters present. But everyone on the boat had been PD, except for the six crew members who had woken up, claiming to have slept through the whole thing. It gnawed at Mulino a little. Maybe the gun had slid off the boat somehow. Maybe it was going to show up in the report tomorrow and the whole thing would be over. Maybe, he worried, his mind was playing tricks on him, and he thought he remembered something that wasn't there. Or maybe something else.

The something else he didn't want to think about. Maybe some cop had heard just enough about Mulino from back in the day. A story about Ebbets Field and the trial room and maybe this detective was due a little payback. Not that any of them knew the whole story. Just the bits and pieces that get passed down as warnings in locker rooms and grimy hallways. Enough, though, to maybe take action. To think it would be a good idea to make Mulino squirm. They didn't know how much he had squirmed back then. Or maybe something worse. Maybe it wasn't some line officer on the ship kicking the gun overboard. Maybe someone higher up was thinking about Mulino too. Maybe there was a reason he was called that night after all. Mulino hurried out of the elevator and into the heat. He had someone to talk to.

CHAPTER SEVEN
PAPER

Leonard slouched by the nautical window and stared past the pigeon shit onto the West Side Highway. He'd taken over Davenport's office because what the hell, he was in charge now. At least until they threw him out. And if he didn't at least stake a claim to the corner office, then he'd be sending a signal that even *he* didn't think that he belonged there. And if he brought this one in, maybe he could stay.

More information on the shooting would dribble onto his computer for the rest of the day. Memos from the Crime Scene Unit, roll calls from the Harbor Patrol, scans of memo books from patrol officers and daily activity reports from detectives, and every scrap of paper filled out by every cop that had stepped foot anywhere near the boat that night. The NYPD ran the full technological gamut. There were the elite security units with retinal scanners, the high-end narcotics squads with fifty-foot cranes mounted with ultraviolet cameras to look into your apartment, and the counterterrorism units with goodies galore. The evidence guys are fully capable of scouring a ship in the middle of the night and sending you a bundled e-mail with eighty-seven photographs to look at the next morning. But in its daily plodding heart, the NYPD is a pen-to-paper operation. There are dozens of carbon paper forms that haven't been updated yet, so every precinct has to keep a typewriter on hand to fill them out. Personnel files are printed on immense rolls of paper, complete with hole-punched perforated edges clinging to a spool as the machine chirps away. The entry-level kid at most businesses keeps a digital calendar, but cops are stuck with memo books where they are supposed to ballpoint everything they do, from collaring a murderer to helping someone down a flight of subway stairs. Mostly the memo books are filled up with the phone numbers of girls who like a guy in uniform. Aided cards, stop-and-frisk forms, use-of-force reports, warrant execution reports: a cop has to write out every one by hand. So even though Leonard would get every piece of digital data sometime today, his file wouldn't be nearly complete.

In a week or two, the actual paper would come in. Leonard could smell the dusty residue of Ms. Mortiz's third grade class whenever he opened a manila envelope from a local precinct. You need the hard copy. Even the pages that they scanned and sent ahead were all only one-sided. Whenever a cop needs to know something but doesn't want someone to look at it later, he folds over a page of his memo book and jots it down on the flyleaf.

He had done the interview too soon, he thought. He didn't know enough. Mulino had been almost too bright and too eager. Showing up in the uniform when most detectives will roll into DIMAC in their sweatshirts. The detective had been smiling, trying to help, until Andropovic used his stupid tapping-on-the-knee stunt again. Leonard made a note to report that to the union.

Mulino hadn't looked like Leonard had expected either. Skeptical dark eyes on an otherwise broad sweet face, Mulino looked almost too nice to be a lifelong cop. He had shot another detective, he was answering for it at DIMAC, and he hadn't hardened into the traditional scowl, even now. The skin around the corners of his eyes was still soft and his hair had only a hint of gray. The guy had spent most of the interview almost smiling.

And the story had sounded good enough. But the story always sounds good the first time. Before you've gone back over it and checked against the logs and the other guy's memo book and the security video if you can get it. It would all turn on whether the part about the gun panned out. If a gun turned up, Leonard wasn't going to bask in City Hall's glow after all. But if there was no gun, it wouldn't matter what Mulino said.

And it still didn't make sense that Mulino was the guy who got this call. Plenty of detectives awake at one in the morning, regular day off or no. And it wasn't like Mulino was some special firecracker, the guy you absolutely need to have when you're stomping around a container ship.

Maybe he would find some answers in the digital production. The least he could do was to start looking. The preliminary personnel records had shown that Rowson had a tussle with Internal Affairs about eighteen months ago. Now the whole thing was spelled out. A summary investigation for improper disposal of evidence—a euphemism for pocketing the profits of someone you busted. Rowson had taken down a small-time fencer of stolen jewelry—stuff that discreet household help tries to sell through private channels because it would attract attention at a pawnshop. The detective had been accused of keeping a couple of pairs of earrings for himself. They had been in his desk, and he'd claimed the whole thing was an accident. He hadn't sold them, so they couldn't bust him for it. The report had hinted that maybe he had been planning on giving them to his wife for their anniversary. They hadn't even been real diamonds, but Brian Rowson probably didn't know that. The investigation had been closed as unsubstantiated, with no trip to the trial room. Instead, Rowson had been transferred to the Harbor Patrol. Somewhere where he couldn't get into any more trouble. From then until the day he was shot he had a crisp and uneventful history.

Nearly getting busted for stealing a pair of earrings, though, is no reason to get killed. And it wouldn't explain why he had been on the boat to begin with. Leonard set down the personnel file and tracked through the roll call. The original would be a thick printout from an antique computer, complete with dot-matrix rendering and a ribbon of holes on the side to hold the paper to the printer's knotty spool. The scan was almost illegible. Every day each precinct churns out this record of who is partnered with whom, which sector they plan to patrol, which car they will do it in, all capped off with the serial numbers of their guns. Harbor Patrol doesn't use cars much, but officers are still divvied up with partners, and as often as not cruise assigned swatches of the waterways.

Nearly every day for the last month, Leonard saw as he scrolled through the roll call, Detective Rowson had been paired with the same cop: Officer Joey Del Rio. They had been all over the city: scouting the East River looking for illegal dumping, Coney Island where a drunk might just slip and drown, and the Bronx side of the Hudson where now and again someone would still leave a body. Most of the other officers would trade partners every few days, but Rowson was paired with Joey Del Rio every day that he wasn't assigned to be the sergeant's driver.

The name of the sergeant caught Leonard's attention as well. Sparks. Of course. It was the sergeant who had ferried Mulino out to the boat. Once or twice a month, Rowson was assigned to drive Sparks. A routine duty for a junior cop, driving the sergeant around. But Rowson wasn't a junior cop any more. It seemed that even though Rowson got to keep his detective's badge, after his IAB investigation he was back to being a patrol officer in everything but title. On the day he was killed, Brian Rowson was RDO—on his Regular Day Off. So was Officer Del Rio.

Leonard checked the assignment for Rowson's weapon. It was a standard-issue nine millimeter. Just what Mulino said he saw, the same gun that almost every cop in the city carries. If Rowson had been out on that boat without his weapon, the gun would be at his house or at his precinct. Doing a search of a precinct locker requires a field visit, and for DIMAC to do a field visit requires NYPD approval. You get your approval from the wrong lieutenant and whatever you're looking for is gone when you show up.

The full evidence report hadn't come through yet, but there were ballistics on Mulino's weapon and effects at least. The techs on board had snapped and bagged the shell, Mulino's flashlight, the small bit of flesh that ended up on the deck of the boat. The bullet itself had probably landed in the ocean after. Little chance that they'd recover it. Not that it mattered; there was no need to run the ballistics to see who had done the shooting.

Mulino's gun was preserved, along with the results of his breathalyzer (he had passed). But there was no photograph of a second gun. Maybe it would show up later today with the full evidence list. Maybe some tech forgot to take a picture of it. But given the dozens of photographs of the scene and the minutiae that had been recovered, Leonard kind of doubted it. He was left with a statement by a detective that he had seen a gun. Not just the shine and the flash of it, not so he could maybe have made a mistake. Mulino said that he had walked up to the body and seen the gun by the dead man's hand. But the photographs from the boat gave no clue that a gun had ever been there.

Except that wasn't true exactly. Leonard scrolled to the end of the file. The pictures of the crime he didn't have any jurisdiction to investigate. The dead sailor that Mulino had stumbled across before he shot Rowson. The kid's head was a mangled mess. A fair chunk had been scooped out from the left temple, but both eyes were still open and the lips were parted as if about to speak. The uniform was tidy and he was lying straight on his back. He may or may not have been shot with a nine millimeter, but he was shot with something. Only one bullet was gone from Mulino's gun. So if Rowson hadn't killed the crew member, or if he hadn't been armed at all, then someone else had been out on that deck. The rest of the skeleton crew—only seven men on the whole boat—had all been below deck and had slept through the whole thing, if you could believe them. It's not as though Leonard would ever get access to them. They were for the NYPD to interview now. If he couldn't prove that it was related to Mulino shooting Detective Rowson, he couldn't force anyone to talk to him.

Mulino had been called after midnight, he'd said. He was sent out with a Harbor Patrol sergeant he'd never met and he'd never been told the color of the day. He received no briefing. He didn't know what he was looking for. Or who. Anything could have been happening on that boat. The detective had had no idea what he was getting into out there.

Leonard stood away from his computer and surveyed the dumpy office. It wasn't much, but he was in charge now. He had a stable of sixty-five investigators at his disposal, but most of them were admittedly burnouts or kids ducking out from work early to work on screenplays or civil service lifers watching their own pensions. Even the best of them were spending two years getting their feet wet before heading off to law schools and corporate towers and bundles of money to assuage the guilt. They didn't know yet that the quest for truth is thick with contradiction. That sometimes you have to bully someone to catch a brute, to lie to someone so he'll confess to being a liar. Even the smart kids could be easily outmaneuvered by a diligent corrupt official or a clever union lawyer. In a few years, they would understand. But he couldn't trust them now.

For two years at DIMAC he had done all of Christine Davenport's heavy lifting. He had pored through the padded hours of the minions of the Consumer Affairs Department and the fake sick days of sanitation officers. He had watched seventeen hours of video footage to see which firefighter had looted a trove of personal possessions. He had drafted her speeches and balanced her budgets. Now he was in charge, but he had no deputy as reliable as himself. His job would be pretty much the same as it had been before.

Except that he would be the target if something went wrong. If the investigation failed, his head would roll. And if Mulino felt cornered, he would feel that Leonard was the one cornering him.

Maybe no gun would show up. If Mulino was making up the part about the gun, then this was a cop who had shot an unarmed man in cold blood. Who could be facing the loss of his job, his pension, worse. Leonard shrugged it off. The cops never take revenge on you. Not personally. That's the first thing they tell you when they train you at DIMAC. Never worry that the cops will actually come after you. Because if you do, you will be paralyzed with fear.

But there is no harm in seeking a little protection. He closed his door, picked up the phone, and called City Hall. Even with Davenport quitting so suddenly, Leonard still had a friend or two left. He had paid out enough favors as the top lieutenant in a couple of different agencies. There are always children of friends looking for jobs, tickets to minor-league baseball games to distribute, introductions to make. All of it the completely-above-board butter that feeds any big organization. And the City of New York is a very big organization.

A soft, bored lifer answered the phone. You have to be pretty high up in the city before they give you someone to pick it up for you. "Deputy Mayor Victor Ells's office."

"Is he in? It's Leonard Mitchell at DIMAC."

"Let me check."

The Deputy Mayor for Legal Matters had been brought into the new regime from the US Attorney's office and had a reputation as a corruption fighter himself. He had led the rackets division in the Southern District, prosecuting a crime family that had controlled every street repair project in Manhattan. Not content to lock up mobsters, he had started going after the executive staff of the Department of Transportation, bagging the deputy commissioner there on fraud and perjury charges. After the election, the new mayor had brought him on board—maybe because he trusted him or maybe because he wanted to pluck him away from a job where he could throw the mayor's cronies in jail. Leonard had always liked him; he was the only person at City Hall he could speak to without getting the impression that he was being scolded for something.

Rumors were that he was eager for the top job himself and was going to challenge his own boss in a couple of years. He would be receptive to what Leonard had to say either way. His patent-leather voice was worth the wait to reach him.

"Leonard. It must have been an interesting day and a half over there."

"Is that because my boss has just quit, or because I've got one detective that gunned down another and swears the guy had a gun that no one seems to be able to find?"

"Isn't it great to finally be in charge of something, though?"

Leonard held the phone away from his face for a moment. He was in charge. Was about to be. And what he was about to ask Victor Ells to do might compromise that, if it went the wrong way. No matter what, he was about to go from being someone who was owed a debt to being someone who owed. But if it all panned out, he would be able to pay it back, and then some.

"Listen, Victor. I have something to ask you. I need to call in a favor."

CHAPTER EIGHT
LEGWORK

As he rounded the corner of the third flight of stairs, Detective Mulino's knee started talking to him. It asked him to find an ottoman or a coffee table to prop his leg up on. No dice. Mulino looked up the landing. The only NYPD building he had ever been in with a working elevator was One Police Plaza downtown. Even here at the OCCB headquarters, right next to the recently refurbished Brooklyn DA's office, it was five flights up if you wanted to talk to a chief. Mulino figured there had to be an elevator somewhere. The chief himself wouldn't take the stairs.

It was a short walk anyway from Gold Street, where Mulino had been stewing for three days. Mulino understood the optics—you shoot someone, you have to turn in your gun and get parked someplace where you can't hurt anybody, no matter how competent you are. If they pin you for it, you stay there. So every customer service job in the NYPD was filled with guys too dangerous to put on the street but too insulated by their union protection to actually fire. Vehicle impound centers. Parade and demonstration licenses. And most of all the Property Clerk, sandwiched between the Eight-Four on one side and the Social

Security office on the other. The dim brick municipal office dug in even as one thirty-story glass condo after another sprouted next door.

There were twenty-six officers in Property, and it was a strict daytime tour, so if you were lucky you didn't have to spend a full hour at the window more than once every couple of days. Because waiting for you on the other side of that window was a thick angry river of the general public, free to make demands on you. There were a few vics coming to pick up a necklace that had been recovered from the pawnshop after the babysitter lifted it, sure, but well over ninety percent of the items vouchered at Property were the effects of people who had themselves been arrested. Lottery tickets that had been scratched but held onto just in case. Half a pack of cigarettes that would have been worth twenty dollars apiece in lockup. A nickel-plated pipe that no one was even going to bother to test for drugs because the perp had been brought in on a stabbing anyway. And each morning after the bail hearings, a swarm of newly released not-quite-criminals crossed Jay Street and stumbled toward Gold to demand the return of their personal scraps. On the first of the month, when the Social Security office next door had checks, they would make it all in one trip. The NYPD sent its worst officers to the Property Clerk Division because it didn't really care how people coming off an arrest were treated. Most likely they'd be back inside in a few months, after their plea, so why not give them a taste of it now.

Mulino had done his hour as best he could. The other cops in Property didn't speak to him at all. He was a probie to them. In a few days, a week maybe, he might be back out on the street—as stale as OCCB felt to Mulino, it would have been a dream to most of these guys. So when each skell at the window handed him a yellow carboncopy voucher, he walked down the stairs to hunt for the envelope himself. And each time the guy said that there were twenty bucks missing from his envelope, Mulino slid over a complaint form and a pen. He didn't ask for any help from anyone. If in a couple of months the

Department frowned on him and decided that he could spend the rest of his career in Property, then he would be one of them.

Or maybe not. Because here in Property, surrounded by officers who had been ratted out or had caught a raw deal or had otherwise been beaten down by the NYPD, Mulino felt the cold disdain of what had happened at the Ebbets Field Apartments more than he ever had at OCCB. These guys had been betrayed, and most of them had been on the force long enough to remember what Mulino had done. They weren't like Sparks, who maybe heard the story along with fifteen or twenty others. When these guys heard that Detective Ralph Mulino was coming in, they knew who he was in a snap.

He turned the last corner onto the landing and shook out his knee. He stopped to catch his breath. He had felt light, walking up the stairway without his gun, his radio, his flashlight, but after four flights he was still winded. He checked that his shirt was tucked in. He pushed into the hallway and announced himself to the admin, a sleek woman who had grown her nails so long that she couldn't possibly use her fingers to type.

"Detective Ralph Mulino for Chief Travis."

The woman nodded. He had been announced downstairs. Mulino walked toward the square wooden chairs, a few copies of day-old tabloids on the end table. Ordinarily he would leaf through them while he waited. Today that wasn't such a good idea.

Whenever he started thinking about Ebbets Field, he always imagined something he could have done. Some way to make it end differently. But it always came out the same. It had been hot that night, not as hot as the night on the ship but hot enough. Mulino had been in OCCB no more than a month and was still taking radio runs, still hoping that he could prove something to someone and move far enough up the ladder to make a difference. He was paired with Chuck Ramsay, a real old-school guy, someone who had weathered Knapp and Mollen and laughed at all the jokers in suits who had never been on the streets but thought they could make judgments. Good for a laugh and an old story, but someone who would never have lasted at the new NYPD, even if they had let him stay.

The call had come in at the Ebbets Field Apartments, on the border of Crown Heights and Flatbush. Twenty-six stories of misery, then, rising above a broad cement plaza that was itself a good twenty feet above street level. Once you climbed the stairs off of Bedford and into the houses, you were in another world. It wasn't technically a housing project, but there wasn't a soul inside that paid market rent. The whole thing had been a boondoggle from the start between a developer who knew someone in the Section 8 office and found a way to make a fortune off of poverty. The Dodgers had left, the stadium had been torn down, and affordable housing was all the rage. But it had never worked out to be anything other than a hellhole, a place where for thirty years the few honest people unlucky enough to be stuck there locked their doors and ran down the stairwells with their eyes to the floor, hoping not to be caught in the crossfire on their way to the street.

The call had been vague, like they all were. Woman in distress. When they had arrived, Mulino and Ramsay had found her hiding in a Dumpster. Jeans, barefoot, topless, she was curled in a ball and bleeding from the head and neck. She wouldn't speak to them and wouldn't unlock her arms from around her knees, the only thing protecting the shame of her breasts from the two cops. Mulino didn't blame her. Ramsay tugged at her arm and gave up. The paramedics could take care of her; he called for a bus and described her injuries. She muttered an apartment number and they muscled their way into the building and upstairs.

They should have just shot the guy when they first saw him. That's what Mulino had come to believe over the past twelve years. The door was open, the man was screaming incomprehensibly, and he was smashing everything in sight with a foot-long claw hammer. The television was in shards, there were dishes in tatters, about seven or eight good-sized gashes in the drywall. If they'd just pulled out their guns and opened fire, they would probably have been able to weather it.

But this was just after Louima, not long past Diallo, and people remembered Baez and the others too. So Ramsay, out of character, had taken it slow. He'd pulled out his pepper spray—they had just upgraded from the chemical mace to the pepper spray, and all the officers had been encouraged to use it. The mace interfered with the nervous system—someone on angel dust wouldn't even notice. Pepper spray swells the soft tissue of the eyes and throat. Even if you're drugged out, you can't do a thing if you can't see and you can't breathe. So after Ramsay had told the guy to stop, and instead he spun around with the hammer, Ramsay had let loose with the pepper spray. When the man went down, Ramsay had worked on cuffing him and Mulino had called in that they had one under and needed another ambulance too.

Months later, in the trial room, Mulino had done his best. He had said he didn't see Ramsay cuff the man; didn't see how he was sitting; had been watching the stairway for the paramedics the whole time. He didn't mention that Ramsay had pulled out a second set of cuffs and shoved the man's face into the ratty carpet. He had pretended he hadn't seen the knee to the back, the twisting of the neck. He had never heard the words positional asphyxia, and he figured that when the coroner came back and said there was cocaine in the man's blood that would be the end of it. But that wasn't the end of it. The paramedic had said that the man had been on his chest and rear-cuffed when they came, and somewhere in the Patrol Guide regulations on pepper spray it says you're supposed to turn someone onto his side, because the coughing and hacking caused by the pepper spray is indistinguishable from the coughing and hacking of suffocation.

So Mulino had done his best, but his best wasn't good enough. For another cop to ever trust you, you have to do more than simply pretend that you didn't see. You have to actively swear that the other guy did everything according to the book. The implicit promise, every time you roll up to the curb, shut down the sirens, and step out of the RMP, is that you will lie to the Grand Jury for the guy next to you. You may not like him, he may not like you, but if you don't both know that you will take a perjury charge before you let the other take a murder rap, then all bets are off. The only way to get through the job is with someone next to you who will give you his full support. And Mulino's mild lie about an averted gaze, when they snipped off Ramsay's badge and swiped his pension, was always considered by his fellow officers to be a betrayal.

"Detective Mulino, the chief is ready for you."

The knee still hurt as he stood up and made his way into the plumb office. Here were oak and teak and tasteful photographs on the walls of Chief Travis handing out plaques to men and women to remind them of their bravery and loyalty. He was in uniform—once you are promoted high enough, once they give you stars, it becomes a perk to wear the bag again. Anyone who can read the code written into the collar brass and buttons knows where you stand: whether you are a patrol officer forced into the uniform or whether you are a commander asserting your authority. Mulino had met the chief only once before, after the investigation in Ebbets Field. This guy remembered him too.

"Detective, I have some bad news for you. I wanted to let you know before you heard it from somewhere else. Evidence is sending its final inventory to DIMAC today from the shooting. Officer Rowson's gun was never recovered."

Mulino looked at the chairs fronting the chief's desk. His knee begged him to sit, but he hadn't been offered.

"I'm telling you just what I told the investigator, Chief. I saw the gun."

"I understand that. I wanted to let you know. As a courtesy. What they found on the ship."

Mulino bit his lip. He had been thinking, during three days of being shunned even by the guys at Property, if there couldn't be another answer. If some of the techs who had come on board didn't also know him. Didn't think that maybe this would be a good way to get payback on someone who didn't truly trust his fellow cops.

"I saw it in his hand and I saw it on the deck, Chief. You want to stop and consider what that might mean? What someone may have done?"

Chief Travis looked across the desk at the detective. Mulino could sense himself being evaluated. He could feel the pity spill forth. They probably had started on the job about the same time. And here was Travis with a white shirt and an oak desk, while Mulino couldn't even sit down without being invited. Travis was telling Mulino, as delicately and subtly as he could, that he simply didn't give a damn about him.

"I'm not handling the investigation, Detective. I'm just letting you know. If you think that the Harbor Patrol cops or the Evidence Control Unit improperly disposed of evidence, you can always go to IAB."

Mulino nodded. That would really seal his reputation. The detective who turned on his fellow cops, accusing them of setting him up because he couldn't be trusted to protect them. He'd try that and cold shoulders in Property would be the least of his problems; he could actually turn up dead.

"Is that all, Chief?"

"I just wanted to tell you in person. As a courtesy."

And that was his signal to leave. Turning on his good leg, leaving the door open for some subordinate to handle, Mulino made his way back toward the four flights of stairs and an afternoon by himself in the back room of Gold Street. Not, he thought, that anyone would miss him if he didn't show. He turned down one landing, then another. His knee was feeling a little better, to tell the truth. No one at the Department was going to check out whether he had been set up. No one at DIMAC cared if they got one corrupt cop or another; every badge was a trophy indistinguishable from every other. If he wanted to clear his name, he was going to have to do it himself.

CHAPTER NINE
THE STREET

The chair was too comfortable for Christine Davenport. A soft leather number designed to put you to sleep, to steal your edge. But she would never lose her edge, and she didn't like it when someone pretended it was possible. She had been waiting twenty minutes, and had long finished the very nice coffee poured by the absent man's secretary.

Making someone wait in your lobby is a weak person's way of showing that you are powerful. Letting them wait in your office alone, the papers on your blotter within reach, was only for a master. Go ahead, he seemed to be saying, step around the desk and see what's in my mail. No one is watching. The place isn't bugged. It's only that you will feel so weak and so small doing it. Davenport set her empty coffee on a convenient coaster and uncrossed her legs. She set the two slim binders she had been carrying with her on the desk. Davenport now had eighty-two documents to go over with the head of EHA Investments.

She stared past the empty desk through the floor-to-ceiling windows; nothing there but the glass wall of the next tower over, bright and shiny and meaningless. Even in daylight the harbor beyond was an oily cipher, a thick band of gray murk. It was a view, but it wasn't a top-dollar view. EHA Investments didn't have a panorama above the other buildings. No matter how he craned his neck, the man she was waiting for could never get a peek at the Statue of Liberty when he was tired of staring at how much money he made.

To the left of the desk, a broad empty space, maybe thirty wasted feet. Davenport knew that it was the empty space, not the fancy furniture, the designer coffee, or the view, that was the showpiece of the office. Real estate in Lower Manhattan still went for almost two grand a square foot. If you really wanted to show that you were somebody, you wanted to waste a decent chunk of it. To those in the know, a half-empty office spoke more than a Kandinsky on the wall. And Christine Davenport was always in the know.

She had pulled the slim batch of e-mails together over two days and talked through with the associate why she had picked them. He was still interested in the drugs, the scandals. She realized when she spoke with him that he hadn't even realized what they had found; she couldn't bring him along.

Sitting with the binders in front of her, the coffee cup long empty, Davenport realized what was off. The place was too quiet. The terminals in the trading floor behind her had all been staffed, and there had been men and a few women running from one to the other, chattering in low serious tones, but there was none of the tumult that Davenport was used to at these places. Then again, she thought, it had been almost fifteen years since she had done this work. Maybe the guys who ripped out their phone and shouted through the walls had all moved on to other industries. Or gone to jail.

She never heard him come in. She sensed he was already next to her and turned her head to see a regal haircut and a three-hundred-dollar tie. Two sets of manicured nails peeked out from the folds of a combed-wool suit. It was the height of summer but he was old-school. The voice was barely above a whisper.

"Ms. Davenport. I am so sorry to have kept you waiting."

Above the offset collar was a thin neck and a jaw that had been the pride of Tower Eating Club in 1964. The eyes were still dazzling: Davenport could tell she was being evaluated. Being judged. The man held out a wiry hand and Davenport stood and shook it. It was strong, but cold. The whole office was cool, and would stay that way through the heat wave. The natural-seeming light came from nearly undetectable sources. It was as though the whole room was a soft little experiment in making a place as unnervingly pleasant as it could be.

"I am at your service, Mr. Holm-Anderson."

"Well, you are charging by the hour, which is very close to the same thing."

The man rounded the corner of his desk and set himself in his college chair. Hard wood all around him. The chair, the desk, the bookcase against the other wall, the one without a view. All real wood and solid. Aside from the window itself, there was no nod to either of the twin fads of glass and steel. Aside from the view, you could have been in the 1950s. There was no computer on the desk. No phone. The 1850s, Davenport thought. He sat with his hands on his knees, his eyes sharp above sagging cheeks.

"Would you like to take a look at what we found?"

Davenport gestured to the binder. Usually, the big shots would be eager to thumb through it. Some of them wanted to get the documents in advance, to start the process of kicking out one miscreant or another, proving how attentive they were to whatever regulation had been broken. But the man just sat there, looking at Davenport and not acknowledging the binder. As though the vinyl was so modern as to be poisonous to the touch. He gave a hint of a nod and Davenport went on. She opened to the first set of tabs.

"There are a number of people at your firm who are engaging in extra-curricular activities frowned upon by law enforcement." These were the drug ones. Guys boasting about what they'd done over the weekend. How they'd spent the money that they hadn't really earned the week before. Holm-Anderson bit a corner of his lip and looked out the window.

"Am I boring you, Mr. Holm-Anderson?"

She could afford to push a little. She had an ace up her sleeve. You always had to start this way. You have to tell them everything. Even when it starts out with something they probably know. More importantly, though, Davenport was watching Mr. Holm-Anderson. When you see how they react to the little stuff, you get a sense of what's coming next.

He held up a schoolmarm hand. "I have been in this business for nearly fifty years, Ms. Davenport. I know what kind of people work here. If I could change human nature I would. I also know that FINRA and the US Attorney would laugh at me if I came to them and said that was all I had found."

"This is all in the spirit of full disclosure."

"Is there more?"

So she went on to the next batch. The guys who had bought up a few thousand shares of a software company two days before it announced a new product. An airline merger anticipated by about a week. The usual litter that suggests someone has a friend of a friend who is willing to whisper a little about something. Enough to revoke a couple of licenses.

But more than that were the shorts. The bets against companies that anticipated failure. One against a drug company days before a patent got invalidated. Another on a natural gas company in the Ukraine two weeks before a pipeline exploded. A short on a construction company the day before its crane had collapsed in Midtown Manhattan. The list went on—a Japanese fishing venture shorted just before it lost four boats in a typhoon, and a clothing label shorted a week before its shanty factory in Bangladesh collapsed. Then last week, a bet against an international freight company, the one that owned the ship Ralph Mulino had shot Brian Rowson on three days later.

Holm-Anderson looked up at these.

"The fund makes money any way that it can. Right now, things are sinking ever downward. Companies are falling. Public opinion is falling. We are as aware as everyone of what has been happening in the city these past few months."

"Mr. Holm-Anderson, there is a question of what people would think."

"We short companies on their way down and we might buy them on their way up. We might try to catch a falling knife or profit from a dead cat bounce; there is no shame in it."

"A what?"

He stopped staring at the numbers long enough to look up at her. His eyes were bright and attentive. "Anything that falls fast and far enough will come up off the ground when it hits. Should you throw a dead cat out a twenty-story window, even that will rebound a bit from the pavement. And when a miserable stock collapses from forty dollars to two, there will be money to be made on its way back up to six."

"But it will fall back down. Not just to two, to zero."

"It's all in the timing."

"You're in it for the short term."

"Everyone on the planet is in it for the short term, Ms. Davenport. The best anyone can hope for is a moment of joy before we sink back into the muck. Over the very long term, the target price for every stock is zero. There's nothing we can do to change that."

"But there is the question of whether they knew, Mr. Holm-Anderson. Whether they were tipped off."

"A typhoon in the East China Sea is public information."

"Let's look to the last set of e-mails."

Delicate and reluctant, he took the binder, licked his finger, and turned the tab. Davenport went on.

"You'll see there is no return address on these e-mails. And they aren't identified as being received by anyone at your firm. We had the vendor run analytics and they came up dry. No evidence of who the recipient was. Except that they are on your server. And all we have for the sender is the country. Yemen. Malaysia. Six from Indonesia. One from Syria. Does your company do any business in any of those places?"

"We talk to people all over the world. We are always researching."

"And you're writing in code like this?"

The e-mails themselves were the real problem. Someone has a few exchanges with someone in Yemen, it could be anything. There are plenty of legitimate reasons to e-mail Indonesia. But when the texts of the e-mails are nothing but slashes and dots, a collection of letters that don't make words, antennae go up. Writing that you think a drug company is going to lose its patent is one thing; writing that "q*--d/ <)dln @a-+ $Dn" is quite another. Davenport hadn't sent them out to be de-encrypted yet. She wanted to see his face when he saw them. To see if they were a surprise to him. But he gave away nothing. Quiet, intent, he could have been reading the phone book.

"What do we know about them?"

"Only where they came from. And that they landed here. It could be anyone at the firm. It could be more than one person." And she looked up, into the bright eyes, and thought, rather than spoke the final threat: *it could be you.*

When you set out on one of these investigations, you always hope you are going to find something, but that you are not going to find too much. Because if you uncover a rogue employee and you wrap him up and hand him to the company in a bow, you can take your check and walk away and everyone will be happy except the guy who has to go to jail. But when you find out that someone who is really in charge has strayed, it makes for a whole other ballgame. You want to know and you don't want to know. Because pretty soon you aren't sure whether you are working to protect them or turn them in any more. But you have to ask.

Eliot nodded. He looked down at the paper. "I can keep this copy?"

"Yes."

"I will think this over. Can I get back to you in a few days?"

"Sooner rather than later is best."

"I understand."

She turned and heeled to the door, silent over the plush carpet. Nothing was patched with tape here. She eyed the frosted office doors as she walked out along the too-quiet trading floor. Heavy masculine names, ringing with self-importance. And one woman's name, she paused a moment to see, Veronica Dean. As Davenport stopped, sensing a fellow soul in a rigid suit, she saw a figure behind the pane. A woman sitting with sure posture, typing rapidly, fixated on her terminal like a racecar driver on the road. *Nothing to see here. Move along.*

Davenport turned out through the trading floor to the elevator, worried that every set of eyes in the place had been staring at her on the way out. As the elevator swept her back down to safety, she caught her breath for what felt like the first time all day.

Eliot Holm-Anderson leaned back in his club chair and traced the e-mails. He looked back to the dates in the section before. The news was nothing more than he dealt with in an ordinary miserable week. Then he flipped once again between the coded e-mail and the short trades. He had caught something in them after all. He fished a pen from a drawer and marked the first of the series. He traced down again. He made another mark. When Davenport had first given him the binder he hadn't seen the pattern in the jumble of trades. He marked again. He was beginning to make sense of it. He turned the page back again. He noted again. It was undeniable what was there. That woman hadn't even realized what she had been carrying around with her. She hadn't connected the dots on her own investigation. He marked the final page. He set down the binder and turned toward the window, looking out into the inky harbor.

It was much worse than he had thought.

CHAPTER TEN

HARBOR PATROL

Detective Ralph Mulino made his way slowly down the switchback wooden staircase toward the Harbor Patrol. The stairway had been built fifty years ago for longshoremen and was showing its age. Never mind his knee; with each creak Mulino worried that the whole thing would collapse. He took a look back up to the street, his car protected, he hoped, by his union decal. This corner of Red Hook, where antique warehouses had been filled with knick-knack shops by eager developers during the boom, had fallen just as fast after. It was already getting so that if you left your car for half an hour you couldn't be exactly sure it would still have all four rims and the battery when you got back, even with the union decal. Maybe it was almost so bad that the union decal made you a target. The Red Hook Houses, once notorious, then stable, and now growing troubled again, were only a few blocks away. But the guys in Harbor didn't look up; the kids in the houses were not their concern. Mulino clattered down to the foot of the pier, walked past the tidy NYPD motorboats and toward the squat Quonset stationhouse that housed the Harbor Patrol command.

The typical NYPD command is loud and messy and filled with

unhappy neighbors waiting to file petty complaints and sleepy officers eager to take lunch. The floors of most precincts are speckled with dirt or blood or bile, and usually heavy doors seal off the public entryway from the cops' haven behind. Mulino's own quarters at OCCB had been a mishmash of pushpin boards advertising months-ago robberies and flurries of daily activity reports and UF-250s and bulletins that sergeants were supposed to read aloud at ten roll calls in a row but never did. When a witness or a victim came to the inner sanctum it would look as though everybody was working. But the Harbor Patrol didn't have the chance to get muddled by intruders, so the officers could keep it police-neat, staving off the squalor that most precincts had long since tired of fighting.

The station was spare and quiet and wide open—beyond a front podium, there were twelve prim desks topped with up-to-date terminals, staffed by young cops transferring their handwritten reports to some centralized database. Working the eight-to-four tour at Property, arriving at Harbor Patrol at quarter to five, Mulino hadn't expected to see Sergeant Sparks manning the fiefdom. But there he was, his collar brass orderly and his sharp jaw crisply shaved. Most precincts have a gate at the front, a clear physical barrier beyond which the rabble cannot go unless summoned. Here at Harbor there was only a blue line painted on the floor. Mulino wasn't the general public, but he hadn't exactly been invited.

"Sergeant, I thought you worked midnights."

"They gave me a promotion, how well I handled everything on Monday."

The NYPD schedule is broken into three eight-hour shifts. The eight-to-four is reserved for guys who have made their numbers or fixed their partners' paperwork or generally kissed their supervisor's ass and put in for daytime so they can get back to Nassau in time for the Yankees game to start. The four-to-twelve is when most of the actual crime happens, when people are off work and the sun is down, but they aren't asleep yet. It's for guys who want in on the action and are still looking upward at their next promotion. The midnight tours are for the hard-core meatheads who can't be trusted not to kill someone or let a new arrest walk out of the precinct. The guys they come across on the twelve-to-eights, it wouldn't matter that much anyway. Sparks had been dumped on midnights just like he'd been dumped on Harbor, and now he was basking in his move up the ranks.

"Good for you."

"You got some business here at Harbor I can help you with? Property doing on-site inspections now?"

Sparks couldn't have been more than twenty-eight, his hair gelled and his shoulders square. Mulino imagined him getting off work, going home to Staten Island, and getting free drinks at his local bar while the girls he went to high school with drew lots to get the chance to marry him. Sergeant by twenty-eight probably means captain by thirty-five, which means by the time his pension kicked in there would be a three-bedroom house in New Dorp and other such luxuries. His chest puffed out and his eyes already on the lieutenant's exam, Sparks wasn't unfriendly exactly, but he wasn't really asking Mulino if he could help him.

"As a matter of fact I'm here about the shooting."

"Not sure I'm supposed to talk to you about an open investigation, Detective."

Mulino looked past the sergeant to the aisle of quiet, uniformed officers, each pecking away at his terminal. None of them looked up, but both cops knew they were watching. The corners of a dozen pairs of eyes straining to see who was going to win this particular little pissing match, wondering whether their sergeant would give in to the detective or make him back down. Sparks was right, they all knew that the Patrol Guide instructions were to keep your mouth shut when anything was before IAB, DIMAC, the Inspector General. But they all also knew that the Patrol Guide went out the window when it came to protecting a fellow cop. Even the newbies, though, could see that Sparks and Mulino didn't consider themselves brothers-in-arms.

"You came up on the boat after, Sergeant."

Sparks looked to the floor. He would play along just enough. "I did hear a gunshot, Detective. I boarded the ship to provide assistance. I didn't know whether an officer had fired or had been shot. Or both."

"You knew Rowson."

"He worked out of this precinct. All these guys knew him. Most of them better than I did."

The clattering at keyboards slowed for a moment. Cops straining to hear. Mulino felt a cool lonely silence. He had been stripped of his gun when he was sent to Property. He was alone in a precinct with thirteen uniformed officers. He was a fellow cop but to some of them, maybe, he was just the guy who had shot their buddy. And if something happened to him, they would all have each others' backs.

"When you came on the scene, Sergeant, you saw Rowson's gun, didn't you."

Sparks took a tiny step forward. Still at his little podium now, guarding his blue entrance line, he spoke slowly, his blue eyes hard on Mulino. "You know, Detective, I really can't say. I got up to the deck and the ESU guys and the EMTs were there, and I saw that you were kneeling, and that someone had been shot. But really, I was pretty much in the back of the crowd. I can't say that I saw anything one way or the other."

It was a practiced speech. One that Mulino knew well. He had given it himself at Ramsay's trial. Sparks knew that. He was throwing it back in his face.

"The kid's locker is here?"

Sparks turned from his roost and walked to the row of lockers on the far wall. The officers kept their noses at their terminals. Mulino wasn't sure if they were really that devoted to their menial tasks or if they were simply terrified of their sergeant. He knew what it was like to be a junior cop, though, to hope that you could just be invisible while the storm passes by.

At the lockers, Sparks turned, his eyes fixed on Mulino's feet, checking to make sure he was behind the blue line. The detective was a civilian to him now. He fished a small key from his pocket and unlatched the cabinet, then reached into a cubbyhole like a magician proving his hat is truly empty.

"I didn't see it on the boat, Detective, but he didn't leave it here. And I'll be sure to tell the investigators and the evidence guys the same thing."

Mulino nodded. As Sparks turned back to the front of the precinct, Mulino scanned the row of rookies. There was one, near the back, trying a little too hard to look like he was working. It was cool in the station-house, but the kid had sweat on his temples, was breathing heavier than you'd think you'd need to sitting at a computer. A chubby face, short dark hair, sort of spacey eyes. Mulino looked down to the nameplate. Del Rio. He looked at the face again. The eyes. He thought maybe he remembered him from that night.

"Officer Del Rio. You came on board the boat after, too, didn't you? You were out there."

The kid gulped and looked up at his sergeant. The glassy eyes clouded over in confusion. Sparks didn't take his eyes off Mulino while he addressed Del Rio. "Officer, you don't answer that question or any other questions until you have permission from me to be released from duty."

Mulino smiled. "You get promoted up to four-to-twelves along with your sergeant, Officer? You do some exceptional work that night?"

Sparks had made it back to his perch at the entrance to the precinct and nudged Mulino toward the door without ever touching him. "I am happy to chat with you a little off the record, Detective. I can handle it. But you don't need to bring my men into this."

"I'm sure you can spare Officer Del Rio from his World of Warcraft league or whatever it is you have these guys doing."

"That's going to be all, Detective."

"Officer Del Rio, you saw Rowson's gun, didn't you? Or are you the one who tossed it off the boat?"

In retrospect it was a bad idea to walk past Sergeant Sparks, but Mulino wanted an answer from Del Rio before the sergeant could coach him. But before the detective was a foot past the blue line, Sergeant Sparks had grabbed his left arm, twisted it to the side, and flipped and pinned him to the ground. Mulino's shoulder ached with pain, but he could feel the sergeant easing up on him. Sparks was not going to pour the pressure on. He was a fellow cop, after all. The sergeant loosened his grip and Mulino snapped his arm free, twisted himself out and sprang to his feet. In the moment, he could always summon the energy back, if it came to it.

He stared down the sergeant, ready to have it out. Mulino could see the recognition in Sparks's face, could see that he knew Mulino was faster and stronger than he looked. That Mulino had probably been on the force long enough to have gotten in a couple of scraps with other cops, and knew how these things went. Mulino knew that Sparks didn't want to risk losing a fistfight on the floor of his own command.

But Mulino knew something else as well. He was a detective under investigation. He didn't have his weapon. He wasn't supposed to be in this precinct at all. If it came down to it, an incident report showing that he'd even been here could be the end of his pension, however the shooting case went down. He backed off behind the blue line. The standoff was over. He nodded to Sparks.

"Thanks for talking to me, Sergeant. I appreciate it. And Officer Del Rio, you think that over. I'm sure someone else will be talking to you soon enough."

"Goodbye, Detective."

Officer Joey Del Rio looked down at his computer. Mulino watched a single drop of sweat spill out onto his keyboard. He backed out of the precinct, his eyes locked on the sergeant's the whole way.

Standing at the lip of the curb overhanging the waterfront, Leonard watched the detective amble up the dock toward the stairs. Mulino had been in and out of the precinct in ten minutes. Still, that was plenty of time to cook up a story with Sparks. No one really got a rip for talking to another cop during a shooting investigation: you weren't supposed to do it, but with the forty-eight hour rule and the tight bonds of blue, there was no way to stop them. And if you forwarded a case to the DA saying you couldn't find evidence of a bad shooting but you could show that the guys had spoken to each other, it wasn't as though they were going to bring charges for witness tampering.

But on another level, it didn't make that much sense. It wasn't Mulino's story that was a problem, and Sparks hadn't shown up on the deck until after the shooting. Mulino's problem was the evidence. Mulino's problem was that he'd said that Brian Rowson had a gun, and as Leonard had learned when the full packet had come in just after lunch, no gun had been recovered. It had been enough to send Leonard into the field, and watching Mulino hail a car service on Gold Street had been enough for him to try an impromptu stakeout.

Mulino stopped at the base of the rickety staircase. Leonard ducked back behind the railing. He could explain himself if he had to, but better just to leave. There was nothing more to see, just a middle-aged man struggling up a couple of flights of stairs. Whatever he had wanted to see had gone on inside the precinct. A search for the missing gun. A hunt for a suitable replacement. The dead cop was already dead. The living cop was still a brother. If the sergeant still had Mulino's back, then the next day Leonard would get a fax with a statement about seeing the gun, how it slipped into the water. Or better yet the gun would appear itself.

If nothing came from the precinct though, even after an in-person from the detective, then that meant that they didn't have his back. That they didn't see him as worth protecting. And that was its own kind of mystery. Leonard slipped into the car he had borrowed for the night from the city, lurched forward into the wicked heat, and turned toward home.

CHAPTER ELEVEN

SHORTS

The numbers streamed past on the terminal, blinking and changing faster than Veronica Dean could keep track of them. Mineral deposits in Asia, recycling plants in New Jersey, a reinsurance company in the City of London. Ten years ago she had kept a tight watch on a few sectors, but as things had gone to hell and back she needed to keep both eyes open. Once upon a time she'd actually gone out to see the companies. Visiting gold mines in Indonesia, impressing the hardened prospectors by not flinching when she was bitten by a bug the size of a sparrow. Standing shin-deep in mud and whipping out a flip phone to tell New York that the reported core samples were all a fraud, that the operation itself was one big swindle, and thereby getting out of the scandal before any of the big investors. Not to mention that she'd made it back to the airport alive after telling the man with a machete that she was on to him and that her investors would be pulling their funding that very day. She was remembering it wrong, maybe. The mud couldn't have been much past her ankles. Still, nowadays she wouldn't even float down to the sidewalks for lunch; the days were spent pacing the pristine carpet and looking out the floor-to-ceiling windows from Wall Street to the two bridges and Brooklyn beyond. A trace of mud was unthinkable.

She had sensed something about the woman who had looked in this morning. Dull. Severe. Some sort of prosecutor or regulator or lawyer coming by to slap Eliot very gently on the wrist and pick up complimentary tickets to the opera, no doubt. There had been enough of them through the oak office over the past few years. Enough at first that Veronica had dared to hope. That maybe someone would find out and then the whole mess would be over. She would be able to speak up. But each one left with a smile and a backslap, leaving Veronica locked down in her own little terror. Speaking up would only make it worse.

Veronica never went into the field any more. She visited her companies over the wires, occasionally calling in reinforcements on the ground, eager apprentices that someday hoped to wield her power. They would fly off to remote mines and villages to stomp around and report back on the facts behind the rumors of foreign speculators. Even these kids had it easier than she did; they could use their digital toys to call in a videoconference at a moment's notice. When she had hit the trails it had been without 3G, without a satellite phone, just her and the toothy man who told her that he had found real gold and dared her to call him a liar.

She was watching one number as it flashed by. Every few seconds a little bit lower. She would have to time it just right. From twenty-two to eighteen, to seventeen, to fourteen. The panic was under way. Panic was something that Veronica understood. Panic was different than fear. Fear would gnaw slowly, cloud your judgment, lead you to do something you knew you shouldn't. Panic was clear and straightforward and meaningful.

Together, all of the prices flowed into unfathomable noise. But if you could pull out one stream of numbers, keyed to one price, and you knew that price's final destination, that was when everything was worth it. She had been watching the news for the past two years as much as anyone. She knew that all was not right with the newly reborn metropolis. It was easy to point to a host of villains—and Veronica knew that as a speculator on the eighteenth story of a Wall Street office, she was everyone's idea of a villain in the new regime. She thought she was part of the solution, or that she could be, if she could come out from underneath the fear. If only someone could give her a chance to explain. The number dipped again.

Little downfalls might be terribly sad for the people involved with them, but for Veronica they were just another opportunity to turn a quick profit. The toothy man with the machete, when his gold mining fraud had been exposed, had jumped out of a helicopter as it surveyed his ruined fortune from a height of eight hundred feet. It wasn't Veronica who'd killed him, she reasoned. She had only let a gullible world know that he had been lying. His own deceit had been his cause of death.

The numbers were dropping further. Twelve, then a huge jump to nine. At seven and a half, it was almost down to a third of the price it had been less than an hour ago. Veronica smiled and leaned into her terminal. There would never be mud on her shoes again. It was time to make some money.

She didn't hear him come into her office. You never do. Eliot's soft pale face barely registered. He always floated in silently, awash in expensive clothing and designer accessories, taking in the world he had built.

"All right."

He was holding a thin vinyl binder, crisp tabs taunting her from it. It looked unusual on him. She had never seen him touch a computer or a telephone. The dull facts of the tabs, the binder, the paper, jarred against his gentle fingers.

"When you have a moment, I'd like to talk to you about some of these."

She looked up. She knew it was a mistake as soon as she'd done it. He had marked up the pages. With a pen, maybe even the calligraphic one he kept on his desk that looked ceremonial. She couldn't tell anything from the markings but she turned her face back to the computer as quickly as she could, hoping he hadn't noticed her fear. This is how they do it. They find a fall guy. Nothing to see here, just another corpse out the window. So if you have to, take action first. Hit back before they even hit you. It wasn't so much about what Eliot knew about her, but what she knew about Eliot.

But don't give any indication. She squinted at her machine, feigning confusion. "Sure. I'm busy until close-of-market on this, but tomorrow morning?"

"That would be fine." He tucked the binder under his sleeve and pirouetted back toward his office, shutting out the howl of the modern machines that worked so hard to bring him so much.

Veronica noticed a single pulse of sweat wriggling down her temple, past her cheekbone and on to her chin. She didn't deserve to be afraid. She had done everything right. No one she had met in the corridors of power was as frightening as the man she had stood down in the mud eight years ago. But deserve it or not, she was afraid.

And she knew why too. She carried all the fear because she was carrying all the risk. It had started so simply, it had been so easy, it had gone so well. But it's the easy ones that hook you. The first one is always free. And before you know how deep you are into it, you cannot turn around.

The droplet skidded off of her chin and onto her desk. It seemed out of place in the dull meaningless office. Too much life. Veronica had never had so much as a plant on the windowsill or a photograph of a pet. The office was angular and anonymous and if she didn't come in one day, they wouldn't need to change anything more than the name on her door. And that day was coming, one way or the other. She knew that much, as her eyes locked in on the machine.

Veronica reached to whisk away the sweat with a tissue and tossed it into her pristine wastebasket. Under the muffled hum of the machine, she gave a short soft sob. She had always been afraid, and she still was. But for the first time in a long while, she was no longer in doubt. She knew what would happen next. She turned back to the demanding hum of her terminal. It would all be over soon.

CHAPTER TWELVE
LEAKS

Tony Licata sweated past the plaza and up the steps to City Hall. When they ask to talk to you at night, you have to go. It won't do to pick up the phone. Licata had always walked to get his stories. When he had started, it had been the only way. He'd been assigned to courts, which meant the first stop each day was the clerk's desk at Manhattan State Supreme to read the filings from the night before. Nothing hits the wood like a lawsuit. One girlfriend suing to get back jewelry that her married boyfriend had given to another girl he was dating. A Queens shoe salesman suing his pediatrician for making the moves on the daughter. You need sex, money, and a certain ick factor that people think they don't want to hear about. But people don't really know what they want to hear about.

Licata would read the filings and tart them up for scandal. Every aggrieved widow desperate. Every girlfriend a starlet in the making; if you find a way to suggest she was a stripper, even better. And every target a Wall Street big shot—you could bust out the dollar signs in the headlines so long as the guy had some kind of connection to finance, even if the closest he came to the big time was manning the residential mortgage servicing desk at the Bank of Nova Scotia.

Now the filings were all online, and most of the shops hired some law-school dropout to read them all at nine o'clock and flag any that the paper could use. The kids didn't understand what made a story worthwhile, so Licata never read what they sent out anyway. They loved rock stars getting arraigned for not paying child support. That's never front page. None of them had read a tabloid a day in their lives before working at one. Licata had moved on to crime, the city desk, but he kept one of the clerks at Manhattan State Supreme on his payroll just in case. They knew their own dockets better than the kids did anyway. Fifty bucks for anything that makes it in the paper. Two-fifty if it hits the wood. Licata could track down the angry plaintiffs and explain that, by cooperating, their case would be worth a lot more money. Bring a photographer if the woman is the least bit attractive. Licata still got a court byline once a month on average. As often as not, they were cases that the kid working for the paper had missed.

But the courts beat was just a side gig to him now, a way to get himself a little extra juice when leaning on frustrated detectives or ambitious deputy commissioners. Information in city government was usually a buyer's market. Or it always had been. The price of paperwork was usually a hearty meal and a couple of rounds at the Blarney Stone. Tony knew which detectives at IAB could be counted on to photocopy their closing reports and slip them under the table while telling raucous stories of locker room antics. Guys who'd been passed over for narcotics or homicide teams and took their revenge on the whole department for sticking them in Internal Affairs. But that was before e-mail, before cell phones, before the department could call a service provider and find out who every detective had spoken to over the past six months. You so much as call an IAB detective and leave a message nowadays and your editor gets a call back from his lieutenant. Guys knew they were being watched: even their print jobs were logged and tallied. It was too much of a risk for a cop to walk out with a stack of papers under his arm nowadays.

So in twenty years Licata had slowly been pushed to the outside. Once upon a time, if one cop had shot another, Licata would get a call from a friendly source and be standing at the scene before the EMTs had swept away the body, taking off-the-record statements from the lead detective. Now he was stuck in line with the cub reporters, trying to put the best spin he could on the dead statements released by the Deputy Commissioner for Public Information. And in that game he was behind the cubs, who thought journalism was about taking whatever information the public officials deigned to release and adding their own clever comments. Kids took press releases and mocked them up on their blogs and said they were journalists. Licata still thought that the purpose of being a reporter was to report—to get information that no one else had access to and disseminate it. But he knew he was falling behind. In the digital age, the information market favored the seller after all. And when the seller called you, you had better show up.

Which was why Tony Licata was hiking up the broad stone stairway into City Hall after sunset. His daily copy was filed; he ordinarily would have been at the Blarney Stone telling a few stories about the good old days himself. Tonight he was all ears.

There was no guard at the front desk; security was set at the perimeter and anyone who made it as far as the plaza was presumed safe to head into the building itself. Licata passed the swinging wooden gate that led to the prim ceremonial Blue Room on his left, like saloon doors you had to pass through on your way to every press conference. But he wasn't going to a presser today; he swung up the marble staircase to the official offices. The hub of the biggest city in the country and you'd think that somewhere there would be an elevator. At the top, he turned left, away from the City Council chambers and toward the executive suite.

The new administration had swept out the old bullpen and re-established the hierarchy of executive administration. No more sea of cubicles for even the most senior officers and the mayor himself; the new progressives insisted on the trappings of authority. Sturdy cherry doors now closed off the populists from the world they promised they were bettering. Tony Licata stepped through the empty antechamber and toward a door left just a smidgeon open, decked with a trim chrome nameplate: Deputy Mayor Victor Ells.

One knock was enough. "Is that you, Tony? Come on in."

Licata pushed open the door and saw Ells posturing behind his desk. A broad man with a politician's smile that you couldn't help but believe even if you knew it was fake. The casually rumpled suit that signaled he was always hard at work, and smooth silver hair—hair that looked as though it had been ironed and pressed. From the beginning, this man had always seemed to be as much in charge as his boss. He had nothing to say from behind a podium, he didn't deliver speeches or even get mentioned in them, but when deputy commissioners needed to quietly resign, it was a call from Ells that would make it happen. The rest of the floor was empty. Even at the highest levels of power, city employees get to go home to their families at some point. Licata stepped inside and took a seat.

"I'm glad you could come by and talk to me."

"Yeah, well it's been a pretty dry week. Only a cop shooting a cop and your office of misconduct is walled up on it."

"I thought they were going to move you over to Sanitation. You could cover the strike."

It was Ells's way of showing that he had sources too. Just that morning Licata's editor had floated the idea of him moving off of the police desk and covering Sanitation. A great gig for the next two weeks if they end up striking. Then you're stuck the rest of your life reporting on whether the snowplows came out on time or not.

"They haven't hung me up just yet. Maybe they never will. If I come in with something worth their while."

"That's right. Give me the hard sell. I invited you here, after all."

Licata always found out the terms up front. When a deputy mayor has a secret, the price is higher than a round of Killian's. "What are you looking for me to do?"

Ells slid a small stapled packet across his desk. "That's Detective Mulino's statement. He didn't know the color of the day. He says he saw a gun, but you know they didn't find one. He was bumbling his way through the whole thing."

Licata didn't reach for the paper. Touching it would mean accepting the terms, and he hadn't been given any terms yet. "And what do you need?"

It was the deputy mayor's turn to lean out, to take in the room. He had a broad smile and a sharp pair of eyes and if he didn't look much like a natural politician, he looked like a natural leader. "You're going to want to sit on this too. You know there have been some rumors that my boss might be hanging it up after the one term. With the little disasters, the crime. It may just be too much for him. I just want you to remember, when the time comes for the right person to make an announcement, who has helped you out along the way."

So, he could get the confidential file from a deputy mayor so long as he promised to puff that deputy mayor up when he took the next step and announced he was running. There were worse things. If Ells won, after all, then Licata would be in a position to get strategic leaks directly from City Hall. Ells knew that, of course. It was all part of the bargain.

"I can live with that."

"I knew you could."

Licata reached across the desk to pick up the file. Ells smiled. The deal was struck.

CHAPTER THIRTEEN
THE CORNER

It woke her sometime after two, thick chemical smoke that stung Christine Davenport's eyes. She sat up in bed. She could barely see through the room. There was no fire, just brutal, mean smoke, smoke that wasn't from burning wood or paper. It reminded her of the smell made when she had melted the sippy cups by leaving them too close to the stove. Her husband was asleep beside her. He barely rolled over. Davenport sprung out of bed and ran to the boy's room.

She turned the corner into the room that wasn't really built as a bedroom. The boy was sleeping, as oblivious to the smoke as his father. She twisted him up to sitting and he blinked awake. It wasn't as though they couldn't breathe, and she couldn't see any actual fire. By this time her husband was standing at the door, waving his hand back and forth like that would do any good. She hefted the boy up, half onto her shoulder. As she turned from the miniature bedroom she saw that the smoke was chugging in from outside. They had left the window facing Perry Street open and something below was burning. Hoisting the boy, she turned to her husband.

"Can you go close that? And check why the alarms didn't go off."

The boy, groggy, swept his head from her neck to her shoulder. There was no danger now, maybe, but she still wanted to get out of the apartment. You never can tell.

"Mommy?"

"Shh. We're going downstairs. We're going to see what's going on."

"What's that smell?"

"Shh."

"Can I have some milk?"

They moved in slow motion, Adam struggling to shut the window and Davenport screwing a lid onto the cup of milk. She tied a pair of proper shoes on Henry and stepped into a pair of slippers herself. They were on the sixth floor. Never use the elevator in a fire. But there wasn't a fire in the building as far as they knew. Still better to be safe. She slipped down the broad stairwell, carrying the boy, her husband trailing.

In the stairwell, safely away from the smoke, she gathered her thoughts and she held her son's hand. The panic was over. Her thoughts drifted back to the worry she had suffered all afternoon. She hadn't been able to read Eliot. Usually, when the tables turned, you knew right away. Once-eager executives suddenly coy, asking immediately if all of this is really necessary. But the man in the wool suit in summer had taken the news quietly. Maybe he had something to hide. Maybe he knew who did. It was something more than walking a midlevel trader over to the feds, but Davenport couldn't tell how much more. That's why she had taken the precautions that afternoon. A place to secure everything she had found so far. To preserve it. Just in case.

By the third floor Henry was up and walking on his own, one hand in his mother's and the other gripping the milk. Their clothes smelled. The entire apartment would have to be cleaned. Another expense. The sleepy overnight doorman was more alert than Davenport had ever seen him as she tugged her son out toward the street. As soon as they turned from the desk toward the exit, they were silenced by the heat and the sound of it.

In front of their building, right below their corner window, a car raged with flame, spitting out the acrid smoke and those thick, slimy wisps that slither off of things that aren't supposed to burn but are nevertheless burning. A twenty-year-old Volvo, car seat in the back. It was instantly recognizable to Christine Davenport. Some sort of liquid, leaking from deep within the skeleton of the machine, dribbled down the street, afire the whole time. Henry's eyes widened at the scene. Adam's eyes traced the smoke as it drifted up through the neighborhood trees into their window, and turned to Christine.

"Chris, that's . . ."

She had the boy in her arms and was already out the front door.

"C'mon. Let's go look at the fire."

There were two uniform cops standing by the front of the wreckage, trying to shoo off sightseers and keep what little traffic was still on the streets to a minimum. It was late, dark, but Davenport hadn't looked at a clock before leaving. She stared at the blistering upholstery, the plastic curling away from her son's car seat through the window. She tried to remember if anything valuable had been left inside. Not that she would reach in to get it now. Even in the vestibule, beyond the door, she could feel the heat. There was no sign of a crash; just the smoking wreck of what once was her car. Carrying her boy, Davenport pressed through the window and walked up to the cop, who gestured to move along.

"That's my car. The smoke woke us up. What happened?"

The cop looked to his partner. The partner smirked, and Davenport sensed he looked a little too happy given the circumstance. "It's her car. You may as well."

The cop scowled at the burning car. "Some animal tried to appropriate the vehicle. Apparently he left his hot-wiring skills back in Brownsville and couldn't get it to start." The cop shrugged. "So he figures that if he douses the whole thing with gasoline we won't find his fingerprints. Genius that he is, he manages to trap himself inside after setting the fire. We have him in the ICU. You gotta tell the insurance we're keeping the car as evidence."

"Oh. Okay. Thank you."

So that was that. The car thieves were on their way back. Some of them were just smart enough to try to conceal their tracks and just dumb enough to almost kill themselves in the process. No one could keep the rush of the real New York from seeping back in somewhere. Davenport nodded to the cops and turned back to her building. Henry's bright brown eyes kept fast on the flames. Her husband had already started his way upstairs, and Davenport walked her son back inside, the last defense from the outside world, and felt safe taking the elevator back to her apartment.

As the smoke emptied from the apartment, Christine set the boy down back in his toddler bed, his smile drifting away as his body gave in to sleep. She sat with him for a moment. She could protect him if it came to that. Maybe she'd take him for an afternoon at the playground sometime. She stroked his hair, stood up, and walked back into the living room. Adam was still uselessly waving at what was left of the smoke when she spoke to him.

"We have to tell the insurance company that they're impounding it."

Her husband too seemed perhaps not concerned enough. "It's okay. It was old. I hope they even give us enough to get another." The car was no use to Davenport after all. It was her husband who drove, on the three days a week that he had to be in New Jersey, living the academic dream of the musty, thoughtful man in a frumpy old car. Maybe he was hoping for another clunker to replace it. He would probably be ashamed to drive something more modern.

She walked past him and set up a fan in the window. Set to exhaust, it wouldn't do much, but it was better than swinging your arm at it. Her husband slipped around the corner from the window and into the real bedroom. Not that it was much bigger than the too-small bedroom. You could fit a bed in it anyway. The smoke was clearing, but the smell still lingered, stark, acrid. A hint of fear in it. Adam called faintly from the bed as Davenport watched the smoke clear. "Are you coming to bed?"

Davenport sat on the sill, looking downward. "Just a minute." She stared out at the melting car, the plastic now burnt away and the metal husk glowing with heat. It was a magic, throbbing sight. A bright-pink skeleton surrounded by quicksilver fire on an otherwise ordinary street. She couldn't turn away from it; the tires popped one by one and the chassis slumped to the asphalt.

Then she looked up and down the street and felt suddenly cold. Two cars down from her burning wreck was a sleek, black SUV. The car after that was an S-Class. The whole block was peppered with luxury automobiles and here she was supposed to believe that the neighborhood car thief had targeted a battered Volvo with an odometer in the high one-fifties.

She stared out at the two uniform cops keeping guard, watching the car melt away. They had been there before the fire department. According to them, a man had been pulled out of the car and taken to the hospital, but no ambulance siren had woken her up. From below, one of the cops saw her looking at him and stared back, offering a firm quiet stare and a thin smile.

The Little Fear hadn't come back after all. This was the real thing. Or at least it was a warning. The real thing wouldn't be only the smell. Whoever it was knew where she lived. Knew her car. Knew she had a son. She slipped into Henry's room and started packing a bag. Her husband's parents were in New Jersey, they could stay there. Cut down on his commute, now that he didn't have a car anyway. Take the first bus in the morning. See if it was too late to enroll the boy in school out there. The boy would miss the last week of camp, another expense down the drain, but now very much worth it. There was no point in waking Adam or Henry, they were useless at packing themselves up anyway. She would stay up, have them ready, shuttle them off to the suburbs until the danger had passed. She would stay behind and finish what she needed to do. She turned to the bathroom and started to peel out her son's necessities, neatly filing away the toothbrush, comb, and soap into tidy plastic bins, planning her own next move as she packed for her careless boys.

The night was just beginning.

CHAPTER FOURTEEN
WARRANTS

It had all finally come in. Bankers' boxes, binders, spools of illegible dot-matrix splatter. Every scrap of paper that the New York Police Department had ever collected on Ralph Mulino, Brian Rowson, or any officer on the scene that night had been dumped somewhere in Leonard's office. At least he had taken over the commissioner's suite, so there was a conference table to smear it over. No one would be having a conference there for a while. From the table, the files metastasized across the chairs, the floor, the shelves. The whole room seemed to be pasted with a thin flutter of paper. You couldn't even see how dirty the rug was.

Leonard had started his way through the mess, but he already knew the most important part. He knew what he wasn't going to find. There was no photograph, no daily activity report, no memo book, no inventory log, no evidence of any kind that Brian Rowson was holding a gun when Mulino shot him. Leonard would have to do interviews for that. He had already scheduled the sergeant to come in the next day. There were some techs coming in, but they would stick to the script. Exactly what was in their written report but no more.

He had already found one thing, though. Mulino had been in the trial room before. Over a decade ago. Leonard reminded himself to put in a call to the trial room to always make sure they give him everything on the subject officer before the interview. He shouldn't have had to wait for this. Leonard had chuckled when he read it. The whole thing had happened in the Ebbets Field Apartments. His own building now. A few floors below him, recent enough that people would remember. But even ten years ago it was a different world, a different building, a different kind of fear in the hallways.

Mulino had been a witness to a higher-ranking officer who had botched an arrest and killed a guy in the process of pepper spraying him. Give the old-school guys new toys and someone is likely to wind up dead. There are pretty clear instructions on the back of the canister of the spray about how you're supposed to treat someone when you douse them. But old-school guys don't read the instructions on the canister. Fortunate, Leonard thought, that Mulino kept his revolver. No telling how many people he would have killed with the nine.

But a funny thing about that old case. Mulino got a decent rip, a couple of weeks' suspension, and he basically kept his mouth shut. He had offered no evidence whatsoever that could help the DA, even though he had to have seen exactly what was going on as Ramsay sprayed and tackled and cuffed the big guy, and then probably kicked him and twisted his neck to boot. The PD usually rewards that kind of silence. They close the wagons and make life a little easier for you. But no one had made anything easier for Mulino. No promotion to a task force, no comfortable desk at 1PP. Just wake up every day and hit the streets.

The scoop on Mulino and the color of the day had been on page three of the *Daily News*. Leonard was glad that Ells had done him that favor. Keep a little pressure on the case. Prep the city for a finding. The detective was sloppy, he hadn't been paying attention, he saw something he thought was a gun. In this environment, no one would raise a stink. The police unions wouldn't hold a march across a bridge in solidarity. They were becoming cowed by the new administration themselves. Leonard turned to the files on the other officers, picking apart their histories. He wanted to be sure on Mulino; he wouldn't draft his conclusions until after another half-dozen interviews and after every piece of paper in this office had been scoured. And he maybe felt bad for the guy. Maybe it wasn't Mulino's fault that he had stayed on the force a little bit long and lost a step along the way. But if Leonard was going to prove himself to Ells and the guys above him, he was going to have to bring in a trophy sooner or later, so he couldn't avoid the one that was tied up on his desk with a bow.

After Rowson's brush with IAB, he had been swept clean and parked at Harbor. And as soon as Leonard opened the files piled around his office he had found more. The command was full of them. Guys who avoided the trial room after reaching into someone's throat for a piece of gum they mistook for a glassine envelope. Guys who had shown their badge one too many times at a bar that didn't think it had to give every cop in town free drinks. One guy who fronted the money on a drug buy and swore up and down the kid had pulled out a box cutter on him, the box cutter never found. All of these guys had been cleaned up and shipped to Harbor to work for Sergeant Sparks. Not a peep from any of them since.

Sergeant Sparks. His history was baffling enough, as well. Until about eighteen months ago, Sparks had leapt wildly through the ranks, had received all the badges and pins that his superiors could throw at him. He had the highest score on the sergeant's exam of his class, not to mention higher arrest totals and a near-perfect physical exam. And then out of nowhere he had been sent off to Harbor. Unlike the rest of them, there wasn't any trip to the trial room or DIMAC or IAB or any of the dozens of agencies assigned to tweak NYPD officers first. Just a sudden detour to a forgotten command, and then radio silence for close to two years.

Maybe someone thought Sparks was good for the troubled kids. The Harbor Patrol was being used as a kind of rubber room to see if Sparks could whip the bad eggs back into shape, or at the very least keep them where they couldn't hurt anyone. But that didn't explain Sparks himself. You don't give up your chance to march through promotions in the Patrol Services Bureau to supervise a bunch of screwups in Harbor without getting something back for it. Maybe he had wanted to go. Maybe Sparks had done something wrong, but had impressed his bosses so much since that they'd just slipped it right out of his file. They were just pieces of paper in a cabinet after all. Whatever had happened, there was a big gaping *why* gnawing beneath.

The office was big, but it was hot and the air conditioning was worse than usual. Leonard unlatched the big semicircular window overlooking West Street and tugged at it. Nothing. Probably had been painted shut decades ago. He gave it another push, his palm on the glass. It wasn't moving. He could sense that he wasn't alone. He was in charge now, for the time being, and had to put up with the civil service lifers floating around him. He let go of the window and turned around.

"What can I do for you, Detective?"

The guy at the door wasn't wearing a badge or a uniform, but with some guys you can just tell. The jacket that doesn't quite go with the pants. The pants that were bought two belt sizes ago. The twenty-dollar haircut that he spent half an hour trying to make look nice for the occasion. Behind him, an obvious lackey. They come in pairs.

"Yeah, Leonard Mitchell? DIMAC commissioner?"

"Acting commissioner. I'm kind of busy." Across the floor, the desk, the table, all confidential NYPD documents. If the guy tried to come in the room, Leonard would really have to ask for ID. The man gestured to himself and the one over his shoulder at once.

"Detective Harrison. And this is Officer Ricci. He's with Warrants?"

Police are used to showing up and telling you what to do. When they start off by asking questions, or worse yet, introducing themselves with a question, it's never good. Usually it means they've been sent to you under duress, to run some menial assignment they think is beneath them. Or they are delivering bad news. Or both.

There was another person behind Harrison. A lanky uniform guy barely twenty years old, his face still red from teenage acne. Over six feet tall but would fall on his face if the big one slapped him on the back. Five years of eating like a cop would cure that. The NYPD does not settle for donuts, what with the junk food of the world on every corner. It feasts instead on Jamaican beef patties, General Tso's chicken, Cubano sandwiches, and Dominican pork knuckles. The kid would beef up soon enough. Shy too, standing tentative at the office doorway, afraid maybe he'd get a shock if he stepped in front of the detective.

"Warrants, huh." Leonard looked over the skinny kid. Maybe he was assigned there, but he wasn't with them. Warrants officers started their day at four, ferreting out guys who had skipped their arraignments. One guy would stand at the front door of an apartment and pound the hell out of it while the partner stood behind the building looking at the fire escape, waiting for a panicked criminal to jump out in his skivvies so they could cart him back before the judge. When you put in for warrants, the first thing they test you for is if you can scale an eight-foot fence in a second and a half. The kid may have passed that one, but Leonard didn't have much hope for his prospects.

"I hate to intrude on you and I know the situation is . . . sensitive." The detective had that slow, fumbling way of trying to sound like he cared. It came off like he was sleepwalking through his job until the matinee started at Shea. "But I'm here to show you this."

The detective pulled out a piece of paper that had been folded, folded again, and then crumpled into his suit coat. Leonard smoothed it up against the office wall. It was a search warrant. From what Leonard could tell, it had been hustled together at six that morning; the NYPD must have wrangled a judge out of bed to sign it. The place to be searched: the offices of the Commissioner to Investigate Misconduct and Corruption. The items to be seized: relevant evidence. Leonard laughed at the last part.

"Relevant evidence? That's rich." He would call the Law Department if he had to. Officers were not going to ransack his offices based on a shaky warrant.

"You can see it's from missing persons." Leonard looked at the bottom of the warrant. So it was. Detective Harrison gained speed. "I didn't want to tell you like this. Your ex-boss has gone missing. Yesterday morning about five o'clock, she told her husband and her kid all in a panic they had to leave the city. We've spoken to them. They said she was extremely agitated. She put them on a bus and then she disappeared. No word from her cell. No one at home. We got video of her getting on the Staten Island ferry at six eighteen last night. We got nothing of her getting off at the other end."

Leonard felt suddenly sick. A twist in his stomach, as though he had eaten something that had come back to life and was struggling to find its way out. This wasn't a teenage runaway case, the cops waiting forty-eight hours to make sure the kid wasn't coming home before they started looking. Leonard had his own problems with Davenport, leaving him stranded at DIMAC and in the crosshairs of the administration. And he hadn't spoken to her since she'd left. He pulled himself up and looked at the detective.

"Why are you on this? Why send warrants? Why not send in missing persons?"

"Like I told you, Officer Ricci is warrants. I'm homicide."

With that, Harrison was already in the office, slipping on a pair of plastic gloves. And suddenly the place was full of them. Rookie cops carrying plastic bags, pretending that the ephemera they were itemizing could be dusted for fingerprints. Guys who had joined the police force after taking sixteen credits of forensic science at John Jay, who barely knew that the technology they saw on television was mainly fake. That a fingerprint isn't going to come up unless the person had been pressing their hand against polished glass or lacquered wood while sweating, that hair doesn't carry DNA, and that luminol picks up about fifty substances besides blood.

The way most murders get solved is that an aggressive detective corners the dead guy's most suspicious friend and badgers him until he confesses. The physical evidence is mainly just for show. Leonard shirked against the wall watching the carnival, the mountains of plastic baggies being stuffed with worthless junk, the papers he had been so looking forward to reading being trampled, the desk being rifled through. He watched the cops load up dozens of file folders and notepads into official-looking cartons. One cop stood dusting the windowsill. The one that Leonard had just tried to yank open for a bit of fresh air, on which he'd probably put his palm right up against the glass. The cop kept at it. If he noticed Leonard watching him, he didn't let on.

Leonard could tell that the whole search was only theater. If Davenport had been murdered in the office, the police would know it by now, and if she hadn't, there wouldn't be anything worth finding. Most people don't hide evidence of the crimes that they are about to commit in their desks. Most people who get kidnapped or murdered don't know in advance. They don't leave clues on their bookshelves. Search warrants are good for getting the guns from a stash house or the kiddie porn off a home computer, but combing someone's workplace is a pretty worthless way to look for what anyone wanted hidden. But searches can have other purposes, and theater has its uses. It can let everyone know that the police are serious. Or it can make the officers feel that they are important. Or it can surprise someone; the search itself can make a suspect nervous enough to blurt out something he shouldn't.

Standing by the wall, watching Detective Harrison chew on a mug of coffee, Leonard realized that the police have more than one way to intimidate you. They may close ranks when you have one of theirs under investigation. Or they may think that you didn't much like the way your boss treated you on her way out the door. Surely you spoke to a couple of friends about what a pain in the ass she was. Surely one of those friends lit up a joint once, or smoked a cigarette on a subway platform, or did some other inconsequential little misdeed that he'd like to have wiped off his record.

Police know that you can make anyone look guilty of anything. They only need to show that you have a motive. No blood? No body? That only shows how good you are at cleaning up the evidence. All they would need to do is start thinking about who might want to hurt Christine Davenport. Who had she most recently betrayed? Who had something to gain by having her gone? Leonard thought over each question. As he did, his stomach grew thicker and tighter. His eyes met the detective's, staring at him over the rim of his cup. He knew that behind the coffee, Harrison was smiling.

Harrison's phone rang and he reached to his waist. He oozed a couple of monosyllables into the phone, his eyes on Leonard the whole time: "Yeah? When? Where? Sure." He pocketed the phone and set down his coffee.

"You wanna come take a walk over to the financial center with me? Harbor Patrol found something I'm gonna take a look at. I figure you may want to take a look at it too."

The blood rushed out of Leonard's head. He nodded at the detective; he couldn't do otherwise. He wouldn't turn the police down now. It would look as though he was holding out on them. And holding out on the cops would have looked very bad that morning. After all, the whole pageant had been planned entirely for him.

CHAPTER FIFTEEN
PROPERTY

Mulino walked the long corridor in the basement on Gold Street, wishing for a little more light. Most commands hold off the spittle and the chaos of an angry world with a firm shield: the desk, the gate, the place beyond which the general public does not go. And behind that door the officers keep their personal sanctuary. At OCCB, Mulino could find any case from the past thirty years by date, vic, or investigating officer in under ten minutes. It was all police property after all, and the police respect their own property.

Everything packed in the basement on Gold Street was other people's property. The officers stuck here had no use for keeping it tidy. Once upon a time, cardboard boxes had been stacked neatly on the iron racks. Now soaked in dust, the racks buckled with rust and the boxes threatened to vaporize at the touch. Every few weeks, someone came by and hauled the contents of another rack to the landfill. It didn't matter, most of the crap that had been down here more than a year would never be found anyway. The labels had peeled, the boxes had faded, and most likely it had been put in the wrong place to begin with. Mulino turned down an aisle, making a go of it, checking the card that had been pawned off on him by the veteran at the desk. Someone had come by looking for his watch, which had been vouchered in 2012. When the news is going to be bad, the most recent assignee gets to deliver it.

Not to mention that he had come in late, and every set of eyes that marked him had read about his DIMAC interview on page three of the *Daily News*. When your confidential statement ends up in the paper twenty-four hours later, they are after you. The meeting with Chief Travis hadn't been the friendly heads-up he thought it had been. It had been a warning. Get ready. This time you're taking the fall. And after the trip to Harbor, Mulino had just about believed it himself.

But he hadn't been ready to give up entirely. Which was why that morning he had parked in Cambria Heights, at a neat brick house with a steeply sloped roof and a lush lawn and aluminum awnings above the windows. The American Dream, inside the city limits. The walkway had been lined with dozens of bodega bouquets, already fading, as though lining the aisle to a grim wedding. He had made the unwelcome pilgrimage, rung the bell, then stepped down from the stoop. Give her a little space.

She must be used to these calls. The flowers had come from somewhere, after all. One cop after another detouring out of his sector, his precinct, out of his borough if it came to that, to pay respect to the widow. The funeral wouldn't be for two days and the line officers wanted to show their support. So did Mulino, but he wanted some answers as well.

She came to the door in neat black slacks and a red blouse, dressed up like you would for a workday in Manhattan. Trim, conservative, anonymous. She was slightly older than her husband had been, her features and body soft from motherhood. Seeing her, Mulino thought of the kids. Best not to mention them. They would be staying with an aunt, a grandmother, trying to keep the school routine together.

"Ms. Rowson."

"Yes."

"I wanted to pay my respects."

"All right. I know."

He could tell she was tired. It had probably been going on all week, he figured, one cop after another telling her how much he cared. How much Brian Rowson had done for the community. How well they supported a fellow officer. It couldn't have been easy to stomach this parade of thick white men coming by to tell her how much they loved her husband. Her husband who had endured it all himself most likely: his locker glued shut with Gorilla Glue at the Academy, the caricature gorilla face slapped over his nameplate; the sudden quiet when he entered a room of laughing officers; the stiff way other cops spoke to him when they first met him, sussing out whether they could tell their favorite jokes without word getting back to their sergeant. Dead, he was one of them, but on the job he had never been.

"And I was wondering if you could tell me something."

Mulino was just another member of the faceless mob to her. Intruding without intruding. Sharing in her grief for a moment and then going back out onto the job while she was left alone again. She was nodding, playing the routine as she had for days. She hadn't even heard him speak.

"Ms. Rowson?"

"I'm sorry. I was. What was that?"

"Your husband, Ms. Rowson. You ever know him to go to work without his gun? You ever see him leave the house without it? He keeps it locked up in the house when he's there, doesn't he?"

"This city, my husband wouldn't walk to the train without his weapon." He saw her catch herself. She had spoken before she realized it. Now she was staring at him, trying to bring his face into focus. He wasn't just one cop in the parade anymore. Mulino couldn't hide his face, the one that had been in both tabloids already, the soft skin around the eyes, the thin lips, not another anonymous cop. He was surprised it hadn't happened when she first opened the door. But she definitely

Andrew Case

recognized him now. She stepped back into the house, ready to slam the door. She paused and iced a question at him.

"What are you doing here, Detective? Why would you come here of all places?"

He looked up, holding the weight of nearly thirty years on the force on his shoulders. "I really am sorry, Ms. Rowson. I really do want to pay my respects. He would have done the same for me."

"And yet you ask me that. You ask me about his gun so you can make yourself feel better. I don't think you should feel better, Detective. I want you off my property."

She didn't slam the door. She was in too much control for that. Mulino heard the deadbolt snap shut with finality. He didn't look over his shoulder. He knew she was watching him go.

It had made him nearly an hour late for the Property Clerk. It's not like they can fire you or punish you any further for that. But the assignment sergeant can make your morning a little more unpleasant. It wasn't Mulino's turn at the window, but for showing up when he did, he had been handed the voucher and sent to the basement to look for a watch that everyone knew he wasn't going to find. Still, he had learned something from the detour. The gun had been real. His mind wasn't playing tricks on him. It had been there when he shot Rowson and it wasn't there afterward. The evidence team wasn't going to vindicate him by finding Rowson's gun on the ship, but no one was going to hang him by finding it in his house this week either. If the weapon was plumb gone, he still had a chance. Someone had been shot on the boat before he got on, after all. Unless they were going to pin that on him too.

Satisfied that he had sat in the basement long enough to seem as though he had been looking for the watch, he sweated back up the narrow stairway and to the two-inch Plexiglas window. The man on the other side was stepping from one foot to the other, red-eyed, eager to get his watch back so he could sell it on the street for ten dollars' worth of whatever was making him feel so horrible. In the background, the scanner droned about radio runs that none of these officers were going to have the chance to answer. A woman in Flatbush saying her husband was threatening her with a knife, sure to turn on the police when they arrived. A man seemed to be trying to break into a house in Cobble Hill, according to a neighbor. When the patrol showed up, he'd prove he lived there and accuse them of profiling him.

"Sir, I'm afraid we did a thorough search of the premises. Anything after two years you can never be sure. I couldn't find this. I did my best."

"No no no no no. You gotta find my watch." The man's thin sockets held eyes that had once been bright blue but were now dull, graying to match his aging hair. Guy couldn't have been more than forty but wouldn't make it another five years.

"I did my best, sir."

"You stole it. I'm gonna go to City Hall. Cops stole my watch, you planned it, I know all about you."

In the background, the scanner sent out another dismal call for help. Mulino turned his head. They were sending out a description. A location. A body. The docks by the financial district. A name he recognized. He slid the paper below the bulletproof barrier.

"I'm sorry, sir. You go talk to who you need to talk to. Your watch isn't here."

The man started screaming, stomping his feet. He banged on the Plexiglas as the officers behind ticked off the word puzzles in their tabloids. Mulino had done his duty and no one needed to address this man again. Mulino walked past the other cops quietly consigned to their desks, turned left toward the exit onto Concord Street, and slipped out.

He had somewhere to be.

CHAPTER SIXTEEN

THE DESDEMONA EFFECT

Leonard had read his share of autopsies: a woman beaten to death with a claw hammer, a man shot eight times by police-issued, armor-piercing bullets. He had seen sudden violent death advertised across the body in mottled blood, jagged skin, and raked limbs. He knew too, that drowning was as miserable a way to go as any. If someone has been in the ocean for a month, getting chawed on by the fish and soaking himself in seawater, he's going to come out bloated and ripe and he won't have any eyes and his tongue will be the size of a subway rat. But when someone is fished from the river the morning after she succumbed, then apart from her skin wrinkling up as though she had taken a long bath, she won't even look tired. As Leonard looked over Christine Davenport's body, displayed on the dock, he thought she was about to sit up and start scolding him.

The sharp suit and polished brogues were saturated but intact. The towel she'd been laid out on was drenched, but her flesh was still bright and her arms and legs seemed loose. Leonard saw for the first time, her clothing pasted now to her body, how thin she really was. She'd worn the bulky suits to intimidate; underneath she was a waif, a hamster of a person who in another era and a different set of clothes could have been a hanger-on at Warhol's Factory. At first Leonard was shocked, realizing how hard she had worked to make her wiry body look intimidating. It took him a minute to be shocked that she was actually dead. When he was, he stumbled, ready to retch, until the homicide detective caught him by the elbow and propped him up.

"Steady, Mr. Mitchell."

Harrison pulled Leonard up by the shoulders. Leonard knuckled his knees, pressed himself upward, and caught his breath. He had managed to hold it down. Just barely. No surprise. Everyone throws up at their first real corpse, whether it's rancid and mangled or quiet and still like this one. It's the thought of death that sickens you, not the stench. Harrison turned back toward the techs. Leonard stared at him. The detective turned his head as he listened to the tech talk, keeping an eye on Leonard. Keeping an eye on Leonard was probably about the most important thing he could do here.

A couple of cops crouched over her, holding up the hands, checking how far the blue tinge had crept up the fingernails, checking off lists that they'd hand over to the ME so that he could write up a report saying what everyone already knew: She had died sometime last night, maybe late. Harrison finished his coffee and kept his distance. He was listening to the kids, but Leonard could tell he wasn't really paying attention. His eyes were scanning the park. Looking for ways someone might have come in, if she were dumped here. He walked away from his crew and back to Leonard.

"You might want to go ahead and have a seat. It will be a few minutes anyway. And it's hot." Leonard nodded, settling into a bench where he could watch the slow pageant himself. Harrison sat next to him. Maybe the cop was trying to console him; maybe he wanted to watch. Leonard was doing his best to keep calm under close surveillance.

Ordinarily there would have been a morning crowd of moms with strollers and self-righteous joggers throbbing over the flagstones, but it was too hot. The evidence team was in shirtsleeves, but sweat still bubbled up from their temples as they knelt next to the corpse. It was a slow heavy heat; the sun wasn't high enough to glare and burn. Instead, a thick, wet haze strangled the half-dozen uniforms pricking the limp figure, twisting and testing the joints.

The boats in the little basin bobbed expectantly, patiently hoping that their masters would take them out for a spin again soon. The pier had been built for the yachts that banks kept at the ready to take clients past the reach of American law. A night with dope and girls, roulette for the squares. The boats were still there—a couple of sixty-footers, some smaller personal vanity craft—but they hadn't seen much action since about October 2008. It would have sent the wrong message.

Harrison turned away from his view of Hoboken and spoke.

"So I'm sorry for you. I really am."

Leonard just nodded, staring off past the body and into the harbor. The adolescents with the blue gloves were finishing up their work. There was an ambulance nearby to transport her; she would have that small dignity. Leonard started to think about anything that he had seen or heard over the last few days. She hadn't seemed afraid. She hadn't seemed upset. She was busy making plans that didn't include him, but busy nevertheless. He turned toward the cop.

"I can't believe this. Just yesterday she was . . ."

But of course Harrison would already know that. By now he would already know the calendar of Davenport's last few days down to the minute. He let Leonard trail off, giving him the chance to finish the sentence if he wanted to. Leonard didn't want to. Instead he looked at the detective, taking in the vacant expression, the hangdog posture, the suit jacket he hadn't taken off despite the heat. Behind Harrison, across the plaza and on a prim deserted sidewalk, Leonard saw another figure, all too familiar.

"So look, Mr. Mitchell. It's just that someone's gotta ask, so it may as well be me. You wanna tell me where you were last night?"

It was bound to come sooner or later. Leonard had known as soon as they had started searching his office. He nodded and stared back out from Davenport into the harbor. "Home. I was at home last night, Detective. I worked late. I went home." No need to mention watching Mulino visit the Harbor Patrol. If push came to shove, he could explain that sojourn as working late.

"And where is home exactly?"

"The Ebbets Fields Apartments. Brooklyn."

The detective tried not to look surprised. Leonard was used to the look. No one expected him, a guy in a suit working on the executive row at a city agency, to be living in Ebbets Field. Not ten years ago, it had been worse than any project in the city. Brooklyn was changing so fast that even the Manhattan Homicide Bureau couldn't keep up with it.

"Ebbets Field? Crown Heights?"

"Not what it used to be. I make a city salary just like everyone else. I went home after work, I closed the door and I didn't go out again."

"A lot of that going around, the last few years."

"And I have a pretty nice view of the city from there."

"It's only that someone has to ask." Leonard could feel the detective's eyes on him now. Watching his expression. Looking to see if he was too calm, not calm enough. That was the way innocent people ended up in prison, he knew. They look as though they aren't being quite honest to a cop who needs to lock someone up pronto. You feel it's so unjust that you scream and maybe he thinks you look so upset that you're faking it. You check out and he wonders why you aren't more emotional, given the loss you've been through. No matter what you do, it makes you look more suspicious. The Desdemona Effect, they call it. The truly innocent people, the ones who don't even know they are under suspicion, are the ones who look guilty as hell.

Beyond the detective's view, the other figure had crossed the street. A guy who was trying to look a little lighter on his feet than he really was. Who walked to the next set of benches, just out of the drama's circumference, and started staring out at the waterfront himself. Leonard couldn't help but watch Detective Ralph Mulino spy on this little scene as the homicide guy kept up his routine, kept not-quite-asking-questions, just to see if Leonard would say something more.

"Sure." Leonard didn't respond. It would make sense to a cop: Leonard got mad at Davenport for stranding him at DIMAC, hanging him to be fired by the powers that be. He had gone to confront her and things got out of hand. The kind of quick savage decision-making that motivates most murders. The kind of thing that most cops think most people are capable of at any moment.

Leonard had a dull sense that there was something he ought to be remembering. Something Davenport had done. Something he had seen. He didn't ask Harrison any questions. Showing curiosity about how she was killed would make him look guilty too. But something was missing, there was a spark deep in his mind fighting its way up, telling him that he was forgetting something important.

"Detective, I didn't do anything wrong."

"Of course not. You just understand I have to ask. I figure it goes without saying, though, that you should stay close, make sure that you're available if someone wants to talk to you."

"I'm not going anywhere."

"Good to know. You have a nice day then."

Harrison turned away and back toward the tech. It had been a soft warm-up of an interview. Just enough, Leonard knew, to keep him worried. They didn't have any reason to look at him for this yet, except for the fact that they didn't have a reason to look at anyone else either. The techs had lifted Davenport onto a gurney and were sliding her into the ambulance. The heat had kept any crowd away; there were no gawkers, and stringing up the tape had only been theater. Harrison scanned the park one last time, taking in the few people who were out, all of them keeping their distance. Leonard saw his eyes settle on Mulino for a moment. Maybe he recognized him too.

Leonard turned away from the scene; it wasn't going to stop getting hotter. He stared hard at Mulino from across the plaza. He had heard somehow about the body. He was gloating, maybe, that Leonard would know how it felt to be interrogated. But that didn't mean he hadn't shot detective Rowson. And it didn't mean Leonard would ease up on him. The best thing he could do would be to head back to his desk and work the case in the relative comfort of semifunctioning air conditioning.

He clattered back toward West Street, past the broad plaza that had come to replace the Trade Center. Just after it had happened, they had built an aluminum pedestrian bridge to replace the one that had collapsed along with everything else. It looked like something you would string up in the back of a traveling circus to take you to the port-a-potties. So long afterward and it was still there, the only way to cross the highway-speed street. Leonard mounted the metal stairs and withstood the overwhelming echo as he crossed back toward Rector.

Passing him in the corridor inside, a woman in a dark suit with alarming fingernails banged shoulders with him as she passed. Leonard turned to see if she would apologize, but she was already gone. No matter that you're investigating a shooting and that you might get fingered for a murder, the little pedestrian indignities never fail to annoy you. He turned down the stairway toward Rector.

On the sidewalk, Leonard jammed his hands into his pockets to think. Harrison couldn't really make him out to have murdered Davenport. She had stranded him at DIMAC, but that wasn't enough to kill anyone. He didn't stand to profit from her being gone. Surely there was a husband. Maybe he had a girlfriend. Maybe there was life insurance. Something nice and quick and clean to divert the attention.

Inside his pocket he felt something. A small piece of cardstock. He fished out the business card. Harrison hadn't given him one: They usually do. He turned it in his fingers; etched into it was a name he didn't recognize. Veronica Dean, EHA Investments.

The woman on the bridge. She had bumped into him just to give him this. And she was walking toward the crime scene. The card was a smooth bone hue, minimalist, Wall Street impressive. But he could feel with his thumb that the other side had been scraped. He turned it over to reveal a frantic ball-point scrawl: *Manna! Midnight! Danger!*

Leonard put the card back into his pocket very slowly. As if what he had been through with Harrison wasn't bad enough. Another warning. Was it because of the investigation of the shooting? Davenport's death? Leonard was a long way from being a quiet bureaucrat doing paper investigations now. Whoever this woman was, and whatever she was afraid of, he was in no position to turn her down. He stood up as straight as he could and took a breath. His neck raw from the heat, he stepped into the overmatched air conditioning of his building's lobby and started putting together a plan.

CHAPTER SEVENTEEN

SOURCES

By the time Leonard had made his way upstairs, the search team was done with his office. The remains of the investigation littered the dull carpet: upturned desk drawers, lazily opened filing cabinets, everything from a shelf or nook that hadn't been bagged up had been left to rot on the floor. Pens, blank Post-it pads, paper clips, and other office detritus swam into a uniform muck. The place was a mess. The paperwork coming in on the Mulino investigation had never been in prim shape, but it was an abomination now. And who knows what the skinny kid who wasn't a real warrants officer yet had seen fit to pack up and take with him.

Leonard swept enough space off of his desk to make room for Sparks's personnel file, hoping to find some reason he'd been sent to Harbor to babysit a school of cops who hadn't quite misbehaved badly enough to lose their badges. But what Detective Harrison had said kept bouncing around his head. He had softened his delivery, but Leonard knew what he meant. *You wanna tell me where you were last night?* The nice way of telling Leonard that he was their best option for this right now.

Outside this room, down the spattered hallways, was a room with sixty cubicles staffed with ambitious young investigators. Each one longed to be the next Serpico, but instead each investigation meant spending six months looking for another witness to a cop's discourtesy. Most of the complaints were really only a sentence long: *He called me "lady" when I hopped the parade barrier. He told me to go whine at the judge when I complained about the parking ticket.* And on like that. Hundreds and hundreds of sick little disputes: Each would have been easily forgotten on a packed subway or on the corner of Atlantic and Flatbush. But because one of the people was a cop, the complaints became official and gave birth to full-blown investigations with sworn testimony, sheaves of records, and a detailed closing report. You could go your whole career at DIMAC and never get a death case. Truth of the matter is that the NYPD doesn't shoot that many people. Not like the cops in Los Angeles, Houston, New Orleans. Every kid on that floor ached to jump into Leonard's seat, was looking for him to trip up and get shipped out. It would open up a chance to take over the shooting. Stand at a press conference with a deputy mayor, someone from the DA's office, and say how none of the twenty witnesses had seen a gun. No gun had been recovered. Mulino was guilty as hell.

Except that Leonard wasn't all that sure. When you've had even a round of soft questioning about a crime you didn't commit, you slow down your own predatory instincts. Mulino was called out to that boat. Rowson himself wasn't supposed to be there. Rowson had a partner too. Officer Del Rio shared his schedule with Rowson, down to the same regular day off. Leonard made a note to bring in the partner. Find out if he knew anything about Rowson's detour. If he had maybe ever been out with him before. Or if he'd gone out that night. It wasn't blaming the victim exactly. Just trying to get the facts. He started to sense what it might be like to get railroaded himself.

The first thing he did was to call Victor Ells at City Hall. If someone really and truly accuses you of a crime, you pack up and ask for a lawyer right away. But if there are just insinuations and soft words from burly cops, you can do worse than have a well-placed friend look into it for you. He'd already asked the deputy mayor for one favor this week. That had been a success. The story had made Mulino look foolish and there hadn't been a rally by the police union. There hadn't been a raft of volunteer statements defending the detective. No evidence officer had called to say he saw a gun but it slipped overboard. By leaking the story, Leonard had learned that Mulino's fellow officers did not have his back.

But City Hall isn't a great place to double-dip. You only get so many favors before they start calling them in. After the morning he'd had, he would have been happy to pay twice. He called anyway. He left a message with the very polite secretary to have the deputy mayor call him back. He left his work phone and his cell number. He said it was important. He then wrote an e-mail saying nothing more than "call me" in the subject line and "it's important" in the body, just in case.

His phone rang before he'd even finished sending the e-mail. He picked up too quickly, he knew, hoping Ells was getting right back to him. It wasn't.

"So you gonna tie up this detective, put a bow on him, and send him to City Hall before my Sunday deadline, or are you gonna be too busy in lockup for that?" Either way, Leonard was just another story to Tony Licata.

"I don't know what you're talking about, Tony. Investigations take weeks, longer. And I don't see myself getting arrested for anything, unless they start enforcing the jaywalking laws again."

"You were questioned this morning in the murder of your ex-boss, weren't you, Len?"

"Some warrants officers came by the office, said she was missing. They found her on the docks while we were in here. I went out with them. If they wanted to question me, they'd lock me in a room for twenty-four hours without sleep so they could tickle a false confession out of me, wouldn't they?"

"They know you're too smart to fall for that."

"And who are you talking to, that gives you this nonsense? Some tech on the scene sees me talking to the detective and tells you they like me for it?"

"You know I keep my sources safe, Len. Like no one will ever know how I got ahold of Mulino's interview."

"Yeah. We're looking into that internally. You tell your source that when we find him we're going to fire him from this agency." This was a game you always had to play. It wasn't that the phones were tapped exactly. You just acted like they were. If anyone ever got questioned about it under oath later on, you could always say something entirely true and utterly misleading. Licata knew the game too.

"I'll be sure to. In the meanwhile, you want to have a beer, talk about your old boss, tell me how much you loved her and would never do her harm, you know how to reach me."

"Don't hold your breath, Tony." And with that he was done. The PD was whispering to the press about Leonard. Just as Leonard had been whispering to them about Mulino. He slid back into his desperate chair. He still had work to do. Even if he couldn't bring himself to read all the paper that had come in, he could put it back in the boxes. Make the place manageable after the warrant team had been through. It wasn't as though he had an assistant to do it for him. At the very least it would distract him from the hot, wet death outside. And from the card the woman on the bridge had slipped him. He didn't need to be reminded that he was in danger, but now he wanted to know from whom. And why. Midnight was a long way off. Maybe he'd take the afternoon off, take a nap, and head out later. He hoisted himself up and rounded the desk. He dragged a few folders off the floor and slid them into the first box. As he did, he saw the first page. A list of all of Brian Rowson's cell phone calls for the past two months. The evidence guys don't mess around. About to slip it back in the folder, he caught himself.

He pulled the paper to his desk and looked down it, at one number that appeared over and over down the page.

Brian Rowson had been calling someone seven times a day, every day, the last few weeks of his life. Leonard tapped the number into his computer. It was the general line for a little investment firm. One of dozens that can spring up or vanish depending on a single year's earnings. Leonard scrolled through the company's website: a corporate name, some photos of men in expensive suits, and meaningless aphorisms. EHA Investments. The name rang a bell. He looked down at the card the woman on the bridge had given him. Rowson probably wasn't managing his 401(k) in a place like that. The woman wasn't going to tell him something about Davenport at all. She was going to tell him something about Rowson, Mulino, and the shooting on the ship. Leonard fished out the rest of the folder and set it on his desk. He wouldn't be leaving early after all.

CHAPTER EIGHTEEN

DOWNLOAD

"I missed you this morning."

As usual, Veronica had not noticed the pale old man in his winter suit and his serene cufflinks. The soft smile didn't make what he was saying any less of a threat.

"I had a doctor's appointment." No one ever asks if you say that. They are afraid it will be bad news. Impolite. Remembering her mistake from yesterday, she kept herself anchored to the terminal, refusing to look at the bright eyes hidden in Eliot's ashen face. If she had looked up, he would have seen her fear, and now all he saw was her concentration.

She was still afraid, but at least she had a plan now. She would need the other one. The investigator at the docks. When she had heard about Davenport, she realized that anything could happen. That it might all be true. All the more reason to avoid Eliot. She had rushed to the scene and caught the man just in time. He had worked with the dead woman. He would be able to help. From here on out, she would not be able to do it alone.

"So, then. Later on today?"

She was still fused on the screen, pretending to catch numbers as they flew past her. "After the markets close, if that's okay."

"Of course."

She didn't look up, but she could see that he didn't have the binder with him this time. It was waiting in his office. She wasn't sure what would happen to her once she went in. He was being patient, toying with her. She knew what had been going on and that made her dangerous. But he could wait to deal with her. His kind always could.

He lingered at the door a little as she kept at the keyboard, trying to look like she was still focused. Maybe he was waiting to see if she would break stride, to see if she would turn from the screen. Most of them do from time to time. The longer she held straightforward, keeping her eyes down and her fingers moving, the more she feared he was on to her act. But she was committed now; if she stopped, relaxed, then he would ask her to come with him right then. From Eliot's posture, you would never know that the lawyer who visited him two days ago had been found dead. Perhaps they hadn't told him. Perhaps he had known for so long that it was old news. It was one of the many things that Veronica knew not to ask him.

The old man turned back to his sitting room. Veronica allowed herself a slight breath of confidence. She looked down from her machine to the hard drive below. If he had seen the flash drive stuck into her machine, it would all have been over. Breathing deeply now, she moved another two hundred files onto the device. In a week, maybe less, there would be a team of forensics guys determining what exactly she had taken. She couldn't worry about that. If she found herself, a week from now, explaining to Eliot why she had been copying five thousand files from her hard drive, that would mean that a week from now she would still be alive. At this point, that would be as much as she could hope for.

She leaned back in toward the humming screen. Midnight was still ten hours away. There was more left to do until then.

CHAPTER NINETEEN
MANNA

Orchard Street south of Delancey was the old part of the Lower East Side, the part that hadn't yet been swarmed with senseless shops selling frilly clothing to people who want to prove they can pay more than you for a skirt. Most of the neighborhood's Jewish haunts had eventually been handed over to Dominicans and now were grocery stores or bars playing the Spanish feed of the Yankees games. A few places seemed to have been boarded up for twenty or fifty years. The boom had reached as far as it was going to, and as it crept backward, a few old storefronts seemed totally safe from renovation.

One of them sported a stenciled plate-glass window, "Men's Suits and Finest Haberdashery," which no one had bothered to throw a brick through even though it had been closed for decades. Maybe eight or nine years ago, someone had hung a black curtain behind the window, outfitted the inside as a bar, and started telling a few friends. Back when the place had opened, it seemed sweet and fun and slightly scandalous to pretend you had dialed back to Prohibition. Days were bright and money was easy to come by, and you had to work to imagine what it had been like during hard times, when sneaking into bars had been the norm. The little bar, without a name on the door but known as Manna to everyone who went, sparked its own little mini-boomlet of fake speakeasies, starting a trend that soon eclipsed it. The place had been abandoned by its former friends; now only the stray tourist even bothered to go inside.

By the time Leonard followed the stranger's directions and showed up at midnight, Manna had been surpassed by even odder and harder-to-find places, entered through the back door of a tool-and-die joint in Queens, or on the seventh floor of an office tower, empty at night, somewhere north of the flower district. And its cachet had faded further now that there was no more thrill in imagining a crime-ridden world. Less of a fantasy, it was no longer any fun to indulge. By that summer night, there were once again whispers that this corner of the Lower East Side might creep back toward the unthinkable. That it might once again become unsafe to so much as wander down the street.

Still the place hung on, its unmarked front door outfitted with a sliding peephole, so that when you knocked, some overdressed twenty-three-year-old could give you the once-over, pretending to check if maybe you were Eliot Ness come to shut the joint down. A few years ago, Leonard Mitchell, a little too square with his bureaucratic posture and his nondescript clothing, might have been turned away. But they couldn't afford to be so picky anymore. In a quieter and closer city, the place was no longer the favored haunt, but had begun, almost because of that, for the first time to feel genuine.

Leonard stood in the doorway. There were only six people in the bar. A couple of tourist kids were nestled in the back. One of them maybe had read about the place in a magazine a few years ago and wanted to tell the crowd back in Dayton that he had been to a real speakeasy. He didn't know how to find the ones that people still went to. Closer to the front, three people, a little older, were drinking white fuzzy coolers in tall thin glasses. Perhaps they had seen some kind of performance art in one of the sweatshops-turned-galleries dotting the Lower East Side. Or they were leftovers, trendsetters who had moved to this neighborhood when it was red hot, had settled in, and who didn't now feel much like picking up and moving to Bushwick. Or maybe they were just thirsty.

Veronica sat in a booth by the front, alone, cradling an amber-red cocktail with her long fingers, the nails still bright and gaudy. She wore the sharp black suit, and her green eyes shone even in the dim bar. Her posture was elegant without being rigid; she was comfortable, looking important. Her chin barely moved but the bartender caught it and swung round to meet Leonard. He gave a look that said he was maybe ready to take an order or maybe ready to throw Leonard out for chatting with a lady who didn't want him around.

"I'll have the same." The bartender checked with Veronica, who approved Leonard with only a hint of a nod. Satisfied, the bartender turned to his work, mashing up a couple of pristine berries. He wore rolled-up sleeves and a banker's eyeshade to play his role to full camp. Leonard joined Veronica on the severe wooden booth. It was uncomfortable on purpose. Sidling on the bench, he set a manila envelope next to her, filled with Rowson's phone records. It was his ace in the hole. In case she didn't tell him enough. But maybe he wouldn't even need to use it.

"Thanks for coming." There was something in her accent he couldn't place. Not foreign exactly. Just the kind of American that sounds maybe like it wants to be foreign. The rounded vowels of the more prestigious zip codes of Connecticut.

"What did you mean by danger?"

Veronica looked toward the window. It was blacked out with a curtain, so there was nothing to see anyway. "I really am sorry about your boss."

"Thank you. But I'd like you to tell me who you are, and what you meant by danger."

She didn't flinch, exactly. She looked down at her drink and she bit her lip and she looked up again, just as the bartender brought Leonard the same concoction. He took a sip of it—something like a Manhattan, but wrongly sweet. Manna made cocktails with loads of fresh fruit, boasting authenticity but leaving you with drinks that tasted a lot like punch. The bar was draped with glistening boysenberries, bright slices of pineapple, and austere pomegranates. The juice of one of them had made it into the drink. Leonard didn't care for it. She spoke again.

"You saw my card. I'm sure you know where I work."

Leonard had done the due diligence on EHA Investments that afternoon. A sleek homepage littered with boilerplate about providing value to clients during restless times. A collection of disclaimers at the bottom. Most of these operations try to look comprehensive and professional while providing as little information as possible. If he didn't know Veronica's name beforehand he wouldn't have found it on their site. Then he'd gone through financial news sites and some of the angrier blogs that had popped up since the recession started. Some people seemed to know an awful lot about EHA. It had made its reputation by betting on failure, short-selling companies on their way under. In the six years since so many firms started crashing and burning, it had been doing very well. It was one way to survive a recession. Some lonely critics singled it out as a vulture, preying on dying firms. But no one had written anything about danger.

"I know a little. I don't know why you gave me your card. Or why you were running to where Davenport was found."

Veronica clipped the edge of her glass with the bright nails. "Davenport came to talk to the head of the company. Eliot Holm-Anderson. I don't know why. We don't do any business with the city."

Sure. Leonard hadn't even paid attention to where Davenport had landed when she had jumped ship. It would make sense. Leaving the city to go to a private law firm, doing internal investigations. These places will pay a lawyer a little money to write a bright report about

their operations so they don't have to pay a lot of money to a federal regulator. Davenport could cash in and still hunt bad guys. And Veronica
was at the place under investigation. It still didn't explain anything
about the cop calling them all day long.

"And so she was going to embarrass the firm? For making money
off of failing businesses? She had evidence someone had done something wrong?

If he pushed a little, he could get somewhere. If someone at the firm
had a grudge against Davenport, you never know what he might do.
Afraid he'd get exposed, or fired, or sent to jail, he could snap. Maybe
her husband didn't have a jealous girlfriend and an insurance policy.
Maybe there were some bad actors on Wall Street that Leonard could
tell detective Harrison about. Every cop needs a lead. And every lead
starts with a motive.

The woman's fingernails curled cautiously around the lip of her
cocktail glass. "I'd wanted so badly to end up there. On the top floors,
looking out important windows. At one point I would have done anything to keep that kind of power."

Leonard leaned back a little. You can get more out of people if they
think you are comfortable. Leaning forward shows fear, anxiety, ten-
sion. Veronica's perfect posture was shuttered around her drink, but if
Leonard could show her that he wasn't afraid, maybe she would open up.

"So what would you have to do?"

"You can't make money being nice to everyone. You know another
firm is oversold in a piece of land, you take advantage. The brokers in
the building across the street might take the hit and have to send their
kids to public school. You can't get hung up over it."

"That sounds like competition. That doesn't sound like danger."

She took a sip of her fructose. "One time, I had been at the firm
two years. I was the most junior person there. I was in minerals. You
fly around the world, to the most godforsaken places where maniacs
are digging for gold. There was an outfit in Indonesia that had sparked

whispers of a serious find. The price of the company tripled in a week. I was sent to the field so we could know what was going on first. A spring day in Aceh is hotter than the worst summer in New York. I spoke to the local techs, re-examined the core samples. The dig was a bust; it had looked good at first, but the samples proved that the find was worthless. A couple of grams of ore; you'd never recover your costs. I met with the head of the company before I called home. He was like a character out of a fairy tale—a tangled beard and knotted ankles and deep sallow cheeks. He begged me not to make the call, to give him one more week. Eliot made a fortune shorting the stock before it crashed, and that man jumped out of a corporate helicopter floating over a five-hundred foot waterfall. I understand hurting people. So long as it's fair. So long as it's according to the rules."

"And that doesn't sound like danger either."

"Because pretty soon they ask you to break the rules."

"Who?"

She shut down. He waited her out. Usually someone will try to fill the silence. But sometimes you need to push a little. She was ready to tell him, but she needed to be asked.

"Davenport found out who, didn't she?"

"It was Eliot."

Leonard reached out and touched her hand. People talk when they think there is someone there to listen. In ten years of investigating complaints, Leonard had learned how to seem like a good enough listener. He spoke slowly, with all the warmth he could. "The rules changed on you."

"Each time it was a little bit worse. But each step was so small. You undercut the enemy. You get the information more quickly. Someone isn't watching the market closely and they make a mistake; you capitalize on it. And the life is good, Leonard. It can seem hard, but it's worth it. For a girl from Howard Beach whose family thinks someone with a pension from the MTA is a success story, Twenty-Six Wall Street feels like the top of the world."

Howard Beach. It would explain the fingernails. The accent and the posture were a way of overcompensating. In a room full of Groton and Deerfield, it's better to seem as though you're overdoing it than to come off like you grew up in Queens. People might not place you and guess you're maybe a Canadian aristocrat, or someone who did his boarding school in Switzerland; they won't ask questions, anyway. But if you open up with outer-borough vowels when the canapés are being passed, your secret will be out. We all have something we are running away from. His head was still tilted to listen to her. His hand was still on her wrist. He wasn't going to interrupt her.

"First we'd milk people for information. Instead of waiting for our lab reports, just find the guy in the field who needs the money most. The FDA is a sieve; there is always someone willing to spill the results of a study before it's public. Technically illegal, technically insider trading, but everyone does it. Like doping in the Tour de France. You wouldn't be in the game if you didn't push the rules a little bit."

"And then?"

"And then it gets worse."

Her drink was almost empty. She was running out of steam, and while she was giving Leonard a very heartfelt confessional, she hadn't mentioned why they were there. He had to dig further. "Veronica. Someone killed my boss. Either I'm in the process of getting framed for it or the person who did it is coming after me next. I don't even know who to be afraid of. But you do."

A long sigh. A drink from the cocktail. Those fingernails getting perilously close to her lips, and the residue of her lipstick on the glass as she set it down. "That's where you're wrong. I don't know who either. But I know why."

"Why, then."

"Your boss brought some kind of list. There was a binder of e-mails. Records of trades. Eliot was—I never had anything to do with it. Eliot had people at the firm who had taken the next step. They weren't just investigating what was going to happen. Who was doing a bad job. They were sabotaging companies. They would place a short, then set off a bomb. It looks like an industrial accident. You don't just predict that something bad is going to happen. You make it happen. People sell the stock and he collects a profit."

"And where were these industrial accidents taking place?" Maybe Eliot was blowing up wastewater plants in New Guinea. People do all sorts of horrible things for money. He was on to something. For a moment, his ambition ran ahead of him. Catching a cop for a dirty shooting was nothing compared to this. For a moment, he forgot that the last person who had learned this had ended up dead.

"Right here, Leonard. Right in New York."

Nothing would have surprised him except that. This was no far-flung conspiracy. The headlines of the past two years were fodder for EHA Investments' flush portfolio. The crane collapse would just be a short on a construction company. You sell a restaurant and then release rats in its basement. That sickening smell from the chemical plant hadn't been an accident. Someone had made money off of it. And the water taxi sinking had meant actual drownings, actual deaths. Not a game to anyone. "You mean the little disasters."

It wasn't quite a nod. "The crane collapse. The water taxi sinking. The rats in the restaurant."

Leonard tested his own drink again. Still too sweet. Now it wasn't even cold any more. "The city has been under attack."

She just stared into her drink. Some things you can't bear to confirm. "What was on the list?"

Veronica shrugged. "I don't know. I just saw Eliot afterward and I know what happens if you cross him."

"So why target me?"

"If you get arrested for killing your boss, then no one will look any deeper. No one will start talking to Eliot."

So Davenport had put enough of the story together to get murdered, probably by someone who now thought Leonard would look good for it. In the next day or two, something linking him to Davenport's death would be found in his desk or his home. If they could kill Davenport, if they could see that the cops were looking at Leonard, it wouldn't take much to manufacture a little evidence.

"Where is the list now?"

"Eliot has a copy. That's all I know."

"But that's not all you know."

A small hint of fear in the eyes, quickly banished. Ignorance now, a wide open who-me gaze of wonder. Leonard picked up the envelope and slid out a page of phone records, neatly ticked.

"You know that I'm investigating the cop shooting. The detective that was killed on the boat. It's what Davenport did until three days ago."

"I read the papers."

"These are Brian Rowson's phone records. The detective who was shot. Five, six, sometimes seven times a day, the last month, he was calling the same number. Do you see that?"

The thin fingers paging through the paper. "He called our firm."

"Any idea why a cop assigned to the Harbor Patrol was calling your investment firm seven times a day? Probably wasn't managing his portfolio."

"I don't know who he spoke to. It could be anyone at the firm."

"But Davenport could have found out."

"Someone was telling Eliot. If the detective was calling the firm, he was speaking to Eliot. Or one of his henchmen. Eliot knew when the little disasters were going to happen. I think he was hiring people to do it. Not just here in New York. He would hint at something that was going to happen. In Yemen. In Indonesia. He would send these coded messages, and then tell the traders what to do. To short a certain natural gas distributor. Or airline. Eliot would only hint at it in the hallways. He'd ask, 'Don't you have concerns about United Drug?' And two days later a poison outbreak. Or a mine, and it would collapse. Something horrible would always happen when he gave the word. Here."

She took out the flash drive she'd been using all afternoon to copy files. Her fingers shook as she handed it over. "When your boss died, I figured she had learned something. So I did some digging. I found what messages had come through to the firm. Some of them are in code. So I looked at the days of the trades too. The trades were always just after the messages. And they are just before something horrible happened. Look at that. You will see for yourself. What Eliot has been up to."

Leonard took the drive. Veronica went on.

"You have to finish what she started. Her law firm won't do it. They were hired by Eliot. Eventually they will just give him what he wants. Someone else will take the fall. She will have more information somewhere. Her home, her office. You have to find it so we can turn Eliot in."

She was right. Davenport was cautious. She would have built redundancy into the investigation. Somewhere she would have kept her evidence. How had Eliot put it together? How much had he profited? Who were the companies on the list of sabotage targets? And if there were any that hadn't been hit yet, how could he warn them, and save himself in the process.

Veronica's second drink arrived. She reached for it a little too eagerly. Leonard took a chance to reason with her.

"Veronica, turn yourself in. Turn on Eliot. There are good cops out there. You'll get credit for turning them in. Whatever you did, you didn't murder anyone. It won't be so bad for you."

She shook her head and reached into her purse. "You're wrong. I can't prove a thing. If I turn myself in, I will never see the outside of a prison. Eliot and the rest of them will make sure of that. They will make it look as though I did much worse things than I did. The only way to stop them would be to catch them in the act, and I don't have the nerve for that."

"And you think I do."

"Your boss found out what they were up to. You could find out what she knew. If you know who is next on the list, then you can be ready for them. Apprehend them. That is the only way you are going to get to Eliot."

Leonard watched her put back the next drink. Veronica was taking a risk just by talking to him. Leonard had grown accustomed to leaks. He couldn't even mention some of his favorite cases, because the only way anyone heard about them was that he had slipped confidential files that were about to be quietly closed to tabloid reporters. The kindergarten teacher with four open investigations for child molestation who couldn't be fired. The EMT who'd been busted twice for doing heroin on the job; the bus driver who slammed the doors on anyone wearing a Mets cap. He had built his favors with Tony Licata that way, right up until Licata was writing Leonard up as a murderer. Leonard understood, appreciated that Veronica was taking a risk. Maybe it was all she could do. He would take her up on it. But he needed to know the terms.

"So I try to find out who they are going to hit next. I learn what Davenport learned. What then?"

"Call me at work. Don't tell me what you found. I'll know you found something out just by the fact that you called. Once you have some kind of evidence, we can take action. Then I'm going to have to disappear."

"Disappear?"

"They will find me out. Eliot has ways of hurting you. I played as long as I could. I'm going to try to get out alive. I was too caught up in it, and I know I have to get out."

"What will you do?"

"I have ways of making money. Enough for the rest of my life. When this is through, I have ways of escaping. I don't mind running away. But I'm not going to try to hunt him down and get myself killed."

"That's my job, apparently."

"I think you want to. And I think you can. And I think that you know that if you don't, you could end up in prison. Or maybe worse. It's more than I'm willing to do. I need to look after myself. Call me when you find out what she knew."

Of course Davenport could have been working on anything. The bank could have just been one piece of it: There was no reason for her to limit her search. No reason except getting murdered. Leonard looked down at Veronica. She wasn't quite smiling. She had shipped off her burden and handed it over to Leonard. Now he was supposed to find out who had killed Davenport so that she could run off to Canada or Belize or Portugal and never look back. He would have smiled in her shoes too.

"Thanks for your warning. And your help."

The eyes were sweet then, sad. "It's something, Leonard. It's all I can do."

"I know." With that Leonard stood and turned. He left her drinking by herself and walked back into the sticky summer night. The sweat that had crystallized cold in the air-conditioned bar blossomed back to life on his neck, back, and arms.

CHAPTER TWENTY
RESISTING ARREST

A half an hour later, he was off the subway and stumbling toward his apartment. He felt queasy, a little from the booze and a little from the manic swerves from the chilly bar to the hot night into a cold subway and back into the swampy street. He was careful putting one foot in front of the other. Not that you can get pulled over in this town for walking while intoxicated, but still. When he came out of the subway, his phone told him that he had missed a call. From Tony Licata of the *Daily News*. He could wait until morning to return it.

The train let him off at the corner of Empire and Flatbush, the park above him, the quickly gentrifying Lefferts Gardens behind. He had two blocks to walk down Empire before turning up toward Ebbets Field. From the subway, the towers twinkled more like projects than ever. The dull cement balconies, barely big enough to stand on, mainly used for drying laundry. The yellow brick, fading to the color of a smoker's teeth. It wouldn't be long before some developer came in and blew the whole thing for condos. Empire itself was a wreck. A couple of fast-food outlets, a hulking self-storage warehouse, and storefront after storefront shuttered and padlocked. The buildings had all been sold, but the new owners weren't quite sure what to do with them yet. The zoning was commercial, the city was trying to designate it as affordable housing, and a small group of angry locals had decided to storm community board meetings and chain themselves to the fences to keep any development from going forward. So Leonard walked past two blocks of forlorn storefronts on a four-lane street, traffic whipping off the expressway behind him. He crossed at Bedford, off the commercial block and on to the empty residential hill leading to the prison-block apartment.

As he closed in on the corner, there was something quietly out of place. He didn't notice at first, and he kept his stride. Then it stood out at him—a little wrinkle in his ordinary view of the world. At the end of the curb, at the spot where the fire hydrant normally guards the last fifteen feet of empty street, there was a parked car. Almost into the crosswalk. It should have been ticketed or even towed for being left in the hydrant space overnight: it was nearly three in the morning. Leonard walked toward the car, cautiously, from behind. As he closed in, he could tell it was a city vehicle from the broad rear bumper and the two or three extra antennae springing from the back. Not a cop car necessarily. Just something official. Something you would use to show that the guy was important. The kind of thing a city official would be driven around in.

Leonard approached more carefully now, straining in the dark to see if there was anyone in the back seat. He circled wide, hoping to look like just another straggler coming home late from one of the many bars people raved about in this neighborhood. He was almost even with the rear seat, far to the side, when he felt safe to duck his head toward it.

A figure in the back jostled, gestured to the driver's seat, and the car started. There had been someone in it after all. Two someones. The lights sprung to life and the car jolted up the hill and Leonard couldn't make out exactly who was sitting in the back, but he thought he could make out a head of smoothly strained silver hair. Hair that looked like it had been ironed and pressed. Hair he almost recognized.

But before Leonard could think about why Deputy Mayor Victor Ells was staking out his block, there was a fresh brusque voice booming from someone crossing the street in front of him.

"Excuse me, sir?"

Leonard looked up. A uniform cop. Alone. Leonard kept his mouth shut. His hands out. He didn't move and he didn't turn away. The guy could ask him questions if he wanted to, but Leonard wasn't about to volunteer anything now.

"Can I talk to you for a second?" A foot patrol on midnight tour was unusual. Even more unusual was the fact that the guy was alone. The only place the NYPD used foot patrols now was in impact zones—collections of four or five blocks that the department's databases promised were hot spots for drug dealing and everything that came with it. The local commands would flood the zones with officers fresh out of the academy—guys who didn't know how to make an arrest and were uncertain with their weapons. The idea was that just by having uniforms on the streets, you would keep people from committing crimes in plain sight. And it worked to a certain extent—the drug dealers moved their operations three or four blocks in any direction whenever the impact zone changed, knowing the rookie cops were afraid to step outside their sector.

But this wasn't an impact zone. As tough as Ebbets had been twenty years ago, Leonard's corner of Crown Heights was now as neatly kept as the brownstone neighborhoods to the north. A nearby street had won "greenest block in Brooklyn" from the Botanic Garden last year. There was no reason for a foot patrol guy in uniform to come up to him. Wary and no longer drunk, Leonard answered as calmly as he could.

"What do you want to talk to me about, Officer Davies?" It always helps to get the name. They know you are looking at their uniform. Leonard had looked at the collar brass too—Davies was identified as being in the Seven-Oh. The local precinct. The place where twenty years ago a cohort of officers raging from their steroid abuse had sodomized Abner Louima in the bathroom. A different city then. That happens, a precinct gets special attention. The Seven-Oh had been under a microscope ever since, and steroids had been all but wiped out of the department. Now it was the cleanest house in Brooklyn, if not the whole city. This guy was thin too. Young and lanky and his blond hair still tousled like a civilian and he didn't have his police posture down yet. Couldn't be more than a year and a half on the job.

"You mind turning around? You got anything in your pockets?"

He was going to be frisked. Maybe this guy hadn't got the memo that they weren't doing so many stops any more. Maybe it was late at night near a place that used to be a drug corner so it was worth checking him out. Or maybe it was convenient to search a white guy every now and again, just to keep up appearances.

"I do mind, Officer. What do you think I did?"

Early in his career at DIMAC, Leonard had been in charge of outreach. Go to schools, juvie centers, homeless shelters, projects. Tell people that if the police mistreat them they have a voice, there is someone that will listen. But tell them too to keep their heads screwed on if the police stop them. Don't swing your arms. Don't run away. You can ask questions, but don't shout or fight back. Ninety-nine percent of the time, if you just keep calm and comply, it will all be okay. You can always file a complaint later. He had always followed his own advice, talking his way out of a ticket when he was pulled over for rolling through a stop sign or crossing the parade at the wrong place. And so he kept his head about himself now.

"You don't ask any questions. You turn around."

The rookies are the ones who play tough the hardest. Davies stepped toward Leonard and Leonard stepped back. He didn't think he was resisting; it was the animal instinct to step away from a too-close stranger. But stepping away from a cop gives him permission to do things. In an instant the cop had locked Leonard's arm behind him and had twisted him up against the wall. Leonard stood still, both palms on the decaying yellow brick that fronted the plaza to his home.

"Like I said, anything sharp on you?"

"No. I live in here. I don't know what you're thinking."

The cop's hands were all over him, up and down his legs, under his arms. Twenty years in this business and Leonard had never himself known what it felt like to be frisked, how intimate the hand against the armpit, the swipe across the belly, the palm just outside the groin can be. Close, intrusive, and hard. A cop is allowed to pat down the outside of your clothing if he has a reasonable suspicion you have a weapon. If he finds something that could possibly be a weapon, he can reach in and pull it out. But if he finds something that might be illegal but can't be a weapon, he is supposed to let it be. He can't make his own probable cause to search your pockets based on tapping them from the outside. Leonard had dinged dozens of cops for reaching into someone's pocket when all they felt was a bag that maybe held some weed, a folded up wad of cash, or some other suspicious but non-dangerous item.

Like a flash drive. Davies had yanked it out of the pocket and held it now in front of Leonard's face. "You wanna tell me what this is?"

"It's computer files. It's my work." Even that wasn't a lie.

"And that work is?"

"I'm the Acting Executive Director of the Department to Investigate Misconduct and Corruption."

"Sure you are." And with that Davies dropped the memory stick to the ground. Probably not the sort of thing that would damage it. Leonard leaned down to pick it up.

As he bent, he felt a dull broad thud across his stomach. Like he had been trying to throw something up and it wouldn't budge. He sucked in a thick breath, then another, before the second blow took him to the ground. He kept his arms down, he kept his legs spread. As he had told hundreds of kids, if you don't resist, if you comply with the officer, then nothing all that terrible is going to happen. Ninety-nine times out of a hundred.

But then there is always that one. Leonard was on all fours, reaching for his flash drive, when the officer stepped on his fingers, drilling them into the pavement. Leonard tried to turn away, to balance with his other hand, but he was pinned and twisting, a rat with its leg in a trap. The hard blows came across his back. Sharp, sudden, heavy with wood. The officer had taken out his baton. This too won't be permanent. Not if he doesn't get your head. The worst thing Leonard had ever investigated based on body blows with a nightstick was a ruptured spleen. The wood cracked again against his shoulders and Leonard gave in, accepting the pain. Even if he had wanted to resist now he couldn't. The only thing left was to take it, to survive. He could feel the blood welling up below his shoulder blades, the pain of the first blow giving way to an ache before the next one even landed. He was splayed and broken and couldn't move his hand by the time the officer stepped off of it. When Davies slid the baton into his waistband, twisted his heel once more, and turned to leave, Leonard curled up on the sidewalk. He watched as the officer walked away into the dark, dusting his hands.

Leonard was just alert enough to see that Davies hadn't written a thing in his memo book, hadn't given a ticket, was leaving no record at all of the beatdown. The cop had just left the memory stick on the sidewalk. Leonard reached forward and got his fingers around it, slipped it back into his pocket. Too busted to even stand up, Leonard propped his head under his arm and closed his eyes, hoping he'd be able to rise in a few minutes.

CHAPTER TWENTY-ONE

A ROOM WITH A VIEW

It was too bright and it hurt too much. Leonard squinted. He wasn't dead. He figured that if he were dead it wouldn't hurt so much. He couldn't move his right arm. He tried to open his eyes. There was a window in front of him and it was too big and the shades were open and that's why it was too bright. Better to keep them closed. Think things through a little.

He remembered the pain in his hand the most. The look of the heel as it dug in. Cops wear sensible, quiet, shoes. But that doesn't mean it's a picnic to get stepped on by one. And that is if Davies was even a cop. It had passed through Leonard's mind, briefly, that he wasn't. That he had been the victim of a random street crime by someone who had found his way into a uniform and a badge. Then why hadn't anything been stolen? Leonard reached into his pocket to see if the flash drive was still there. But he didn't have a pocket; he was wearing a hospital gown. His arm stung as he reached. He curled back up in the bed.

His shoulder had been wrapped with an Ace bandage until it bulged under his gown, so tight on his arm that he could barely feel his fingers. The pain now was concentrated in his back and upper chest; he felt as though he could feel every blow of the nightstick again, across his clavicle and through the knotted flesh. There weren't any broken bones or he would have been in traction.

His eyes had adjusted enough that he could open them. He could feel dry gobs of sleep crusting each eyelid. Instinctively he reached up with his right hand, but the pain caught him. Instead he cleared his eyes with his left. He must have been out for days. He blinked and stared out the window just past the foot of his bed.

It was a magnificent panorama. He was only seven stories up, but facing east. There was nothing between his hospital room and the water. He could see the merry traffic fluttering along the FDR, the rocky sea wall beneath it, then the broad East River and the Queensboro Bridge. Someone had picked him up and shunned Kings County, up the road, or even Methodist in Park Slope, and dumped him onto the doorstep of a Manhattan hospital. He would have to figure that out too.

Leonard had always been impressed with his view out of Ebbets Field, onto the park and the sea of Brooklyn ahead of him, but it was nothing compared to what the hospital room offered. His own view petered out with the hill beside the park, the East River miles away and blotted out by a series of low-rise housing projects. Now he could barely move with the pain, but at least he was looking directly out over the water. Every New Yorker's dream. He was somewhere on the East Side, high sixties. He had been beaten up on the streets of Crown Heights and had woken up in one of the best hospitals in the city.

He sat up. The pain wasn't so bad anywhere but his back and the one hand. He couldn't even feel the bruise that used to be on his hip. Aside from the thud across his shoulders, he felt kind of rested.

Leonard looked around his room. There was another bed, but no one in it. The whole room was dead still, plain white, and alarmingly empty. The only times Leonard had been in a hospital room was as a well-wisher. Rooms that had been stuffed with cards and flowers and people patting a shoulder or wrist. He realized when he looked around his cell that no one knew he was here. His clothes were folded neatly on a squat inde-structible chair by the door. Other than that, nothing. He pivoted in bed. He might as well try to stand. He might as well try to feel like himself.

He put the pants and shoes on without trouble. His undershirt stretched over the bandage, but he couldn't force his arm through the button-down shirt. And forget about the jacket. It was okay. He could manage in a hospital with a T-shirt on. He slid his hands into his pock-ets. The flash drive was secure in his left. The cop hadn't even taken it. He figured he could go out into the hallway and ask a nurse how long he would be here. He still had work to do, after all.

As he stood up, he heard the door open behind him.

"It's good to see you're doing better." It was a deep, gruff, familiar voice.

Leonard turned around. It was a man wearing a beaten tweed jacket and slacks that didn't quite match, no tie. It was a face that seemed familiar, but coming out of consciousness as he was, Leonard couldn't place it. The man was holding two cups of designer coffee. He held one out to Leonard.

"This is a lot better than what comes out of the machines. I didn't know how you like it, so I got it both ways. Me, I'm not particular, so whichever you don't want I'm happy with."

Leonard stepped forward, still in a daze. The face came into view. Those soft creases around the eyes. Leonard was awake enough to rec-ognize it now. He took one of the cups of coffee. The back of his neck pinged with fear. He thought about trying to leave. But the man in front of him had a gun on his belt, and he was on the seventh floor of a hospital. He wouldn't get far. He swallowed and spoke.

"Thank you, Detective Mulino."

"Please. Call me Ralph. And have a seat. I've got just a few ques-tions for you."

CHAPTER TWENTY-TWO

UP TO SOMETHING

The coffee was still hot and rich and gave a little life back to Leonard. Mulino sat in the squat chair, the picture of calm. Leonard boosted himself back up on his bed and looked over the cop's shoulder, trying to see if there was a nurse or a doctor in the hallway. He might already be trapped.

"We were worried about you for a little while."

"We?"

"I was worried about you."

"That's very nice of you. The last two cops I spoke to, one accused me of murder and the other beat the crap out of me."

"You're saying police did this to you?"

"Why would I tell you, Detective? You wouldn't believe me anyways. Your friend Harrison wanted to lock me up for killing Davenport."

"Yeah. Harrison closed that case already. Turns out your boss was a jumper."

"What?"

Mulino shrugged. "The woman wasn't shot. She wasn't injured at all. She had taken a couple of Valium. You know your boss to take Valium, on a regular basis?

"I wouldn't know, and I wouldn't ask." He bit his lip.

"They have footage of her getting on the Staten Island Ferry. They don't have any footage of her getting off."

"Are you in homicide all of a sudden? I thought you were reassigned given the shooting." Leonard instinctively checked Mulino's waistband. He still had his gun. That didn't mean he was out of Property. He certainly wasn't working the murder case, or the suicide, or whatever it was called now.

"The grapevine reaches all the way to the basement of Property."

"That's a pretty full boat for people to not notice a jumper."

"People pay attention to their own affairs."

"Still."

"Drowning was the cause of death. So either someone throws her off the ferry—struggling with her while she's screaming—or she jumped. Which do you think is more likely to draw attention?"

"She didn't kill herself."

"Well, you can take it up with Harrison. Case is off his docket and the city doesn't need to record it as a homicide when the numbers come out."

Leonard could see how it made a certain degree of sense. Davenport was languid, cold, and ambitious. She had left a job where she was the center of attention and joined the faceless rat race. Maybe that had been enough to drive her over the edge. Maybe after one whole day. At least if you were a police officer worried about the homicide rate, you could make yourself believe that. But Leonard couldn't. She had a husband, a son. And Mulino didn't know what Leonard had been through. What he knew Davenport had learned. And what had happened to him to bring him here. Once upon a time, Leonard would have been afraid to bring it up. But he wasn't afraid of as many things anymore.

"A cop could have taken her."

"What?"

"No one pays any attention when an officer frisks someone in the street. Makes an arrest. The doorman to her building wouldn't remember a cop coming by. Cops can walk someone along a crowded room and no one pays attention."

"And they just throw her off the ferry."

"Or he takes her somewhere."

"A lot of people on the ferry would see that."

"There is a difference between seeing and noticing, Detective. We see things every day that we don't notice. He walks her off quietly. Takes her on another boat. Or to the shore."

"You get some rest. Your theory needs a little work."

"Okay, Detective. But the suicide needs work too. She had too much going on to kill herself."

"Like what."

And with that Mulino had stumped him. Because Leonard couldn't tell the detective what Veronica had said. What Davenport had found out about the investment company. The little disasters. He trusted the detective a little more than he had when he'd interviewed him. But not that much more.

"I can't tell you that, Detective."

Mulino stewed. He looked closely at Leonard. He bit his lip.

"All right then. We'll leave it at that."

Leonard spoke despite himself. "She was up to something. She had an investigation going on. I learned something about it. And the next thing I know some officer from the Seven-Oh shows up on my street and beats the crap out of me."

Mulino leaned back. When a detective doesn't believe what you're saying, he doesn't make a show of pretending he does. Mulino spoke in his slowest, sweetest voice, which still wasn't very slow and wasn't at all sweet. "This is what I actually came to talk to you about. You actually see this person?"

"Yes. Officer Davies. From the Seven-Oh. You can go look him up."
Mulino nodded.

"Look, Leonard. I have my own problems. As you know. I came here
to talk to you because I wanted to let you know that I was totally honest
in there when you interviewed me. I waited on that ship until I was absolutely sure. And I'm being railroaded for it and I don't think you mean
to be doing it. But you're a part of it. So if you tell me there is someone
out there in the department doing you wrong, it's not like I don't believe
it. But my first thought when I hear about a cop beating you up at three
in the morning is someone found a uniform at a fun shop."

Leonard shook his head. His word wasn't good enough. And why
should it be, anyway. This detective had no reason to trust him. Just
before all this had happened, Leonard was the one accusing him of
doing something wrong. And, frankly, Davies as an impersonator made
a certain degree of sense. The pain was spreading down his back again.
He must have been given a painkiller in his sleep. It was wearing off.

"Okay, Detective. I understand. I haven't finished your case yet.
You said your piece. But Davenport had something on these cops. You
should care, if you think you're being railroaded. Maybe she was on to
something. I'm just putting my case together from the evidence that
comes in."

"If someone killed your boss, he did a great job of making her look
like she did it herself."

"You've mentioned."

"Someone is going to come and talk to you about this thing too.
About you being in here hurt. It isn't going to be me. I just came by to
check in on you. You've been out three days, this morning is the first it
got announced you were here."

Leonard looked up at the detective. "What do you mean?"

"Just that. Head of DIMAC found on the street and taken to the
hospital. No one heard from you for days. You were here. I hadn't
known and I figure I'd stop by."

"You're not investigating this."

"I'm on my meal from Property. I gotta get back to 100 Gold."

Mulino stood up, shaking out his bad knee. He took out his card. "I know you have some ideas about Davenport. I don't know, myself. Maybe I'm not supposed to talk to you. But I figure you are interested in the truth same as anyone." He handed the card over and Leonard pocketed it.

Mulino turned and walked down the hallway. Leonard watched him leave. Mulino would go back to the outside world and to his normal life. Maybe it was a life filled with petty crimes, dirty streets, and fights with kids who had stabbed each other over how to split up the dime bag. But as a detective, those were fights Mulino would get to win. Even in Property, he got to hold a little bit of authority over the rest of the world. And he'd head out at the end of his tour and drive out to Long Island where his own family was probably waiting, safely walled off from the world he worked in all day, with Turkey Tetrazzini and a game of Chutes and Ladders. That was over for Leonard now.

As he watched Mulino leave, he thought of one more thing. It had been in the papers, that he'd been hurt. Until then, nobody knew. Nobody knew if he had even survived. Now whoever had done it could find him. And a hospital guard would wave through a badge just like anyone else. No one ever asks questions. Leonard set down his coffee. He stood up. His shoulder hurt like hell, but he didn't have much time. He walked out into the hallway of the hospital, leaving his view behind.

CHAPTER TWENTY-THREE
FLIGHT

The quiet of his room gave way to the steady clamor of the ward. Carts bouncing along regulated hallways. Professionals clattering away at patient machines. Relatives of other inmates ducking their way into a room. But all Leonard could hear was the noise inside his head. The police thought Davenport had killed herself. A police officer, or someone who was trying very hard to look like one, had assaulted him and left him for nearly dead. And now it was in the paper. Bylined by his old friend Tony Licata, probably. Anyone looking for him would suddenly know where he was. He wasn't only worried about keeping himself from being arrested now. He had to keep from being killed. His shoulder hurt and his shirt was too tight, but at least he had his street clothes on. The suit was ruined, but it was never all that nice to begin with. He started walking down the hallway to his left when he saw them rounding a corner behind him. Two uniform cops. One of them was Officer Davies.

"Mr. Mitchell?"

Leonard didn't turn his head. Maybe they'd go into the room to check if it was actually him. It would give him a little more time. He picked up his pace. Run full speed in a hospital and someone is likely to tackle you, but a brisk walk was safe. He shuffled through the slow crowd, residents and patients giving him a bit of human cover. Everyone on the floor was in some sort of a rush. He saw a suite of elevators about twenty feet in front of him. He didn't hear any running; he picked up his pace.

The other cop was talking, the one he didn't recognize. "Mr. Mitchell? We'd just like to talk to you."

He'd reached the elevators. He didn't have time to wait for one. The footsteps were gaining. They were fit from daily trips to the weight room, but both carried eighteen pounds of gear on their gunbelts. They weren't as fast as they thought. Leonard slipped around a woman in a wheelchair and opened a door into a stairwell. He heard the cops pick up speed behind him.

His shoulder seared and his back ached and he ran as fast as he could. He was down one flight when he heard a pair of shoes clatter onto the stairs. Just one. The other had taken the elevator and would be waiting on the ground floor. Leonard shimmied as best he could past the sixth floor, the fifth. He would have to try something else. He burst out of the stairwell and onto the fourth floor.

Leonard turned left and took off at a run along the hallway. The wall to his right offered a mural of an absurdly bright blue sky, a crooked rainbow, and odd shapes that could be flowers or clouds or dinosaurs dancing through hallucinogenic green fields below. Fewer people here, and they looked hollow and shell-shocked, wandering aimlessly around the forced cheer. The children's ward. Where the burned or beaten get swaddled with Silverex and Bacitracin and the parents blame themselves. There was a second bank of elevators just ahead of him. A man stood inside it looking very much like Leonard, except that he was holding his entire fist in his mouth, eyes squinted shut and teeth just starting to cut into his own flesh. Leonard slipped in the doors just as they closed; he could hear the clatter of Officer Davies behind, losing steam. And as bad as his day had been, the guy in the elevator with him had it worse.

Leonard stayed alert as the elevator hit the ground floor. The other cop would be at the end of the hallway, straight ahead, maybe two hundred feet away. Officer Davies might have called him on the radio and he might already be on his way. The man next to him was still chewing on his hand, crushing shut his eyes, trying to forget whatever horrible news he had just been given.

The doors opened to the crowd of a busy hospital. No officer in sight. The stunned man made no effort to get out, so Leonard pushed his way into the mob and started to float with them toward the main entrance. The other cop was waiting for him there, scanning the faces as they left the building. Leonard could see that he wouldn't get far. He turned back toward the elevator. He couldn't go back upstairs. He pushed past the crowd and pulled open a door into another stairwell. Going down. He didn't have anything to lose.

He thought about where he would go if he got out. If the police were looking for him, he couldn't stay at home for long. He couldn't go see friends, coworkers, anyone who would show up in a background check. They could put a tap on his phone, a track on his cell, a trace on every bank transaction, leading them to him like so many electronic breadcrumbs. The cell phone tracing would be the hardest to shake. He could throw away his MetroCard, shred his credit cards, live off whatever cash was left in his pocket, but soon his cell phone would be a homing beacon. He pulled it out of his pocket and saw that he had missed seventy calls over the past three days. His voicemail was full. People were trying to find him, but he didn't want to be found just now. He had to ditch it.

He slunk down the bright concrete stairwell. Painted white, purely utilitarian and spotless. The door at the bottom had a heavy square of fortified glass in its center and a painted warning on its body: Staff Only. The door had a fire bar on it. Leonard hoped that he wouldn't set off an alarm, ignored his pain for a moment, and pushed through, ready to run at the sound if it came. But the door swung open and the hallway kept quiet; he was still safe for the moment. He was in a broad cement hallway, empty buckets and neat mops aligned by the wall. Darkness at the end. He crept along.

At the end of the hallway, he saw a red exit light above another door. He pushed it open and found himself in a small garage filled with service vehicles. Ambulances, patrol cars, a couple of trucks. He walked up to an ambulance and tried the back door. It was open. He slipped out his cell phone and slid it under the cushioning in the side bench. Deep, so it couldn't shake loose and so whichever paramedic sat on it wouldn't notice it. Tossing it out a window or leaving it in a garbage can would have given the cops a static point to trace, and they would have found the abandoned phone in an hour or so. This way, whoever traced him would think that he was zipping around the city at seventy miles an hour.

He turned away from the vehicles, out of the garage, and toward Seventy-First Street. He stepped clear onto the sidewalk. No sign of the cops. They had only covered the public exits. He started west. The street on the north end of the hospital was narrow, and shaded by imperial buildings on both sides. He would take the subway back to Brooklyn; he had already decided where he would stay. He looked up as he neared York Avenue.

A heavy black sedan was parked on the corner of York, about twenty feet ahead of him. The lights flashed on as he approached. The engine hummed to life and it started toward him. He turned and ran back toward the hospital. Someone was following him still. He ran past the garage—the doors had locked shut behind him. At the corner he would be at the FDR. Maybe if traffic wasn't heavy, he could dash across to the walkway on the other side. A car couldn't make that leap. Then maybe he would swim the East River.

The car sped past him and turned up onto the sidewalk, blocking his way. Leonard spun back and looked behind him. There was nowhere to go. He ran toward the car, thinking he could leap the hood and keep on his mad dash to the river. The door opened and a familiar figure stepped out. A sleek suit. Serious posture. And a fierce pair of green eyes. Leonard stopped. Veronica spoke.

"Leonard, they are looking for you everywhere. You aren't going to make it without help. Get in and let me take you somewhere safe."

CHAPTER TWENTY-FOUR

THE SEVEN·OH

Detective Ralph Mulino was startled by how calm the cops were when they came back. Minutes before, using the bathroom after leaving Leonard Mitchell to his recovery, he had heard a commotion on the floor. Looking out into the hallway, he had seen two young officers—patrol rookies—flinging themselves toward the stairwell. He had remembered being that eager once himself, always wanting to be the first on the scene, the kid to make the collar. The sucker. He wouldn't join this race, but he nodded acknowledgement to the cop by the elevator, going ahead to cut the suspect off at the ground floor. Mulino had nursed his coffee in the dull waiting room and was standing to leave when they huffed back up.

When they approached, the elevator cop was collected, pristine, and the one who had taken the stairs heaved and whimpered. Mulino marveled that with all the new technology and all the best tactics, the NYPD couldn't keep its officers in shape even six months into the job. Everyone can do the obstacle course in six minutes when they have to take the POPAT at the academy, and then when they're out in the field, they can't run up and down a few flights of stairs without panting.

"Detective," the elevator cop said.

Mulino looked at the kid's badge. He glanced at the collar brass—the Seven-Oh. A neighborhood precinct in Brooklyn. That didn't make sense. These guys weren't even on the right side of the river. Mulino looked back up at the kid's face, remembering the nameplate.

"Officer Davies. What brings you to the hospital?"

He recognized the name when he spoke it. Davies. The Seven-Oh. Just like Leonard had said.

"We were asked to bring a patient in for questioning. He did flee the premises. Someone will apprehend him at his house."

"I only have the one coffee, or I'd offer you boys one." Something about the rookie cops didn't strike Mulino as quite right. They weren't afraid enough. They had come across a detective almost by chance, and they were shrugging off the fact that they had just lost their man. If Mulino had lost a footrace thirty years before, and he'd turned the corner to find himself face-to-face with a sunburst blue badge, he would have dropped to his knees and begged forgiveness. Maybe it was just the generation. Or maybe Leonard had been telling the truth. This was the guy who had sent him here. His uniform certainly looked authentic to Mulino.

The one who had taken the stairs was still catching his breath. "That's okay. We have to go inside and tell the nurses to give a call in case he comes back." They started to walk past him toward the nurses' station.

Mulino looked up and called after them. "Your suspect came from in there?"

The elevator cop turned around. "Yeah. Guy who got picked up in front of Ebbets Field a few days ago. The detective squad wants to talk with him. Something about a body washing up in the river."

Mulino stared after the cops. Davenport had been investigated by Manhattan Homicide. The precinct of location always catches the crime. The only thing the detectives in the Seven-Oh might want to talk to Leonard about was how he'd ended up in a heap on Bedford Avenue.

And if he told them the same story that he had told Mulino, these guys wouldn't want their brass to know about it. If there was any brass for them to tell.

He thought about what Leonard had told him. It was all coming together. Davenport investigates dirty cops, dirty cops fight back and kill her. He hadn't liked it much himself when he heard they'd knocked Davenport down to a suicide. It had sounded to him a little too much like 1PP wanted one fewer tick on the dial, what with crime on the rise. Christine Davenport had made plenty of enemies at the NYPD over the years. But he still couldn't imagine police officers kidnapping a city official and hoisting her over the side of a boat. Yet here was Officer Davies, going to the very hospital that was treating Leonard for the tune-up. Maybe Leonard hadn't been so wrong to be afraid. Maybe he had clammed up to Mulino because he was afraid of him too.

Mulino sighed. He had learned a lot more that week than he had wanted to about the wrong side of the police department. He fished into his corduroy jacket pocket and read over the report from Harrison. The more he read, the more it seemed like a whitewash to keep the murder rate from getting any higher. He thought about what Leonard had said about people averting their eyes. How they don't get involved in police business. Maybe a cop could drag a screaming woman off of a boat after all. He had seen people look away from worse. He folded the report and put it back into his pocket. He had to get back to Gold Street. After all, he was going to be late coming in the next morning.

CHAPTER TWENTY-FIVE
ESCAPE

The car squealed south on the FDR and Veronica threaded into the wave of traffic before taking a breath. Leonard curled himself into a ball in the front seat. Now that he wasn't worried about being caught, the pain was back. He started to stretch out as Veronica eased off of the accelerator. His feet had just reached the floor when she spoke.

"Look behind us. Is there anyone?"

Leonard slid around and checked the road. The hospital towered behind them, the United Nations ahead, and the traffic buzzed on both sides. But nothing unusual. A sunny summer afternoon commute.

"No. I don't think so."

Leonard slumped back round to face forward. He pulled the seat belt shut. Veronica sped past a taxi and cut in front of it. Her fingers were taut on the wheel, the fingernails digging into the leather. The road curved east and the on-ramp to the Brooklyn Bridge appeared. He looked up at the bridge and over to Veronica.

"How did you find me? How did you know I would be coming out the back?"

"It was in the paper. The investigation is ongoing. I was planning on checking in to visit you. They have cops at the entrance, and when I said I was coming to see you they tried to stop me. If you were coming out that way you weren't going to make it. You were either going to be coming out of that garage or you weren't going to be coming out at all."

Leonard nodded. He had been even closer to getting locked up than he thought.

One hand on the wheel, she reached across him to his wounded shoulder. "How do you feel?"

"I'm okay." Five minutes earlier, Leonard had been afraid for his life. In the chase, with his instincts running full throttle, he had forgotten about mere pain. Now the beating was talking to him again, reminding him. As they took a broad turn up the bridge, Leonard saw the fresh bright downtown sparkle in front of him. Magnificent glass condominiums rising sixty stories, the newly finished complex of towers, all scoffing at the mere Woolworth Building, a stone relic chugging along into the twenty-first century. It all seemed stained somehow, false. A glittering future that had been imposed upon the city, laughing at people who had liked things the way it had been before. Thinking of it slipping back to that raucous past, Leonard felt almost a hint of relief. They swooped onto the bridge.

"Do you know who did this to you?"

He turned to look at her. Her eyes were steady on the road, watching the hum of cars pressing their luck along the bridge. She was the one who had told him what Davenport had really been up to. That Eliot Holm-Anderson had been betting against companies and blowing them up. That the little disasters weren't just the by-product of a swiftly collapsing city but acts of affirmative sabotage. That Davenport had known. Veronica had trusted him with dangerous information, so it was only right that he trust her back.

"I was beat up by a cop."

"What?"

He told her the whole story. Coming home at night. Seeing the car; Victor Ells. And Officer Davies. "Mulino doesn't believe me. He thinks at best it was someone who bought a fake uniform. But I'm pretty good at spotting that."

Veronica pulled the car down the long exit off the bridge. "Why would they assault you? You had only just spoken to me. You hadn't found anything out yet."

"I wonder about that." They wouldn't have known about his talk with Veronica. But they would have known he was investigating Mulino. And they just might have known that he had his doubts about whether Mulino had done it. About whether the trophy was worth it after all. Leaking the interview to the papers had been a test balloon. It wasn't great for the cop, but it didn't lead to marches in the street demanding his head. And if your jury pool is skeptical of your best evidence, you don't have a case. Just maybe, word had got out that Leonard wasn't as convinced as he was supposed to be that Mulino was the fall guy. And if the cops came after Leonard for that, it would mean that they were laying the trap for Mulino after all.

They were on the surface streets now, cruising along the mid-afternoon glut of Brooklyn, meandering on Atlantic Avenue toward the arena, the hub of Flatbush, the noise. "They aren't going to stop looking for you, Leonard."

"I know that. I got rid of my phone." It wouldn't only be the dirty officers who were searching now. Someone would manage to put a warrant out for his arrest. Leaving the scene of an accident, trespass, material witness. It didn't really matter. All they needed to do was to say that they wanted to talk to him, they had come after him in the hospital, and he had run away. Any cop that came across him would pull him in on the warrant, no questions asked. It wasn't the kind of thing you could talk your way out of. And once he was in custody, he'd eventually get brought to the people who were looking for him. And at that point, it would get ugly.

"Good. Smart move." Veronica circled around the library and turned the car down Bedford. "I'm going to bring you home. You shouldn't stay long. The cops will look for you there. But you should have time to change your clothes and take a shower."

"Thank you. Thank you for all of this." His shoulder had started throbbing again, a mean solid pain.

"I wish I could protect you, Leonard. But I'm in danger myself. If Eliot knew what I was doing . . ."

"I'm grateful, Veronica. Really."

"If you get enough to turn them in, I can help you. Davenport came to Eliot. And she had found out enough. She had found out what he was doing. And you found out that Rowson was calling EHA. There are cops who are in on it, who know when the next little disaster is going to happen. You need to find the connection. How did he hire them? Who picks the targets? Who tells Eliot what they've picked, when they're attacking? How did they get paid?"

They were nearing his apartment. "And most importantly, Leonard, who are they going to hit next? I know some people in the FBI. They would be more than happy to take Eliot down. But we need to know more. We need to tell them what the target is."

"How am I going to do that?"

"Davenport was investigating the firm. She found out enough to confront Eliot. Enough to get killed. Maybe they killed her because she was going to expose them, but maybe they killed her because she knew something. If anyone had figured out who they were going to hit next, she did. You have to find out where she would have kept it. Let me know when you have that."

"I don't know how I'm going to do that."

"You're going to have to try."

They pulled up to his building. The street was calm, the usual midafternoon bearded bicyclists parading their authenticity. He already knew where he was going to go. Somewhere that, until today, he most likely wouldn't have been welcome. Where he would never have wanted or tried to visit. But the situation had changed; he might need help from a crackpot. He was starting to feel like a crackpot himself after all.

"Thank you again, Veronica."

"You have to be careful. They are going to be looking at who your friends are. Who you send e-mails to. Don't go anywhere obvious. Don't even tell me."

"I know."

"Good luck."

Leonard opened the door of the car. He gritted his teeth and walked toward his home, sensing the quiet danger that now surrounded him.

CHAPTER TWENTY-SIX

SEARCH AND SEIZURE

For once, the elevator worked. When Leonard reached his floor, he rounded the corner to find his door sitting wide open. Glued to it was a bright-orange placard, NYPD's standard issue to let the unwary know that their apartment had been subjected to a legal search. Leonard had investigated dozens of complaints from unlucky residents who had come home to ransacked apartments, unable to tell which of their missing possessions had been seized by police as evidence and what had been swiped later by scavengers. At the bottom of the sticker announcing the search, there was a phone number to call to have police technicians come and replace the door if the Warrant Squad had to take it off the hinges or bust it in. Leonard knew that the number in fact rang to a cubicle in One Police Plaza that hadn't been staffed in seven years. He had investigated those complaints too.

The door hadn't been knocked in and hadn't been taken off; it swung listlessly into his apartment. The search team had done everything proper, going to the management office and showing the warrant. At one point, the office had probably been on a first name basis with the warrant guys, maybe had a full-time assistant super assigned to opening apartments for the cops. It would have been a dangerous gig. Nowadays it probably was a novelty. Or just coming back into style, like the rest of it. Leonard wouldn't have to call the number at the bottom of the placard. The open door meant that if the cops weren't still inside, they hadn't bothered to close it when they left. They never do.

Leonard toed open the door. His apartment was a mess. The couch askew, his mattress flung to the wall, jars of mustard spilled from the refrigerator onto the cheap tile. The police never precisely clean up after serving a search warrant, but there was an added note of malice in how thoroughly Leonard's apartment had been tossed. And what had they been looking for, after all? What evidence could they find here that he had killed Davenport? If that was even what they were after.

He turned to his desk. His computer was gone. Maybe some enterprising neighbor came by and hauled it off after the cops left the door open. Or maybe that's what the warrant team wanted Leonard to think. He slid his hand into his pocket, where he impossibly held the flash drive from Veronica. He wouldn't even be able to look at what was on here.

Turning back to the door, he tried to peel off the placard. It was stuck with industrial glue; it wouldn't budge without steel wool or a plaster scraper. His neighbors would see the signal of shame for however long it would take Leonard before he could come back. And Leonard didn't know when he was coming back. He had only just figured out where he was going next.

Leaving the sadly swinging door, Leonard pieced through the apartment. He fished a duffel bag from the general wreck of the floor. The police had sought him out at the hospital and had already been here once. They would come back soon enough. He pulled a change of clothes from the floor and stuffed them in the bag. He needed to see what was on the drive Veronica gave him, and he needed to find what Davenport had been working on. There was no time even to take a shower. He was hitting the road.

CHAPTER TWENTY-SEVEN

THE LONG WALK

Live in this city long enough and pretty soon you will go on a long walk. The first one is romantic. Maybe you thought it was sweet and crazy to stroll from Chinatown across the Brooklyn Bridge with that girl who had read that same book you had, which you thought meant she understood you so well. Maybe you traced the Battle of Brooklyn, or you got convinced by some athletic friend to stomp the length of Broadway. You made it almost all the way to Thirty-Fourth Street before you wore out and took a train home.

The next long walk took you by surprise. You were in your office playing Snood, and the lights went off and you clamored downstairs to the news of the Great Blackout of 2003: The subways were out and you were told to get home to avoid the inevitable looting and panic. So you ditched your dress shoes for ten-dollar sneakers purchased from an instant entrepreneur, passed the ice cream stores and butcher shops offering catastrophic discounts, and went to the roof of your building to watch the chaos unfold. But instead, you shared with your neighbors a bottle of wine and a gorgeous uncluttered view of the starscape.

Or the time the snow swept in so quickly that it threw the subway out of whack and you had to sludge home. You were only two stops away, but your numb toes took hours to stomp through the drifts. Later you boasted to friends that you were caught in the Blizzard of 1996, 2007, 2010, pretending it was much harsher than it really was.

Of course, if you were downtown when the buildings came down, if you were in your office and heard that a plane had crashed and went outside to stare up at the commotion, because that's what New Yorkers do, and you had seen a scorched fifteen-foot piece of metal tearing a gash in the middle of Greenwich Street, and blood and steel and people twisting their way down, then you were in the greatest long walk of all, with Armageddon over your shoulder, a rain of leases and promissory notes and litigious letters collecting into forgotten piles at your feet.

Leonard had been on plenty of long walks.

But that day was different. The subway was working fine. There was no shared catastrophe. After jamming together a change of clothes, he unbandaged his shoulder and checked the mirror. His back was a map of welts, purple rising among the shoulder blades. He wrapped only half of the bandage back on and left the rest in his sink. He took a last sad look at his little apartment before venturing back out for his trek up Flatbush, past the zoo, past the museum, past everything.

Leonard couldn't help but notice the garbage. The trash bags were set out up and down the street, bundled and bursting. There were far too many of them; the corner bins were swelling and even in front of the local businesses, there didn't seem to have been a collection. Then he got it. The sanitation talks had broken down and the strike had begun. The supers had put the loads out as usual, but no one had come to pick them up. Not on the collection day, and not on the day after either. Garbage on the streets; just one more little disaster to add to the pile.

The Premier League bars and snout-to-tail restaurants that lined Vanderbilt Avenue quickly gave way to a McDonald's, a gas station, and the bright fences sealing off the new arena. Only a few blocks and the whole thing emptied out into the Whitman housing project. Not like Ebbets Fields. Whitman was downtown but still harsh, true misery that its brownstone neighbors pretended not to see.

Then Leonard wasn't quite anywhere exactly. The Navy Yard was a place, but it wasn't exactly a neighborhood. Close to it all but still in the middle of nowhere; the only corner of Brooklyn that the developers had yet to reach. The last place where the land was still cheap. Leonard knew the address by heart; he had seen it neatly blocked into the sign-in sheet every month at the DIMAC meeting for years.

Leonard stood next to a weary brick building, across from the Navy Yard. The Yard itself had been spruced and polished: now there was a museum, a playground, and a sea of industrial microsites. But Leonard's destination was here, on the other side of Flushing Avenue. No one had renovated this place. It had once been a warehouse or a mill, had been abandoned for years, and would stay cheap until the market caught up with it. For now, the stairs were worn and unlit, the walls were thick with decades of dinge, and Leonard didn't even stop to consider that it hadn't been necessary to buzz before walking in the front door. He was headed up to the third floor. He passed painted steel doors that hid entrepreneurs who couldn't afford the cost or the attention of the Navy Yard. Someone was probably stapling together bags to be hawked as real Givenchys on Canal Street. Someone might be using another floor as a stash house. And some were worse.

He reached the third floor. His back hurt and his legs were tired. He was sweaty and there was a metallic smell in the air. His shoulder throbbed so insistently that he swore he could hear it. He looked around, sure that he hadn't been followed. There were no lights or windows in the stairwell; it felt as though night had come early. He walked down the hallway and found the number he was looking for.

He banged on the door.

He stood still in the empty summer afternoon, listening to the straggling noise behind the door. It swung open and revealed a marathon woman in a silk suit. Roshni Saal. The head of the August 15 Coalition. She looked over Leonard's beaten face and his soiled shirt and smiled.

"If it isn't Leonard Mitchell. I always knew you would come around to our side."

"I need a place to stay."

"Of course you do. Come right in."

CHAPTER TWENTY-EIGHT
NO END OF MISCHIEF

The room was wide and bright, floored with worn wooden planks and walled with stubborn bricks. Broad windows that long ago gave some respite to employees chained to heavy machinery now let in swaths of sunlight. But it was just as hot as it had been outside. The building too old for central air, the room too large for a window unit to do any good, the heat only intensified in the offices of the August 15 Coalition. Leonard could feel the sweat creep through his hair now, his clothing already spent.

Roshni didn't seem to mind the heat. She was thin beneath the suit, comfortable displaying power. Leonard looked past her into the broad clean office. Across from the iron windows sat a row of four or five computers. Neat workspaces without any workers at them. A bookcase against the rear wall. A broad open hardwood floor, not a speck of dust or a rug to disturb the look. And she seemed to be alone in there.

"The papers said you were in the hospital. That an investigation was ongoing."

"I was beat up by a cop." He didn't have to worry whether she would believe him. "I was in the hospital and the guy who did it was there. I had to run. They have been to my apartment. I don't know where to go. I know that I sound paranoid."

"So you figured you'd come to the person you always thought was paranoid?"

She closed the door behind him. The room was too neat, too empty, too clean. His city office was always cluttered with boxes of files destined for storage, unkempt folders on desks. The offices of the Coalition were a museum, the still hum of the four terminals the only sounds.

"Where is your staff, Roshni? Why is it so quiet?"

"I am my staff. Those computers are set to search every publication in the world, in any language, for mentions of police and death. If someone dies in police custody in Kazakhstan, they will find it. And then I make the indictment and put it on the list."

"There isn't anyone else?"

"I don't need anyone else."

It didn't sound like much of a coalition to Leonard, but he was in no position to criticize. He walked to one of the terminals and sat in a stern chair. Roshni stood watch. It wasn't that she was talking down to him exactly. But it sounded as though she was quite convinced she knew so much more than he did.

"You were assaulted by a police officer. You were hospitalized. You have now fled the hospital without being discharged. No wonder they are looking for you."

"They think that I killed Davenport. Or they want to make it look like I did. I didn't have anything to do with it. I thought you'd understand."

One of the computers let out a quick ping; Roshni brushed past Leonard to check on it. She stared deep as she read the news story that had flashed up. A teenage boy in Papua New Guinea had snuck into the cottage of a woman suspected of witchcraft. To please the town's elders, he had beheaded her in her sleep. The national authorities had swooped in, and sometime between the time he was arrested and set to be arraigned, he had been found unresponsive in his cell. Roshni set to work on a new indictment. Of course, like the rest of them, it was just a piece of paper from her printer. No one in Papua New Guinea was going to arrest a police officer on this woman's say-so any more than the Brooklyn DA would. She kept speaking to him while she did.

"Of course I understand. But who else will. I came to your meetings every month to tell you what was really going on. And you humored me, but you didn't really believe me. And I wonder if you believe me even now."

Leonard slouched into his chair. He fished the flash drive that Veronica had given him out of his pocket. He set it on the cheap folding table in front of him.

"I think I believe you now. I think, actually, it's worse than you think. We should look at this."

Roshni finished with her indictment and sent it to print.

"And what is supposed to be on that?"

If it had been anyone else, Leonard would have worried that he'd look crazy if he said what he was about to say. But she already believed things that other people thought were crazy. It's why he had come here to begin with. "I think these cops are behind the little disasters. I think they are working for a bank. Trying to move the price of stocks through sabotage. Terror for profit. The bank hires them to go sink a water taxi and the bank bets that the water taxi company's stock will tank. And I think that Davenport was on to them."

Roshni was massaging her right hand with her left. The hands were lean and smooth. Her teeth were neat. Her eyes were set deep but watched Leonard carefully. She looked at the floor when Leonard was done.

"So maybe it's true after all."

"What is?"

"The biggest short. There has always been a rumor. People do plenty of bad things on Wall Street, but there have always been stories that someone is out there making his own destiny. There is an easy fortune in villainy, and men are capable of no end of mischief after all. If you knew when the bad guys were going to strike, or how they were going to strike. Or better yet, if you just became one of the bad guys yourself."

"A rumor?"

"Going way back. Bhopal. The *Exxon Valdez*. Imperial Sugar. Just weeks before each of them there was a massive short on the company involved. Six days before the Bhopal disaster, someone bet seven million dollars that Union Carbide's stock would collapse. You can always go back and say something is a coincidence. But you could also imagine that someone is out there betting on catastrophe and then bringing catastrophe to bear."

She took the flash drive and slid it into the machine. It burst to life, sprouting communications, photographs of targets, and pages and pages of intractable code, asterisks and slashes and nothing resembling words at all.

"It's going to take me a while to put together what's going on here. Who gave you this?"

"A friend. Someone who would know. It's what Davenport was working on."

"Well, if this is what I think it is, your friend is in danger. Whoever has been doing this has been at it a while."

Leonard tugged at his bandage. He couldn't help but rib her. "Sure. A grand conspiracy. Next thing you are going to tell me is that someone bet against the *Titanic*. Or that this pop-up investment firm caused the Triangle Shirtwaist fire."

"Leonard, on August 27, 2001, someone placed two large anonymous shorts—one against United Airlines and one against American Airlines. No short of airlines in general. No reason to think those two airlines were going to suffer any particular harm. Unless you were planning to cause that harm. We think that there are people out there destroying the world because they hate our way of life. Or they don't like our morals. But almost every time, you can trace it back to someone who is making money."

She dove deep into the screen now, scanning through police personnel files, schematic drawings of a restaurant basement, a license for crane inspections from the Department of Buildings records. The pages swarmed by one after the other. First there were pages of e-mails, all written in code. Then there were pages mapping out what looked like shipping routes, each with a logo and the words "SKS Containers" plastered in a sleek corporate font across the bottom. The next few pages were more coded communications. Then a photograph of a container ship, then a map of its route, pinpointing its final leg across Buttermilk Channel. Roshni sat up.

"They had been planning to sink the ship, Leonard. The one where the cop got shot."

He held his bandage tight and clipped the fasteners into place.

"How?"

"I don't know. I'm going to have to decode this. It could take all day."

Leonard remembered what Veronica had told him. That they needed to find the next target. The container ship had been the last one. She had pulled records from the firm, she had learned what was going on before, but she didn't know what Davenport had found since. Davenport's investigation was somewhere. Either in the hands of the people who had killed her, or stashed safe.

"Roshni, I'm going to have to go out. This isn't complete. Davenport kept searching after this."

Roshni scrolled through to the final screens. Records of trades. Short sells of the crane manufacturer, the restaurant where the rats had turned up, and the private water taxi line. And of the shipping company. Just two days before Mulino had shot Rowson on the boat. She looked up at Leonard.

"They were planning something on the boat. Rowson was there to sink it; he had killed the deckhand. But Mulino shot Rowson and that was the end of it."

Leonard nodded. He had been right. Mulino had been on the up-and-up all along. More than that, he had been breaking up something serious. He probably hadn't even known what it was. Rowson had flashed his gun, had been trying to escape. And once Rowson was dead, why not pin it on the detective. If Leonard had enough to go on, he could bring it to Mulino. But he didn't have enough to go on yet.

Leonard felt a swift pain in his shoulder. He touched his bandage and felt that it was wet. Probably sweat but he couldn't rule out blood.

"I need to change. I need to go out."

"There is a bathroom in the hallway. But be careful if you leave. If whoever is behind this knows what you're up to, they won't hesitate. I'm going to try to look at the code."

Leonard nodded and stood. He walked through the quiet hallway and into the bathroom. Old-fashioned black and white hex tile on the floor fading to gray and gray. Once the developers get ahold of this building, the whole place will be rubble, then glass and steel, and then no one will remember. He took off his shirt and unwrapped the bandage. It wasn't doing him any good anyway. He changed his clothes. Her story was hard even for Leonard to believe, but at least someone was on his side. At least someone believed him. He had found one ally in Veronica and he now had another surprising one in Roshni.

There was more to do. Veronica had told him that Davenport may have learned something. It was worth a shot. But he couldn't even stand up without stumbling toward the wall now. His head, neck, and back shouted at him to get some rest. To wait a few hours at least. He would ask Roshni if he could sleep awhile on the floor. He would go back out after sunset.

CHAPTER TWENTY-NINE
THE *JOHN MARCHI*

Ralph Mulino's knuckles nearly burst as he squeezed the railing of the Staten Island Ferry, looking at the Statue of Liberty and behind it, the morass of the Jersey City shoreline. The impudent clock, ninety feet tall, perched on the edge of the shore proclaiming a single word: Colgate. As though this crowd could be duped into changing their toothpaste in exchange for being told the time. As though anyone on that ferry didn't know the time down to the minute. Each of these commuters had boarded at six eighteen, as each one had every day of his career, and each would disembark at six fifty-two, no matter what the Colgate Clock did or didn't say.

It was the first time Mulino had been on the water since the night of the shooting, and he hadn't started to like it any better. Sure, it was a smooth ride over the harbor, but that did not put him at ease. He was on the *John Marchi*, a new ship brought on when they upgraded the fleet seven or eight years ago. It was named for a Staten Island legend, a man who had served the island as city councilman, state assemblyman, state senator. He'd even beaten John Lindsay in the '69 Republican primary for mayor, only to have Lindsay double-cross him as an independent in the general. The name reeked of local pride, and reminded everyone on board that while one of the places it docked was lower Manhattan, the other place was home.

It was a bright new boat with sleek modern seats and plenty of room to look over the deck, but Mulino was still on the water, and he still hated being there. If you're on a boat, there are only so many places you can go. If things turn sour, there is no escaping back into an alley, there is no getting in your car and speeding away. Mulino had learned again just a few days ago how limited your options are on the water.

He scanned the rows of passengers. They planned their breakfast and their workday around the ferry schedule, and huddled alone during their thirty-minute trip. It wasn't that long ago that most people on the ferry read the tabloids, rustling real leaves of paper in the twilight. But as Mulino looked up and down the ship, he saw that nearly half the commuters were staring at one kind of electronic device or another. The dedicated office drones were settling up their last batches of e-mails while the pure nine-to-fivers updated their fantasy baseball teams or twinkled bright candy or gems into place.

People hated to be disturbed during a ferry ride, a private little reverie taking place in front of a hundred others. But Mulino would do his job. He fished the photograph of Davenport out of one pocket and his detective's badge out from under his shirt. He straightened his posture and set out for his first victim—a woman whose face was happily buried in an e-reader, glad the other passengers couldn't figure out what kind of books she was into.

"Excuse me, ma'am."

The woman didn't look up. A New Yorker's reaction. If you don't pay attention to someone, eventually they'll leave you alone. It works with unwanted men trying to pick you up in bars and with panhandlers. Not so often with the police.

"Ma'am, I'm Detective Ralph Mulino, NYPD. You mind if I ask you a couple of questions?"

She snuck a peek to make sure he really had a badge, then looked fearful. Everyone has something they'd just as soon not tell a cop.

"What is it?"

He held out the picture.

"Were you on the six-eighteen on Tuesday? Any chance you remember seeing this woman?"

The lady looked over Davenport's picture. Davenport stood rigid, the national and state flags draped behind her, smiling too brightly, the way people do in their official work portraits. The lady shook her head.

"No. I was on the boat. I didn't . . ."

And before she could trail off, Mulino was off to the next one. There were at least three hundred people on the ferry, and it would be docking in only twenty minutes. He didn't have time to linger with people who had nothing to say.

The next one was a stiff-looking guy in a suit who didn't want to talk to him and hadn't seen Davenport. The one after that was wearing flip-flops and had a trim beard and was probably a tourist seeing the Statue of Liberty the cheap way. The one after that was another stiff guy in a suit, as was the next one and the following twenty or so.

Mulino had long ago grown used to the fact that police work, at its essence, was profoundly boring. Asking a hundred or so people the same few questions about the same photograph, only to be told by every one of them that they didn't know anything, was not even close to the dullest thing he'd done as a cop. Mulino had interviewed witnesses who only remembered the first two letters of a license plate and the fact that the car was maybe gray, leaving him to make six or seven hundred house visits in Forest Hills, New Rochelle, and Throgs Neck. He had called upon two hundred hardware stores in Brooklyn to ask which of them might have sold a couple of rolls of a particular kind of cable exactly six weeks before. At least these people on the boat were as captive as he was. At least he knew he was going to be through with them, one way or another, when the ferry landed.

"Oh, yeah, I saw her."

It was a woman in a red suit, dark hair short, and an expensive-looking bag at her side. Someone who ranked a little above the middle management functionaries that typically crowded the ferry. Maybe an ad executive or a boutique lawyer. Maybe the kind of person who works downtown, but not the kind that usually lives in the quiet of Staten Island. Mulino couldn't help but wonder what she was doing on the boat.

"You did?"

"Yeah, it was interesting. She was sitting with a cop. She kept looking over her shoulder, like maybe someone would notice. I thought she was under arrest."

"A cop?"

"Yeah. He was wearing his uniform. Young guy, dark hair. I don't know, a cop." Almost no civilian can tell one rookie cop from the next. Mulino had himself been indistinguishable from a couple of hundred others once, coming out of the academy. You don't want the world to think of you as an individual; you want them all to see the uniform first, the badge second, and the gun third. You never really want them to see your face at all.

"And what happened then?"

"As the boat slowed down, you know, before we docked, the cop stood up and told her to come with him. She started to push off at first and then he grabbed her."

"Push off?"

"You know. You see a ton of people in the city. Crazy or whatever. He grabbed her and pulled her in. I don't remember if he cuffed her."

She hadn't been handcuffed. The marks would have been there the next morning when her body was found. Mulino knew just how much a pair of solid handcuffs can drill into the soft tissue. The cop who took her would have known that too.

"What else?"

"I saw one guy get arrested on the ferry once and he fought off the cops and two other guys that were just riding the boat jumped on him and started punching him. Undercovers, I guess. Everyone looked away. This woman didn't want to be there, but it wasn't as though she was kicking and screaming. I didn't think much of it."

"Thank you."

He kept going, eventually finding a good half-dozen who had noticed Davenport get removed from the ferry by a cop. Like the first woman, no one had thought anything strange about it. Why would they? No one cared: these little dramas go on all day long in New York, and the audience usually keeps its distance.

Just as the boat was nearing the dock at Staten Island, one final witness, a cheap-looking man in a cheap-looking suit, told him one thing more. He had been at the front of the boat, and had seen her get walked off just as it was about to dock, just like everyone said. He had been up smoking a cigarette himself, hanging just off the front starboard where they might not bother to stop you.

"But then it was really the craziest thing."

"What's that?"

"The cop led her away, he gestured to the guys who tie the boat on and he took her down the ramp before it was really steady. He had to duck her into the gate. Just like that. Before anyone else got off. Before the boat was even at the dock all the way."

The ferry slowed as it pulled into the landing. It nudged gently up against the pier, heaving back a quick little rock of relief. At most, the space under the gate was only about three feet high. The cop would have had to tug her down and duck under with her to get her through. Mulino looked up and saw the camera pointed at the bow of the boat. It doesn't start recording, though, until the boat locks into place. A little energy-saving measure. In a minute, the gate would spring open and the whole crowd on this Ferry would heave off. Mulino only had a few moments left for questions.

"How did she look as she left?"

The man thought for a second. "She turned around and she just had the widest eyes. She just looked at me. I thought she said something, but I couldn't make it out. And the cop kind of tugged her around and walked her down the pier."

"Any idea what she might have said?"

"Like I said, I couldn't really hear it. And you don't think, you know, when you see someone get arrested. But at the time the way her mouth moved, what I really thought is that she was calling out, 'Help me, help me.' But you know, so many people are just nuts. What are you going to do?"

CHAPTER THIRTY
DUTY

Joey Del Rio looked up from his terminal to find Sergeant Sparks staring down at him. Joey hadn't noticed him show up, wrapped up as he was in entering the week's daily activity reports into his computer. Harbor Patrol had it good, with computers and everything. Back in the Four-Six, Joey had to tally the DARs by hand, and copy them into a logbook every week for his sergeant. The Harbor Patrol had its downsides, most of which involved the fact that Joey very easily got seasick, but the computers were nice. The sergeant didn't say anything.

"What is it, boss?"

"What do I have to do to get your attention?" The guys with a little military, Joey thought, were the worst supervisors. Sparks was okay, but he was in the reserves, and every couple of months he went out to the Catskills or wherever with his army buddies and they built rafts and ate MREs and whenever he came back he always had a hard-on for protocol. For mopping the floor of the precinct twice a day even though no one ever came in, for making sure the laces of your uniform shoes were tucked into the shoes themselves after you changed out of them to go home. For all the administrative bullshit side of the NYPD. He was a badass, Sparks, but Joey would just as soon have taken it a little easier most days.

"You have my attention, Sergeant."

"I just got a call from our friend."

"No, Sergeant. Find someone else. I'm off tour in thirty minutes."

Sergeant Sparks never got angry. Instead, he started to speak more slowly and he lowered his chin. Like he was displaying his unhappiness with a small child who was mildly retarded. He was speaking very slowly to Joey now, with his chin nearly touching his chest.

"You are going to go off tour when I tell you to go off tour. You accepted the special assignments. And I don't have to remind you what you were given in return."

Joey gritted his teeth. When Sergeant Sparks had first come to him, almost a year ago, he had been desperate. He had been taking in extra money working security for an underground card room. Frisking the guys that came in. Advising them what to do in case of a bust. The undercover that came and played had never even sent a team to bust the room—he had just notified IAB that Joey had been working there.

Sparks had straightened it all out, but the price got higher and higher. At first there was extra money for the work, and the jobs were easy. Then they kept asking him to do things a little bit worse. Damage property. Hurt people. And by the time he realized that Sergeant Sparks owned him, it was too late. The NYPD remained a paramilitary organization. If he tried to rat out Sparks to his lieutenant, he would take the fall with him. Maybe even instead. Ever since what had happened to Brian on Monday, Joey had sworn he wasn't going out on any more of the special operations. But Sergeant Sparks did not see eye to eye with him on that one.

"Please, Sergeant. No one ever said it would be dangerous."

"It got dangerous."

"Well, isn't that your fault? Wasn't the detective supposed to come out after it was all done?"

Sparks looked at the floor. It was the first time Joey had ever seen him look vulnerable. "I did everything I could to slow him down. I told you both to be quick. I told you we were coming. He was getting suspicious, the way I drove the boat. He jumped on board as soon as we got there. I couldn't hold him off any more than I did."

"You didn't hold him off long enough, did you? You didn't hold him off long enough to keep Brian from getting killed."

"We're almost through. The whole operation is coming to a head. But tonight we need you. We're relying on you."

There was no one else in the precinct. Joey thought, just for a moment, about what would happen if he drew his gun on the sergeant. He might have surprise on his side. He might get his shot off before the sergeant did. But even if he did, what then? How would he explain to the Firearms Discharge Control Board why he'd shot his direct supervisor in the middle of a station house with no civilians for a mile around? And if he just refused the sergeant—he wasn't sure exactly how Sparks would pull it off, but he knew that the NYPD wouldn't stop to mourn the loss of Joey Del Rio very long.

"What do you need me to do, boss?"

CHAPTER THIRTY-ONE
WAITING

It was warm and soft outside, the kind of summer night where you start out sixteen and stay up late and pretty soon you're thirty-four with a kid and you don't know where it all went. Leonard was worse even than that. His body ached in a thousand places. He had fled a hospital without getting discharged. He was probably wanted by the police. His only hope of coming through was to get the proof that Christine Davenport had been putting together. Proof about the cops. Proof about Eliot. He stepped up from the Wall Street subway and walked toward number Twenty-Six. With his change of clothes he was presentable, but only barely. Even with the badge, he would arouse suspicion if he tried to go in. He would have to wait for Veronica out here.

The monuments to capitalism past—the stock exchange, the Federal Reserve—loomed larger without the daytime crowds, and Leonard felt suddenly small beside them. He was reminded that he was only a petty bureaucrat, someone with maybe a little power over those even pettier. To the gangsters who flashed in and out of here all day, Leonard and the cops were both equivalent suckers working too hard for too little money. Whether he ran a city agency or pushed paper around the back rooms, at the end of the day, he went back to the Ebbets Field Apartments and the banker went back to Rye. They had no trouble keeping the streets clean here, sanitation strike or no.

Leonard had just seen how the strike was hitting everyone else. He had cut through the Whitman Houses on the way to the subway. Black plastic bags had been torn open and shredded through the courtyard, spilling spoiled fruit and coffee grounds. The fresh rot had been blown into piles.

But on Wall Street, the trash wasn't so bad. The corner bins were overflowing with the soda cups and fast-food wrappers, sure, but nothing had burst and spilled across the sidewalk. The street was already quiet. Fifteen minutes after the closing bell, the subways were crammed with administrators and traders and all manner of support staff. When Leonard had passed Trinity Church, the eternal traffic of Lower Broadway still slogged toward downtown tunnels, but Wall Street itself was dark and still and silent. Throughout the rest of the night, the others would trickle out, never lingering, heading to celebrate at a discreet underground club or just meandering home. Leonard saw a figure in the revolving door. Veronica was on her way out. She saw him. Her fierce green eyes, for the first time since Leonard had met her, flashed with a hint of fear. Maybe she was just surprised to see him; she looked at him and spoke.

"You've changed."

"I got some clothes. I'm staying with a friend."

"Don't tell me who."

"I've seen your file. They were trying to sink the boat. I don't know what Davenport showed Eliot, but if you're right, she had something more. She knew where they were hitting next."

Veronica looked inside her building, back toward the elevator bank. "You have to hurry. Eliot spoke to me again this afternoon. He called me into his office. I think he knows that we're onto him."

"Okay."

"You have to stop the next attack. You have to find out what the next one is going to be. You're in danger. We both are."

Leonard steeled himself despite the evening swelter. "I'm going to Davenport's."

"The police already searched it, I'm sure. If there were anything there, they would have found it."

"The police searched for evidence of her murder. They weren't looking for what I'm looking for."

"If you find it, come by to tell me. Here at the office. Anywhere. I'm worried about Eliot. About what he knows. The sooner you find anything out, the sooner we can act. And then we'll be safe."

Leonard nodded. A slim breeze drifted between the heavy, old buildings.

"Okay." He turned away from her. He could hear the thin clatter of her heels on the broad flagstones, making the deep, full city sound like just another medieval village. The sound of a bored tourist on her way home from checking the Duomo off her list.

Leonard set out north from Wall on another long walk, this one to Davenport's apartment. He walked softly on the cobblestones himself. The click of Veronica's footsteps faded away and Leonard made his way up Nassau Street. At night, total silence here. Or at least it ought to have been. He stopped when he thought he heard another pair of footsteps behind him. He turned around to see only the thick and still darkness. His imagination. He set back onto his walk, pretending he didn't hear the other footsteps start back up again.

CHAPTER THIRTY-TWO
REAL ESTATE

Christine Davenport had lived with her husband and child in what had once been a quiet apartment building on Perry Street. Some couples, some families, people doing just well enough to put down roots in what wasn't exactly the heart of the village. At one time, the old units could see unobstructed over low, abandoned warehouses. Then developers began to take advantage of favorable zoning laws, tax breaks, and river views to raze the last light industrial pockets of Manhattan and push the new Village all the way to the shore. The old tenements and townhouses, where the alcoholic artists of the 1920s had sung each other miserable poems, had long since become single-family residences. The only place for apartments was west. So they had risen, cold metal and sharp glass that blotted the water from the windows of the merely well-off. It was a neighborhood for those who were rich but not banker-rich, people with enough money to do everything except stop developers from putting up a forty-story rhombus between themselves and the river.

The new units blocking the precious view were stocked with hedge funders and tech tycoons. They insisted on kitchen counters made of Italian limestone that chipped if you cooked on it, couches made of gauzy fabric that stained if you breathed on it, and other luxuries that showed off your wealth but made your life generally uncomfortable. Davenport's tidy two bedroom, a pretty nice place in most of the city, would look almost dumpy by comparison. Leonard had been there once, had met her husband and kid and seen what was left of her view after the last condo had gone in. A sliver of water and a bit of Hoboken were on display to the south if you tilted your head just the right way.

She'd been dead almost a week. The cops would have already done a search, like Veronica said. He'd put on a good face for her, but he wasn't all that hopeful he'd find anything. If the official verdict was that she was a jumper, though, Leonard still had a chance. The NYPD doesn't send its firecrackers to suicides. If there had been a knife or a gun stuck under a pillow cushion, they would have found it, but if Davenport had hidden something to stay hidden, it would still be there.

Leonard stood in front of the stout brick building after his weary summer promenade. Even after midnight, people had been out on the streets, drinking beer in paper bags, listening to baseball on the radio. The old New York was beginning to show its face after over a decade in hiding—a city that was middling poor and a little on edge but sparked with life. People complained, but walking the length of Broadway on a summer night, Leonard had seen that there was a song in the city as well. New York was finally having a little burst of freedom, or maybe, Leonard thought, it was only having a rebound from the past twenty constricting years. Maybe New York had grown so safe, so sterile, and so cold so quickly that it had hit a wall, and the only thing happening now was to spring back.

The boom had been bad for street life; people had stayed inside, checking their stock portfolios at all hours and rubbing their hands at the paper value of their apartments. Now that the bust had finally settled in, people cut their budgets and split a pizza with their friends at a

park. They stayed out late. The cops had better things to do now, with
street crime creeping up, than to smack down on open-container laws.
The quality of life, long kept in check by wealth, was returning.

But not to Perry Street. Tucked away from the main drags of the
Village, extending to the water, it was still and quiet and too clean. At
nearly one in the morning at the tail end of August, the building was
dark upstairs. Davenport's lobby was bright and spare, trying to keep
up with the pristine neighbors—white walls, white couches, powerful
light. The apartment building as art gallery, minus any art. Leonard
swerved through the doors and was met with the weight of overpow-
ering air conditioning. He suddenly could feel his sweat start to freeze
in place.

There was a saggy doorman inside, reading the *Post* and listening to
a radio at the same time. A guy who had spent a lot of time plopped in a
chair like this doing just about nothing—he'd once been in pretty good
shape, maybe, but now bulged in the waist, legs, and forearms. His eyes
were clear and his hair was thinning and he drank from an oversized
Styrofoam soda cup. Maybe he'd spiked his Pepsi to get through the
night, and who could blame him. The radio droned with baseball—
the Yankees were on the West Coast, which meant the game would last
well past one. The guard looked up at him, and Leonard held up his
badge, nonchalant.

"Follow-up on the Davenport suicide."

His jowls sagged as he looked up from his paper. "Uniform guys
have come already."

"We have some new intel on a possible fraud. City Hall stuff."

"Lady's already dead."

"It might implicate some other people." Leonard stepped toward
the guard, giving off his best air of shared confidence. "I'd appreciate
you keeping this quiet. It's sensitive. If the wrong people find out, they
might start destroying documents."

"Uniform guys already took her computer."

"We have some intel." Leonard could tell that the guy had been a cop once. He was heavy now, but even a few years in the NYPD can get you set up with the kind of work he had, which you can then keep for life. "Where were you on the job?"

He chuckled. "That was a long time ago. I did six years in the Seven-Seven. Found out I wasn't going to make detective and didn't want to keep walking around waiting to get shot."

Leonard's old neighborhood. Back before the bakeries and the cocktail lounges and the sustainable seafood shop had driven him just outside of its boundaries and into the Seven-Oh. "I know the Seven-Seven. Before they redrew the precinct lines. Prospect Heights."

"We called it Crown Heights then. Cause that's what it is."

"The rough side."

"Both sides of it were rough then."

"I suppose they were."

Leonard smiled at him. People love to talk. People love to believe that their memories of the good old days—or the bad ones—still mean something. That what happened to them is relevant, which means they must be relevant too. Once you get someone to think you're on the same side, warm, together, maybe they stop asking you questions.

Leonard could sense the guard looking him over. Wondering if maybe Leonard wasn't dressed up enough to be a cop. Remembering all the task force guys who would go to church in their Jets hoodies if their wives would let them get away with it. But Leonard knew that the guard would let him pass. It was either that or call a precinct to check him out, and calling a precinct would always be too much work for a guy waiting for his retirement by working overnight security. The guard nodded, swigged his soda, and lifted his paper back up to his eyebrows.

Leonard walked past him to the elevators, which had been redone a few years ago but already looked tired. People put up all-white interiors and it looks cool and minimalist for a moment, and then smudges start to show, hands propping people up against the wall when they come home drunk, someone bringing their kids over to their friend's house for brunch, a patina of grime covering the elegance, unless it is constantly scrubbed, repainted. All the sorts of things that building management is likely to cut back on when the place is undersold and understaffed. The elevator dinged and Leonard stepped inside.

CHAPTER THIRTY-THREE
COLD

The elevator doors sprung open and Leonard walked out into the pristine hallway of the sixth floor. The apartment was unlocked. The cops had probably left it that way. He slipped inside.

The place was a mess. Leonard had heard that Davenport's husband and son had left in a hurry, and hadn't taken much. Whatever they left behind was tossed in a few different heaps in a few different rooms. The smaller bedroom, a closet with a window really, was awash in little-boy clothes hiding sharp plastic toys, traps to the unwary. The broad kitchen opened into an oblong living room, all of it strewn with papers. The husband was a professor, Leonard knew, and it seemed as though every book in the place had been opened and shaken and tossed on the floor, just to make sure no secret suicide note had been tucked inside one. At the far end of the living room was the view Leonard had once seen: a tiny balcony just big enough for maybe two people to squeeze out on, and floor-to-ceiling glass walls that gave Leonard the sense that he was going to fall at any moment. He slid open one of the doors and stepped out.

Heat seeped into the apartment—every indoor space in New York competes to be colder than the next in summer, driving you to sickness when you come in from the comforting swelter. Leonard stood on the balcony. Looking south, he could make out the harbor by the financial center where Davenport's body had been found, the two piers jutting gently into the Hudson.

He turned back into the apartment. The mess that had taken over the floor was everything that had already been looked at. He had to see what had been left in place. He started in the boy's bedroom. It was incredibly small. There was a toddler bed tucked against one wall. It barely fit. The boy was five, he would be getting to be just too large for this. And the next size bed wouldn't fit in here. Leonard lifted the mattress and looked below. He sorted through the dresser, the colorful little-boy underwear and a collection of soccer jerseys. He tapped the sides of the dresser for hidden space. Nothing. He felt rushed, antsy, as though something was coming. He reminded himself not to hurry. He breathed deep. No one knew he was here except for the guard downstairs. And the guard downstairs didn't care.

There was nothing in the boy's room. He wandered back out to the living room. The books were a mess. The couch had been overturned, then set back. He checked between the cushions but there was nothing there. That's what the cops would have done. Sitting on the couch he looked past the stone countertop and into the kitchen. A dozen cabinets, a thousand places to tuck something.

He passed a block of knives untouched on the countertop, the refrigerator decorated with careless magnets, a vase that probably very recently held flowers, disposed of by a forgiving cop. He opened cabinet after cabinet. Plastic kids' cups and sturdy plates dominated. Leonard shook a few of the thermoses for sounds that something had been left inside. Nothing.

He opened the fridge. It was empty, the gentle cool a small refreshment on a long night. The same with the freezer. Not even a tray of ice cubes. He closed the door and stared at the fridge, a half-dozen magnets making a minor constellation on its face.

The magnets. There was a full plastic alphabet, but then something else. Six metal disks, too utilitarian to be some sort of game, pinning no shopping lists or school lunch calendars in place, parked in a line across the right side of the door. Leonard picked one off the fridge. He turned it in his hand. Davenport was smart enough to know that the best place to hide something was in plain sight. He tugged at the magnet, but it was solid, just a piece of metal left on the fridge for no particular reason.

Leonard snapped the magnet back onto the fridge and looked at the other five, close. Smooth uneventful little circles, one after the other. Except one. One had a faint crease down the middle of it. Leonard plucked it from the fridge. He snapped it apart. A flash drive presented itself out of one arc. It was a clever little hiding place. Once upon a time, you couldn't even wave a flash drive near a magnet without erasing it. He would take it back to Roshni and look through it. He slid the magnet into his pocket and breathed out. He was almost there. If the drive had Davenport's investigation on it, the whole thing would be solved. He could show it to Veronica and together they would expose Eliot's scheme.

He turned back to the room, and found himself staring down the barrel of a Glock nine-millimeter handgun.

CHAPTER THIRTY-FOUR
GRAVITY

Behind the gun was a young guy with a chubby face. Clean-shaven, short curly hair, sort of spacey eyes. Leonard would have thought he looked like a sweet kid if he weren't holding that gun. Leonard recognized the nameplate from the stacks of paper he'd been reading.

"Officer Del Rio. Welcome to the neighborhood."

"Don't do anything stupid."

"I won't do anything stupid. I won't shoot anyone, for example."

"We should have got you long before this." That wasn't any surprise. Leonard had figured it was the Harbor Patrol who had been after him. This guy at the head of the line.

"You didn't feel like bringing along your pal Officer Davies this time? Or is he even a real cop?"

Officer Del Rio pointed the gun to Leonard's pocket.

"Take it out."

Leonard reached toward his pants. "I'm going to move slowly. You asked me, so just keep your cool."

His shoulder hurt as he reached in. He slid his hand into his pants and pulled out the magnet with the flash drive inside. He lifted it out and held it between his thumb and index finger.

"Hand it over."

"Or else you're going to shoot me? You'll walk out of the apartment and leave me here dead? Do you think that security guard downstairs won't be able to ID you? I bet you showed him your shield. Gave your name. He's going to come up here and find a body and tell the DA that Officer Del Rio of the Harbor Patrol followed me in. Give them your Tax ID and everything."

"Now."

Leonard set the magnet on the marble countertop. The cop held his gun on Leonard as he leaned in. "Stay still." Del Rio kept his eyes on Leonard and reached onto the counter. Leonard thought for a moment about making a lunge for it. His shoulder hurt too much for him to move quickly. He might have talked Del Rio down from just shooting him outright, but he didn't want to press his luck.

The cop reached for the magnet with his left hand, keeping his right trained on Leonard. He pulled it to his edge of the counter. Leonard saw his eyes dart down to it. He was maybe four feet away, and behind the kitchen island. If Del Rio was distracted, Leonard might have a chance. He figured that if he could keep the cop talking, maybe keep him thinking about more than one thing at once, he could confuse him. That would be a start.

"Why are you doing this, Joey? Who are you working for? You're a cop; you aren't supposed to be out running around killing commissioners and robbing people."

"That's right, I'm a cop. It used to mean something, to be a cop in this city."

"And you don't think it does anymore?"

Del Rio scrunched up his nose and Leonard saw his pasty cheeks quiver. The cop looked suddenly so young. "It used to be they let us go out and do our job. Keep crime down and everyone is happy with you.

Then we are watched by everyone. We are watched by DIMAC. We get watched by the feds. We aren't supposed to be cops anymore. It's like working at the post office."

Leonard smiled. Del Rio couldn't be more than twenty-five. The new administration had stepped up enforcement against the police, had watched them a little more closely, but this guy had never known a world where the cops could run through the streets cracking skulls and not pay a penalty for it. "Someone's been feeding you that, Joey. Someone has been telling you about the good old days. The 1970s, before Frank Serpico and all that. You weren't even born. It wasn't how they tell you it was, you know."

"No, I mean just now. The city starts falling apart because the mayor won't let the cops do their job. And then who gets the blame. We do. I'm sick of it. We're all sick of it. So if you want to know why, well we're just letting you know what it would be like without us."

"But you tried that. You tried just not doing anything at all. And it didn't work. So you had to start going out and making the crime. What does that tell you, officer? Who is keeping the city safe from you?"

"You keep quiet."

Leonard remembered that Del Rio had a partner. One he was paired with every day of patrol. Most likely he had been with him on his fateful day off too.

"The whole precinct was in on it, wasn't it? You were sent out to the boat with Rowson. What were you doing out there? How did you end up getting away?"

"I don't need to answer any of your questions. I'm not at DIMAC getting investigated. You impersonated a police officer to break into this apartment." Del Rio stared at Leonard. Leonard could see the cop's hand start to shake. The cop was attacking him, the natural pounce of someone who was worried. Who was afraid.

Leonard stayed calm and spoke slowly, his eyes on the gun. He had to rattle the officer. "Who sent you out there? Did you do them all?

The water taxi, the crane, the chemical spill? Do you even know who's behind it?"

"I know why we're doing it. We're doing it to make the world safer. You get a little taste of what life is like if the police aren't there to protect you and you're all going to come running back into our arms." The same tired rhetoric. The animals are taking over the city. Leonard could tell just from listening to Del Rio who had been feeding him these lines.

"No, Joey. That's just your sergeant talking. You're doing it because someone at an investment bank has been betting against those companies. Hoping their stock price will go down and then hiring Sparks or whoever he works for to wreck them. You're just a tool in your own little conspiracy."

Del Rio stammered. Leonard watched him work through it. Of course Del Rio wouldn't have known anything. He would have taken orders from someone, likely Sparks, and never thought about who was running the show. From Del Rio's perspective, Sparks would have been a guy who got him out of a jam and asked him for some favors. No one would tell the muscle that they were rigging stock prices for an investment company they had never heard of. They'd come up with a story the cops could believe if any of them ever asked. But given how close they had been to being fired, how much they owed to Sparks, it was more likely that none of them had ever asked. Del Rio's grip tightened on the gun and he stared dead at Leonard. "I know everything I need to know."

"Did you kill Davenport too? Are you going to phone me in for impersonating a cop, have the Sixth Precinct come by to collar me? They'll get here, and as far as you know that flash drive has evidence tying you to a murder. Do you think Sparks will cover for you then?"

Del Rio stared at Leonard. Leonard realized that he was bruised and his clothes were ragged, and he didn't look like someone who could be trusted. But he could see Del Rio start to puzzle it over as well. To wonder, maybe, if he was being set up himself. If Del Rio and Rowson had been out on the boat together, then something had gone very wrong. Del

Rio had already seen someone get killed as part of this operation. As the cop stopped to consider, Leonard could see his grip on the gun grow lax and his eyes glaze in a moment of distant contemplation. He stared down at the little flash drive, then reached to pick it up with his free hand.

A moment was enough. Leonard feinted to his right then swung back toward Del Rio's hand and threw it onto the marble countertop. Forget hitting the body, just take out the hand with the gun. The gun went off, but the bullet clattered past harmlessly. It hit at least three walls before it stopped—one thing they don't tell you when they sell you expensive tile for your backsplash is how well bullets will ricochet off the product.

Del Rio screamed. Leonard thought about nothing but the cop's hand. He held it on the counter and twisted his body away from the barrel. Del Rio managed to launch two more rounds before Leonard had climbed all the way on top of the island. Kneeling, Leonard had a good view of Del Rio's face; he winced as his shoulder seared, but he managed to land a punch. Del Rio screwed up his nose and swung wildly with his free hand. Leonard dodged it and ground his knee onto the officer's pinned right wrist. That was what made him let go of the gun, screaming and wailing and grabbing his bent palm with his good hand.

The cop had managed to flick his wrist while dropping the gun, so it swung off the counter and onto the floor. Leonard was still on the island, pinning Del Rio's arm and shoulder below his knee as the cop twisted away from the countertop. Del Rio turned to lunge for the weapon and Leonard slid off the counter and into the officer, the two of them balled on the floor, swimming among books and papers and loose clothing, both out of reach of the gun. The magnet sat harmless on the countertop. Del Rio slid on his shoulders, stretching his foot toward the weapon. Leonard tugged him back and thrust his knee into his gut. Del Rio gagged for a moment, then gasped as he looked up.

Leonard wasn't in the kind of shape that the cop was; sitting at a desk doesn't prepare you for someone who hits the weight room twice a day. Plus he only had one good arm. He was the underdog, but when you're the underdog, you can take bigger risks. You can do things that otherwise maybe aren't fair. So he yanked on Del Rio's hair, twisting back the cop's neck, and landed a pair of blows below the ribs. Del Rio lost air quickly, gasping. Leonard grabbed the back of the Del Rio's head and slammed his face against the marble countertop. Being a little bit unfair has its advantages.

Leonard tried to slip around the cop toward the gun. Del Rio tripped him. As Leonard fell, his hands hit the pistol, sending it sliding across the floor toward the open door out to the balcony. Del Rio started past Leonard, Leonard grabbed Del Rio's knee, and they both spun down to the ground. Del Rio was on top of Leonard, swinging at his face. The cop landed a few pretty strong blows, and Leonard learned that when the guy takes a full swing, getting punched in the face can really hurt. Not to mention that when you're lying down and get hit, the back of your head hits the floor, and in a nice apartment like Davenport's that means hardwood, with an emphasis on hard.

Leonard was pulling up from the blow and Del Rio was reaching for the gun when Leonard grabbed at the cop and something slipped out of his belt. A canister a little bigger than a tube of lipstick. His pepper spray. Leonard didn't have time to think, he just let loose with it, squeezing the top and letting the stream take its course. By regulation, you are only supposed to shoot one burst of pepper spray, for one to two seconds, and then assess whether it is having the desired effect before firing again.

That, of course, is the regulation if you are a police officer pepper spraying a non-compliant civilian. But Leonard was well past the world of regulations. He squeezed, and when Officer Del Rio shrieked, he pressed harder still. Leonard got closer than the allotted three feet. In fact, although he didn't feel great about it, he shoved the canister in the cop's mouth and sprayed some down his throat. If Leonard had found out that a cop had used pepper spray on a civilian like that, the officer would have ended up with a pretty big rip. As it was, Del Rio was rolling on the ground coughing, and it wasn't clear whether the red gobs dribbling down his face were spray that hadn't made it down his throat or his own blood. He was on his hands and knees now, blinded by the spray, trying to breathe.

Sprawled on the floor, writhing in pain, Del Rio lunged wildly, trying to corral the gun maybe. Wheezing from the pepper spray, his eyes starting to swell shut already, it was useless. Leonard walked past the cop and picked up the gun. He had never held a gun before. People who talk about guns always say that they are heavy, and so Leonard was prepared for the gun to be heavy. But even knowing that a gun is heavy, when he picked it up it was still heavier than he thought it was going to be, all dense packed metal and also heavy with what it can do, what it means to be holding a gun over a man who is incapacitated, who couldn't fight back, who was now at Leonard's mercy.

Del Rio wheezed. "Don't kill me."

"I wasn't planning on it."

He looked up. He couldn't see, but Leonard could tell that Del Rio was tracking his voice. Leonard was standing by the open balcony door, holding the gun, testing its weight, pointing it at the floor. Not that Del Rio knew that.

"I don't know anything about a bank. Sparks got me out of a jam. I owed him."

"And Rowson? And Davies?"

"He's got about a dozen cops. He pays us extra."

"He pays you extra to let the chemicals out of the plant? To sabotage the crane? To sink the water taxi?"

"Everyone was supposed to get off that boat okay."

"It sounds so innocent when you plan it."

The cop took two very deep breaths. Leonard could tell he was struggling, but that he had plenty of strength left. He was in pain, but cops can still operate when they are in pain. If he could see, if he could breathe okay, then Leonard wasn't out of the woods, gun or no. Del Rio heaved up to his knees and spoke.

"I'm sorry about all this. I never wanted to hurt anyone. But you should have stayed out of this. It wasn't your business."

"You're in the house of the woman whose business it was. And her business was my business."

Del Rio was crouched on the floor. As soon as he'd finished speaking he thrust his hands over his eyes. That was going to make it worse. He was going to rub the oil right into the cornea. What he really needed to do was flush both eyes with water, but Leonard wasn't about to tell him that. It was in the Patrol Guide, and if Del Rio didn't know, maybe that was just one more reason he got picked for these kinds of jobs. As Leonard walked closer, though, Del Rio pounced. He had been listening to the sound of his footsteps. Leonard had no reflexes to lift the gun and shoot at Del Rio. His arms were down. His finger resting far from the trigger.

But he could step out of the way, and when Del Rio jumped and Leonard swept to the side, the officer sailed through the open window and onto the balcony. Before he could stop himself he was up in the air, his body over the ledge, his feet twirling behind him. His hands swarmed around, looking for something to hold. Leonard swung toward the cop; he didn't want to kill anyone. He caught Del Rio's arm and the cop gripped his wrist. Leonard was yanked toward the ledge by the other man's weight, and his torso bruised suddenly against the railing. Leonard was bent over the edge, Del Rio holding his arm desperately with both hands. The cop's face was speckled with pepper spray and his eyes were squinting shut with pain. Leonard heaved a moment upward, trying to bring the cop back inside. His shoulder soured and his arm was weak and limp. He looked beyond Del Rio toward the quiet street. The cop grunted, grabbed Leonard, and started to pull upward.

The pepper spray had been smeared across the cop's hands and streaked onto Leonard's arms. He could feel it start to sting, but more than that it was oily, slick. As Del Rio lifted one hand, the other slid down Leonard's wrist, and even as he lunged again for the cop it was too late. Just below him, Del Rio looked as though he was hanging still in space, his mouth smeared with the spray and his eyes fierce, blinded, and cruel. He seemed to hover for a moment before streaking six stories downward. Leonard looked away, and when he turned back he saw Del Rio sprawled in the empty street. The whole block was deserted. If the guard saw it, he would already be on the phone. Otherwise the body might lie there all night. Leonard looked again as something caught his eye. Del Rio's body, splayed on the street, still had a gun in its holster. The one that Leonard had wrestled away from him was a spare. An extra police-issued gun. Cops don't carry spare firearms. But there was one weapon from the Harbor Patrol that had been missing for almost a week. And it was just like the one that Leonard was holding now. It was Rowson's gun.

Leonard jammed the gun into the back of his pants and pulled his shirt over it. Nothing much was concealed—if a cop were walking behind him he would see the outline in a second. Sticking the gun there was the second-worst option, after just walking down the street with it in his hand. He had to get back to Roshni's office. And now, with a dead cop to deal with, and proof that the cops were the ones that were after him, Leonard felt pretty sure that going out into the city with a gun was safer than going out without one. His hands were searing from the pepper spray. He soaped them up and washed them at the fancy sink. There were no towels and he had to wipe his hands on his pants. He collected the flash drive, he walked to the elevator and shot downstairs.

He couldn't go back out the lobby. He thought about going to the second floor and taking a fire escape. He pressed the button for the basement and hoped for the best. The elevator opened into a garage filled with sleek little sports cars. Leonard saw a dim red light in the corner of the garage. A fire exit. He jogged past the late-model designer toys and toward the door. He pushed the bar, ready to run if there was an alarm. There wasn't. Another part of the renovation they had skimped on. The door opened onto Washington Street, the gaudy new condos and the water beyond. To Leonard's left was the edge of Perry Street, where he knew Del Rio was lying dead. He didn't hear sirens. He didn't hear anything at all. He walked right, went up a few blocks, and started to make his way up to the subway, ready for a short ride and another walk back to Roshni's office. He had Davenport's final collection of evidence tucked safely into his pocket and a dead cop's gun tucked into his waistband.

CHAPTER THIRTY-FIVE
EVIDENCE

The subway was too cold. People who had been out enjoying the frivolity of a New York summer night in thin gauzy clothes were shivering home on the train, sweat freezing on their necks. The MTA blasts the air conditioning in the summer, trying to prove that it is providing a service, and half the time you end up sick.

But Leonard couldn't stop sweating. He was perched in a corner seat, across from the conductor's booth, squirming so that no one would notice the gun. He couldn't be sure he wasn't being watched. He couldn't spot anyone who looked like a plainclothes. The people on the train, after midnight on a weeknight, were mainly kids, people in their twenties who were now rocking back and forth trying to keep from passing out or peering deeply into electronic gadgets. Maybe a half-dozen, maybe more. They seemed pretty harmless themselves, but you never know who might suddenly step on board.

The girls were in black, and not much of it, showing their navels and shoulders, parading their youth and glee. One of them danced in place, swaying in front of the guy she had gotten on the train with, as he sat with one hand on the railing and the other on her ass, holding drunk and steady, as though trying not to puke on her black-on-black stenciled skirt. The car was clean and fast and quiet—graffiti and soot and blood had yet to find their way back to the subway, and it hummed ruthlessly downtown toward Brooklyn. No one got on at Wall Street, and as the train sped into the tunnel, Leonard figured for the moment he was safe.

He would load up the flash drive at Roshni's; if it told him the next target, he would tell Veronica. Del Rio hadn't known anything about the bank, about Eliot Holm-Anderson, but then again, why would he? If he had been hired just to do the dirty work, why would Sergeant Sparks tell him who they were working for? Instead Sparks had given his minions a cover story. Make people afraid to walk the streets at night, to ride the water taxis, the subways. Make them believe that the restaurants are foul and that the buildings are stuck together with silly putty. And then they'll come crying back to you. Then this whole experiment will get turned around. Another iron fist will land in the mayor's office and dole out another set of medals to the cops who run through the streets shaking down kids.

It was an easy train to get on—an easy story to believe. Leonard himself had started to believe it himself. For a time, he had started to think that the gleaming city of the past ten years, with a new skyscraper on every block and a suspicious cop on every corner, had been the better one. He had begun to doubt the fresh, darker, looser city that was poking its head back above the parapet. Until that night. Until walking to Davenport's and seeing the messy city at play once again. Del Rio and the rest of them thought they were cleaning up the mess, but in fact they had been setting the stage for an even bigger one.

The train roared into Brooklyn as Leonard's sweat eased away. The kids were still lounging and fondling each other, headed deeper into the borough to crash in their shared sublets on Flatbush or their parents' place in Midwood. Leonard was the only one to get off at Borough Hall; downtown Brooklyn died at night. Staunch municipal buildings set off against quiet townhouses where comfortable professionals stay as close to Manhattan as their pay scale allows. No matter how far the city fell, Leonard thought, crime wouldn't swarm back to Brooklyn Heights anytime soon, so they didn't have his troubles. As he walked up the stairway from the subway and was met again with the heat—past one in the morning and still thick, heavy, wet—Leonard realized that no one had his troubles.

CHAPTER THIRTY-SIX

NIGHT

Crossing Cadman Plaza, Leonard could see the garbage strike taking its toll. The bags that had been tied taut and placed carefully on the curbs already bore telltale gnawed holes, and small puddles of gunk seeped out of them. The headquarters for the Office of Emergency Management were still pristine—OEM had some way, in the crevices of that place, to take care of its own. But everything else—the court, the muni building, the McDonald's that fronts the expressway as you turn toward Flushing Avenue—was piled with trash. The neat bundles had descended into scattered piles of wretched-smelling refuse and torn plastic. Even this late the air was still hot, and the urban reek that usually only lingers in alleyways and less desirable subway stations had become pervasive.

Leonard didn't smell so great himself, he realized. It was nearly two, and the best he had to look forward to was crashing on the hardwood floor of Roshni's office and trying to make sense of this all in the morning. He wasn't sure even that she'd be there to let him in. She hadn't given him a key. At least he had the flash drive. He hoped there would be something on it. Some kind of valuable news.

There was no one on the street. He wandered down past the on-ramp to the expressway, to avoid the Whitman courtyard. The toughs in there would have been able to spot the gun in his jeans, making him a legitimate target. He passed into the blocks surrounding the Navy Yard, abandoned for the night, crossed a deserted corner near the warehouse, and stared down the sickening road.

The sidewalk was sticky with ooze. Busted trash bags poured across the asphalt, leaking plastic containers, wet crinkled wrappers, and mottled sludge that had once been food. The scene was much worse than when he had left. It was the middle of the night and no one lived on this street; the trash hadn't been tossed from nearby apartments. Up the road, Leonard could hear a diesel rumble and a familiar hydraulic hiss. He stepped onto the sidewalk and into the doorway of the Coalition's building. It was dark enough that he could hide, so long as no light shone directly at him. He breathed deep and held still. The sound of an approaching truck wouldn't ordinarily fill him with fear. Ordinarily, though, he didn't break into buildings to steal documents and throw cops out of windows. There was nothing ordinary going on that night.

The truck turned the corner toward the trash-speckled street. A sanitation rig, all right. The kind driven by the guys who were on a full-on strike. The kind that no one believes is out of the garage. And here it was, carrying a full load down to the Navy Yard. As it passed the warehouse, the belly of the truck heaved upward and the flaps at its rear sliced open. A thick wave of trash gushed straight onto the asphalt, coating it slick and warm. The load spent, the truck roared on, righting its payload and gliding toward downtown, light on its feet now that it had released its burden.

Leonard stepped out of the doorway. Someone was dumping trash on purpose. Maybe certain neighborhood bosses had paid off their local council members to arrange for a few runs to ease the misery of the strike. Maybe the people running the basketball arena or the arts complex had found a way to get their special pickups. But what would be the point of spreading it all over the road? Who were they trying to punish? Wouldn't somebody notice, with the drivers allegedly out on strike?

Leonard pushed through the doorway. No buzzer, no lock, just like this morning. He hiked through the dark stairwell to the steel door hosting the Coalition offices. He tried the handle. Nothing. He bunched his fist and banged the door. Three, four times, hard. Hoping he wouldn't wake up the guys loading glassine envelopes downstairs; they might come out shooting. No answer.

There was nowhere else safe to go. He slouched, his back against the door, and slid to the floor. He was exhausted. He smelled. His shoulders were throbbing and all he wanted to do was sleep. He cradled his head into the doorframe, a steel pillow, and was almost asleep when Roshni, groggy herself, opened the door. He slid almost to the floor, catching himself on the doorframe before he banged his head.

"Leonard. Did you find anything?"

He turned to his knees and reached into his pocket. What to tell her? By now someone would have found the body. It would be over the radios. If she knew what kind of danger Leonard had brought with him she wouldn't let him stay. Accessory after the fact is a real crime when the fact is a murder. And Leonard himself had to worry about more than just the cops from the Harbor Patrol. The whole force would be out after him. Someone would be talking to the doorman. They'd be getting a description. Not long after that . . . He didn't like to think about it. Better to say nothing. For her own safety, after all. He pulled out the flash drive.

"We have to take a look at this."

CHAPTER THIRTY-SEVEN

SPARKS

First Rowson, then Del Rio, Sergeant Sparks thought as he stepped onto the dock. These new officers were eager and hungry, but they couldn't keep their cool. It was hard enough training them to be cops. Getting them onto bigger projects, getting them to keep their heads on under pressure, was almost impossible. It was a risk they'd both taken. They knew the drill. Rowson had a family, but the NYPD had good death benefits, they'd be well taken care of. Del Rio was just a kid, dumber than a sack of hair really, but they'd give him a hero's funeral. Getting killed on the job was the best thing that could happen to him. The way it went down, people would think the kid was breaking up a robbery or something. Posthumous promotion to detective and a thousand cops who never knew how slow he was saluting him.

There were a few of them left, but Sparks wasn't even sure he could trust them. Not after what just happened. He'd sent Del Rio after the investigator for a reason, but the investigator had turned the tables on them. A shoddy, sloppy civilian. It was an insult to the force to have someone like that best a uniform. Someone who didn't have posture, didn't have form, didn't have self-respect. Not like the police. To Sparks, that was what the project was all about, after all, teaching the city the value of respect. The money was the least of it. No matter what the man who was paying him thought, to Sparks that was just a means to an end. A way to get the people back under control. And here was the evidence that they were necessary, a civil servant sneaking into an apartment after midnight and killing a police officer. Someone who carried a badge himself, no less. Shameful. No wonder crime was on the rise.

And who knew if Mitchell had found something. Sparks had the team search the apartment but you never know if everything is there. If the investigator knew, then Sparks would have to act quickly. There had already been too many mistakes. Del Rio had let Rowson get shot. Setting up Mulino for it by taking the gun had been gravy, but there was nothing on the wires about Del Rio having two guns on him. Del Rio didn't even know how to wipe someone out and plant a gun on him properly. And it meant that Mitchell now had Rowson's gun. That wouldn't do him any good. It would only be a matter of time before the apartment was dusted for prints or the security guard sat down with a sketch artist—now every cop in town would be looking to take him out. The guy wouldn't be able to cross the street without being shot. It was one less thing to worry about.

He stood at the base of the pier. Spindling out from the Harbor Precinct into the bay, the lights of the Verrazano signaling the way home to Staten Island. He walked down the scraggly wood toward the edge. The NYPD ought to renovate the docks. With the money being spent on iris scans and fingerprint sensors at One Police Plaza, it was a travesty that the special patrols in the outer boroughs had to suffer like this. A board creaked and nearly gave way; proof of his point.

It didn't matter if Mitchell had found something at that apartment or not. Sparks would have to finish the job tomorrow, and he would have to do it alone, but after that, the people would come round. The fear that he had lived in for the past two years would fade, and he would be able to go back to the bright shining life he had been promised when he first put on the uniform.

Sparks stepped toward the last few feet of the antique dock. The water was still. He reached the edge of the pier and hauled in the little dingy. He pulled back the tarp and checked on the bricks. Tightly wrapped plastic packages, ready for their duty. He counted them, as he did every night. The full load was there. Time was short. He looked back up at the bridge. The Verrazano, the greatest bridge in the city, but the one that snobs in Manhattan don't even bother to know exists, stood triumphant over the channel. On the edge of the pier at the Harbor Patrol, Sergeant Sparks folded a tarp over enough Semtex to bring it down.

CHAPTER THIRTY-EIGHT
IDLEWILD

Leonard Mitchell, soaked and broken in the tatters of his work uniform, couldn't help but notice that Roshni appeared pressed and fit, still in her silk suit, long after midnight. She had slept in the suit, or maybe she hadn't slept at all, instead pacing through her near-empty office waiting for the computers to spew out another faraway tragedy. The cool metal glow from the screens enchanted the office, otherwise dark. Sitting at one of them, looking over his shoulder at her before slipping in the hard drive, Leonard wondered at her poise. Imperial cheekbones, stone-dark eyes, and a twenty-first century indeterminate skin tone. He had always considered Roshni Saal a zealot. But didn't he need a zealot now? Hadn't the hour grown desperate? The machine caught the drive and buzzed awake.

Leonard felt slow and sick and hot and tired. "Roshni. Is there anywhere in here I can clean up? Is there a shower?"

"The bathroom is in the hallway. There's a sink."

He had seen the sink. It wouldn't do him any good. He could splash enough water on his face to keep him awake for half an hour, but if he needed to go back out in the world and not stand out like a homeless man, he would need another plan. He thought as he shuffled in his chair. As he did, Roshni stepped away from him disapprovingly.

"Where did you get that?"

"I told you. I went to Davenport's apartment. I found what she had been working on."

"No. Not the hard drive. That."

The gun was still crammed in the back of his pants. He marveled that he had made it on the subway ride and the walk here without it being spotted. Now he was alone with someone who could maybe help him. Would maybe be his ally. And she had spotted it right away.

"I told you that I'm in danger, Roshni."

"You don't have the gun because you're in danger. You are in danger because you have the gun."

In one sense this was true, but Leonard couldn't tell her that yet. He still needed her help. And as much as she didn't like cops, he was pretty sure she didn't think killing one was the best plan. He could explain that to her too. But he wouldn't be able to explain away the dozens of officers who would come to arrest them if they knew he was here.

He lifted the gun and set it slowly on the counter, the barrel against the wall. "I'm pretty sure that this belonged to Brian Rowson. The dead detective. The police took it from the scene so that they could frame up Mulino, and they were going to use it to frame me up tonight."

"Mulino killed that detective on the boat. Whether or not he had a gun, Mulino killed him."

"Maybe. But if he was set up, don't you want to know why? Don't you want to see what they are planning to do next?"

As if on cue, the computer gave birth to the hoard of files on Davenport's little drive. Some of it they had seen before. Plans for the crane. A schematic showing how to get into the restaurant where the rats had been let out. A series of codes to the security doors of the chemical factory. And e-mails sent to someone at EHA, explaining all of it.

Now decoded, except for the recipient. Brian Rowson had been writing EHA to give a quick little heads-up to the money people that the job was about to be done.

But there was more. Davenport had added to the trove of documents she'd been given by the bank. She had tapped in or broken into the NYPD computers herself. Leonard had seen the scraps of the IAB investigations, but this was new. A digital dossier on all the Harbor Patrol cops and a few more, showing what they'd been accused of, how they had been cleared, and their new assignment. Del Rio had been busted for working at a card game. Rowson had stolen the earrings. Davies had shot a man's dog when executing a search warrant. Each investigation had started honest enough, but each had been dropped before it was done. And at the end of each file was the same neat signature closing the case and reassigning the officer. A signature that Leonard couldn't believe that he recognized. The officers had mostly been reassigned to Harbor, under Sparks's command. The few that hadn't—Officer Davies and another—were assigned to the Seven-Oh, just like they said. Only they too had special notes regarding an assignment to Sergeant Sparks.

"Sparks has a small army of officers. A whole command that will do whatever he says."

Roshni was standing just close enough to see, but far enough to show her disdain, for the gun if not for Leonard.

"I see."

He turned to the next file. Payment records. Wire deposits. Every two weeks, ten days sometimes. Tens of thousands at a time. The next page showing the account holder: James Sparks. So the sergeant was at the center, after all. Not just sending his officers out to bust heads. But getting paid for sabotage. There was nothing on where the money was coming from. Nothing to show that EHA was bribing the officers, that it was dictating what buildings to wreck and which businesses to destroy. Another page. The e-mails they'd seen before. These to EHA, telling them that jobs had been completed. Davenport had cracked the code that had been used. The e-mails where short and plain and had been sent just hours before each of the little disasters. One had been sent the night that Mulino had shot Rowson on the container ship. The last one.

"How did she get all this?"

The room was quiet, and even this late, it was sufferingly hot. The open windows offered feeble hope of a breeze, not enough to counter the glow coming off the computers. Never mind that there wasn't any wind, the streets outside were slowly piling up with garbage, and the wet, heavy air from the outside injected just as much misery as the wet, heavy air inside.

"I don't know how she got it. But we have it now."

And the last set of documents came onto the screen. Something new. Blueprints, designs. A path into a basement. A computer-generated lobby design, maybe from a real estate firm. Except this one was highlighted with red arrows and cross-signs, pointing out sight lines and emergency exits. The next page, a map of the basement. Six markings on it, each noting "structural support" and "carrying capacity twenty-six tons." Each marking followed by a bright-red *X*.

The schematics were all marked with the logo of Idlewild Construction. One of the many that had been busy hoisting buildings during the boom, only to slow down during the slump. But Idlewild had been back in the game quicker than most. It had a few new buildings to boast of. Like the one they were looking at the blueprints for. Leonard wouldn't have to look up the stock price to know it was booming. Or to know how quickly it could drop after the wrong kind of news.

Roshni said it first. "It's a demolition plan. It's a map of how to take down a building."

Leonard nodded. Davenport had found the next target after all.

"Roshni. You're going to have to help me. I know someone who can put us in touch with the FBI. We can give them the documents. They can investigate. And they can stop this."

The third computer down the line chimed forth a small cold noise. Roshni walked over to it and peered at the screen. A woman in Moscow had died of diabetic shock on the way to the precinct after being arrested at an anti-government protest. So much unfairness in things to keep track of.

Leonard was scrolling through the pictures. The plan was detailed and precise, the building familiar. It was obvious in retrospect, the perfect target.

"Roshni, look." She turned from her printout and stared at the plans. Page after page of schematics.

"Oh, Leonard." Roshni stared at the diagrams. As Leonard scrolled the pages, the whole plan came into view. A final slide: the basement floor. Her walnut eyes open wide, she leaned over his shoulder. "Leonard, you can't go to the FBI."

Leave it to the zealot to be rational. Because Leonard was in no position to call this one in. After what he had done that night, he couldn't walk up to the NYPD, the FBI, and show them what he'd found. He'd be in solitary before they ever looked at the file. But there were places to go other than law enforcement. He tried to sound reassuring when he spoke.

"I have someone who can help. Someone who knows about this all."

"That isn't it, Leonard. Look."

She scrolled to the top of the page. Printed in neat small letters above the schematic was the phrase "Target Schedule." And a date.

"You see, Leonard, there just isn't time. That isn't even tomorrow anymore. That's today."

CHAPTER THIRTY-NINE

SKETCH

Ralph Mulino kept a chair by his workspace to prop his right knee up. It hurt if it wasn't elevated, but he couldn't turn into one of those people that went whole hog and actually put his feet up on the desk. Carving out a private workspace in Property had been challenge enough. He'd had to agree to an early tour, and had been at Gold Street before six. He would lose even this meager perk if anyone thought he looked sloppy. He was piecing together a picture of the cop he was looking for, based on the people he had spoken to on the Ferry. Medium build, curly hair. A couple of people had mentioned that the cop had funny-looking eyes, but no one could quite describe why. It was a picture of an ordinary rookie, like a thousand others who had come out of the academy and got fed into a precinct to figure out for themselves if they were going to be the right or the wrong kind of cop. Most officers know within a year, and most stick with their choice their whole career. If this guy was sneaking off the Staten Island Ferry with people who turned up dead not so long later, though, he was more than the ordinary wrong type of cop. Mulino sipped on his coffee and turned the portrait around on his knee.

"Did you hear?" It was one of the newly reassigned officers. You never ask what they did to get dropped here. Some kind of Russian name. Mansky. They make Russian cops now. Once upon a time, Mulino smiled to himself, they didn't even have Russian criminals.

"I didn't hear anything." Mulino swung his knee down from his chair. Standing in the doorway, Detective Mansky couldn't have been more than five-foot-two but had a thick neck and shoulders that could lift a truck. He had been at OCCB too. All of twenty-five years old, he already had his detective's badge and was ready at a moment's notice to go out on the street and start busting heads. Probably had busted one too many before getting word he was going to the Property Clerk. Mulino remembered what that felt like. Mansky had a copy of the *Daily News* in his hand.

"A cop got killed last night."

He dropped the paper on Mulino's desk. The massive typeface screamed out: COP DROPPED SIX STORIES. The obligatory photo of the body in the street, far enough away and covered with a sheet so that it still seemed tasteful. So you couldn't see the blood or the pieces of tooth and the arms bent the wrong way like it must have looked when they first found him. And an inset picture—the academy graduation photo of the poor sap. Taken just before he threw his cap in the air and set out for that miserable first assignment standing security in Times Square. Fourth of July if you're the summer academy, New Year's Eve if you're the winter. Either way, the Force gets to show you that being a cop means standing around somewhere uncomfortable for hours while other people get to have a good time.

Mulino picked up the paper and stared again. He knew that photo. He had spoken to that cop. The curly hair, the silly grin. The kind of spacey eyes. He should have figured it out to begin with. He nodded to himself; he didn't want to tip off Mansky that he had seen any-thing in the story other than what everyone else could find. Mulino looked down and confirmed the officer's name. Joey Del Rio. The Harbor Patrol. He picked up the paper.

Detective Mansky shrugged at him. "Don't bother asking or anything. I've already read it."

"Thank you, Detective. I'll get it right back to you."

Mulino opened the paper and looked at the inside story. The cop had been thrown out the window of the apartment where Commissioner Davenport used to live. He scanned down the page. They had a sketch here too, based on a description given to them by the guard at the building, who said someone who seemed to be a plainclothes cop had been up at the apartment.

Mulino looked over the sketch. That one looked pretty familiar too. It was a face he'd seen a lot recently. Mulino sprung up from his seat and ran out of his office.

CHAPTER FORTY

AWAKE

Leonard stared into Joey Del Rio's face, awash in pepper spray, sus-
pended in the dark. The cop was floating, holding steady as though he
were bobbing in surf. He cocked his head to the side, squinting through
the pain, and he whispered. Leonard leaned out over the railing, straining to hear. He wondered what was holding the cop in the air—he
wasn't hanging on the railing and there was nothing but dead air below
him. As Leonard moved closer, Del Rio smiled sickeningly and grabbed
his arm. The cop's face suddenly contorted, and as Leonard looked
down, his arms caught, he was staring at Roshni Saal. They both flew
over the edge together. She grabbed Leonard tight as they fell toward
the sidewalk below, coming at them quick, hard, and final.

Leonard shot up onto his hands and knees on the floor of the
deserted office. His breath was fluttering and he couldn't slow his heart.
He had slumped off of the chair and onto the concrete floor sometime
in the night. The dream had seemed all too real. Del Rio's face was too
much like the one that had actually sped toward death the night before.
Roshni didn't know the danger she was in by helping him. Leonard's

body was still sore, but his head was suddenly, brutally clear. He was still hot. He was thirsty and he had slept in his clothes. But he was a wanted man with a murder to solve, so there was no time to rest.

He stood and looked around. It was early, not much past six, but daylight already was scorching the office. It was hot and bright and would just get worse from here. The computers were humming away, scouring the world for little tragedies. The one he and Roshni had been staring at before he crashed was still open, Davenport's data still up. Idlewild Construction. A new building, one he and Roshni had both recognized. A series of schematics. It was happening today.

He had already started to put together a plan. But he was sweaty and his clothes were old, and he wouldn't be surprised if you could find blood if you looked closely at them. Roshni herself was nowhere to be seen. He felt a quick jolt, a sudden convulsion like you sometimes get on the verge of sleep, and it snapped him awake. His first thought was the weapon; he looked to the counter. It was still there. Next to it a cell phone. Next to the cell phone a written note. A four-digit security code and a single sentence. *I can always say you stole it from me. Good luck. Roshni.*

So she wasn't going to be part of his plan after all. Maybe it was the gun. Or maybe she had checked the news this morning. It was certain to be out there by now. It wouldn't have taken her long to put together what had happened. Either she didn't want to join him because she was afraid for her safety or she didn't want to join him because he had killed someone. Or both. It didn't really matter. But she was willing to help a little. To leave behind the phone. He had ditched his own so he wouldn't be traced. The police wouldn't think to track hers. Or maybe they had been tracking it for years; keeping up with activists and critics was part of their business. But they wouldn't know it had anything to do with Leonard Mitchell. Leonard turned on the phone and entered the code. It sprung to life, fully charged. He scrolled through the apps and found at least one thing that was sure to be useful. Maybe even more useful than the gun.

The gun was necessary, even if Leonard looked guilty as hell with it prying open the back of his pants. He untucked his shirt. As long as he stood very straight, the shirt would drape over it so you wouldn't notice. He checked the time on the phone. Nearly seven. He had only been asleep three hours, but he felt more refreshed than ever before in his life. He had a purpose now. He slipped the phone into his pocket, secured the gun, and stepped out to meet a ready world.

He set out for the subway, crossing toward Whitman again, careful to stand rigid so that no one could make out the silhouette of the gun in the back of his pants. As he approached the project, the smell of rotting trash was now constant. Overnight, more loads of garbage had been dumped helter-skelter across the sidewalks. Heavy black contractor sacks had been ripped open by rats or vagrants. Kitchen refuse spilled open into the street, strewing empty cartons from microwaved meals, specked with hardened bits of melted cheese.

Leonard walked into the Whitman courtyard and the scene was worse. At the base of the building, on the two sides where anyone still lived, people had simply thrown their trash out the windows. Along the curtilage, ramparts of waste had piled up: broken beer bottles, diapers leaking stool, shoals of plastic packaging, greased paper towels. It all seeped into the abandoned flower beds clinging to the building. Leonard couldn't pass by without starting to retch. He walked through the underpass with the tail of his shirt over his face and mouth, hoping to catch a whiff of the expressway and the relatively pleasant diesel exhaust. He remembered that he couldn't hold up his shirt without exposing the gun and let it drop.

The residue of poverty lay crumpled alongside the gutters of the building—condoms, sure, and a couple of spent shells, and torn pieces of clothing, broken CDs, and a dog collar. No needles to speak of; the cops put enough heat on the residents to ensure that drugs were kept indoors. Leonard crept past the courtyard. It was still and quiet, no sign of cops filing past to figure out who may have dumped a body in the river. Not yet. The streets were a mess and those unlucky enough to be out and about were stumbling through the general stench.

Leonard crossed the street and headed toward the subway. He had a dead cop's gun and a missing woman's phone. The only thing he had that was his own was his badge. He had the rest of the day to stop a disaster and clear his name. He would need help, and the people most likely to want to help him were dead or vanished. He pulled out the phone and thought a minute. There was one person he had to call before heading out into the world.

CHAPTER FORTY-ONE
WALL STREET

Wall Street was in full gear by ten past seven, but not with bankers. As Leonard stepped out of the subway, the corner of Wall and Broad bellowed with the breakfast-cart men, the shoe shiners, and the parasites who hawk statuettes of the Twin Towers wrapped indecorously with a pink ribbon. Every day these stalwarts ply their trade with the sunrise. Leonard watched the parade from above the fray on the steps of Federal Hall. No one looks up in New York, especially not on Wall Street. He stood behind the statue of Washington, checking the crowd to see that he hadn't been followed. It was safe to use the phone, at least for the moment. Scrolling through it that morning, before making the phone call to set his plan in motion, he had seen that Roshni had a membership at a fancy gym. The silk suits had to come from somewhere, and wherever that was, it was paying for a raft of little luxuries. The gym was only a block away. Veronica's office was just up the street.

He set out through the crowd. Stiff carts were piled with thin coffee and thick donuts, the small men inside them sweating onto their tin floors. Bored cops with M-16s stood in front of the Exchange, assigned to elite units with hubristic names—"Hercules," "Samson," "Archangel"—wishing desperately to lean toward each other and gab about the Yankees like everyone else. And hurried men in blue trading smocks, their oversized numbers pinned to them like tags on so much livestock, snuck cigarettes before dashing inside and running madcap from one terminal to another at the behest of the suits floating around them. A short lull in the carnival, before the whole thing started up again inside. No one had looked up. No one had noticed him. He was safe for the moment as he sidled through the revolving door.

The gym was howling with noise—the midlevel functionaries who keep the Street rolling and can't step out for a long lunch spend their morning pedaling or running or treading to prepare themselves for a grueling day sitting at a desk. Leonard took out Roshni's phone and walked toward the turnstiles. He acted as casually as he could while scanning the phone and grabbing a towel. A profile blinked up on her display, a picture of Roshni in the top left corner. Leonard prepared for a minute to explain—plenty of people show up for their trainers looking disheveled and broken, trying to nudge themselves back toward looking like the person in their picture. But not too many show up about six inches taller and the wrong gender and race. But the woman just nodded at the beep and barely looked up from her copy of the *Daily News*. The cover sported a body lying on Perry Street, covered in a sheet. And an insert of a cop's academy photo, his curly hair popping out from around his hat, framing his spacey eyes. The byline by Leonard's old friend Tony Licata. Leonard stared at the ground and double-timed his steps into the showers.

They would have some kind of picture of him after the fold. A sketch if they had spoken to the guard, or a photo and his name if they had lifted prints. There would certainly be a description of what he was wearing. He made a quick adjustment to his plan. Getting a shower would not be enough. Leonard looked around before sliding the gun into a locker. No one had noticed. He wriggled out of his clothes and laid them on top of the weapon. He turned off the phone and left it in the locker. He padded toward the shower and turned it on.

After two days where he felt as though he was one step from living on the street, the shower was pure bliss. The blast ran his sweat off of him, the grease behind his ears slid away, and whatever had collected under his fingernails and between his toes rushed down the drain. The wound in his shoulder seared with pain as the water rushed over it. He stretched his arm. Only when it was fully extended did he feel any pain. He indulged in the water as it brought his skin and sinuses back to life. But he couldn't linger.

He toweled off and combed his hair. He opened his locker. The cell phone would only take him so far. The clothes were rancid and probably part of a description to boot. He looked down the row of lockers. There was no one in the room. Only about half of the lockers had locks on them. He tried one of the open ones, then another. Nothing inside. He opened the third one and saw an undershirt, a pink dress shirt, a suit. The uniform of a man too important to lock up his clothing at a place like this. Leonard checked the suit; it was a 42. Maybe a little bulky, but he couldn't be picky. One quick glance to be sure no one was watching, and he slipped into the outfit. He turned to his own locker and grabbed the cell phone and the papers from the Harbor Patrol. He was pretty good at getting a suit on quickly. As soon as he had the coat on, he twisted over and tucked the gun into the back of the waistband. A cop's favorite place to sense a bulge. A suit jacket covered it better than his shirt had, but still not well enough. He pulled a pair of shoes from the stolen locker and started to slip his feet into them. They were too small.

"Hey."

A soft little man, a few inches shorter than Leonard, stood wrapped in a towel, about four feet away. Leonard looked up. He looked out the door of the locker room. He might be able to make it, but he didn't have any shoes on.

"That's my suit, man. What do you think you're doing?"

Leonard played dumb. It could buy him twenty seconds, no more. "Really? I didn't even notice. I guess I'm thinking about too many other things."

"You just put my whole suit on. What do you mean you're thinking about other things?"

The man was too surprised to be suspicious of Leonard. He walked just close enough, and Leonard reeled back and landed a roundhouse, hard but a little high. He had to swing with his left hand and he only grazed the man across the forehead. The banker dropped his towel and splayed naked on the floor. Leonard ran to his own locker and whipped out his beat-up shoes before dashing out into the gym. No time to put them on. The man was already standing up running after him.

"Hey! That guy stole my clothes!"

Leonard ran out into the gym at full speed. People's arms were glued to their ellipticals and their eyes were pinned to the morning news, so he had a jump start before anyone heard the shouts from the locker room. Or before they saw the naked man running out after him, jiggling too much to be a regular.

The woman at the front desk was looking up from her paper now. She was the only one between Leonard and the revolving front door. His shoes in one hand, he barreled toward her, the naked man gaining behind him.

"Sir, you have to stop. I can't let you—"

He feinted to the left and she took a step to stop him before he doubled back to the right and hurdled the turnstile into the gym's lobby. He rushed through the front steps and out into the busy street. His feet hurt on the pavement, and he was already starting to sweat again, but he couldn't turn back now. His shoulder was a dull ache, without the stinging pain that had been shouting at him for the last two days. He rushed around the corner to the subway, darting through the crowd. He had left the phone behind, but at least he still had the gun. And the evidence from Davenport's apartment.

A new migration was starting outside on the street. Bankers sweeping softly from the trains to the towers on leather-soled shoes that never seemed to touch the ground. Crisp ironed men bounced from subway to revolving doors, wearing suits and ties in the summer without breaking a sweat. Leonard barreled through the crowd as though he were just another merchant trying to catch the bell. Even the heavily armed cops patrolling the stock exchange barely looked up at another man in a suit rushing down the street. They were on the lookout for terrorists, and only terrorists. Minor crimes like snatching a wallet or bilking investors or ripping off the local sports club wouldn't register with them, particularly when the guy who is being chased down the street doesn't look much like an Arab.

A man in a suit can get away with anything in New York, even elbowing past crowded commuters while holding his shoes in his left hand. Leonard slipped down into the subway and reached into the wallet of the stolen jacket. There was a MetroCard. He slid it through the turnstile just as a train was pulling in. He slipped onto the train and found a seat in the corner. He looked out the window to see if the woman from the gym or the naked banker had followed him this far. He was safe for the moment. He put his shoes on the floor. His badge rattled around inside one of them. He smiled. He was lucky not to have left that behind either. He settled his feet into the shoes and leaned back into the bench. He positioned himself in a corner, head down, doing his best to look like a tired but hardworking professional, and meeting no one's gaze. Now he was just another anonymous man in an ordinary suit heading uptown on the express train.

He stepped out of the uptown train at Union Square and jostled through the crowd and over the stairs to the downtown platform. He would rejoin the street with a new cohort of commuters, none of whom had seen the barefoot man only minutes before. He would be just another man in a plain gray suit. Of course, he thought as the metal extension of the platform scraped into place with its abominable hiss, he would be the only suit on Wall Street who looked an awful lot like the picture of a cop killer in the paper.

CHAPTER FORTY-TWO
VERONICA

When he climbed back out of the subway, the parade was in full force. Leonard was mystified at the men marching toward their corner offices. There was not a glint of perspiration on the razor chins; the haircuts remained unmatted after twenty minutes on the train; the cuffs peeked neatly out from under the suits. The choreography was precise, balanced, and keen. The bodies were angular, the shoulders wide. These boys would hit the gym during lunch to watch cable news and retreat to their desks for the afternoon to make the predictions of their favorite talking heads come true.

It all happened without dirt, without blood, without any of the grime or grease that clung to the municipal machine. These private sector guys, Leonard thought, never sat across a gray table in a dim room with a thirty-year-old tape recorder to question a florid man in a blue suit about what he had done in the darker corners of a breaking city. The crumbling tendrils of East New York and Highbridge, to them, had been cleaned and packaged and cut into tranches to be sold to development funds, and if there were still people living out there and calling it

New York, well, it was no concern to the cogs climbing the towers on Wall Street. These men, pulling electronic trinkets out of their pockets to check the time despite the Tag Heuers on their wrists, had never crossed a river since coming to Manhattan, and didn't know or care what lay over the bridges and through the tunnels. They were living in the city that was still booming; the last four years were, to them, a wrong turn that they would soon pay someone off to correct. They had never seen the general public. Leonard pressed his way through them and toward Veronica's building.

The elevator took forever. Leonard had his back against the wall to keep perceptive neighbors from peeking at the back of his waistband. He had swept in with the badge. The man at the desk had barely cared. In his suit, with his badge, he could have walked through any lobby in the city. Here on Wall and Broad, the firms were mainly interested in sealing off the inner sanctum from tourists, and couldn't be bothered to stop a skinny white guy in a twelve-hundred dollar suit from roaming around wherever he wanted, even if the suit was stolen and, if you looked closely, he was armed. Plus having the guard call upstairs would have meant that they'd know he was coming, and Leonard's plan demanded surprise.

The elevator stopped at another floor and another lackadaisical burnout stumbled toward his cubicle. Leonard reached into his pocket to check on his evidence. It was dry and secure. He realized, as he patted it, that it was just as dangerous as the gun resting upon it. He stood up, settling his shoulders back and breathing deep. For the first time in a week, he was clean and showered and dressed with a crisp professional flair. His hair was combed and you couldn't tell from looking at him that he had killed a man the day before and had a gun tucked into the back of his pants. As the door chimed open and ushered him into the expensive anonymous lobby, he realized that he fit in perfectly.

Perched at a lush desk was a small woman in a large suit looking bored in her elegant prison. The kind who had come to New York ten or fifteen years ago from Omaha or Spokane or Albuquerque with the idea of hitting the big time in some creative career: actress, painter, videographer, it was all basically the same. Most of them took temp jobs of one sort or another and by the time they figured out they weren't destined to be profiled in the Arts and Leisure section, they were professional administrators, keeping the wheels of the big city running without ever figuring out what was going on behind the nearest set of closed doors.

"You weren't announced."

Leonard flashed the badge toward her. "And I'm not going to be."

It was the woman's chance to play tough. "I don't care if you're the FBI or whoever. I'm supposed to call before I let anyone back." Leonard took the phone from her and slid it back to the cradle. He set his badge on the desk and reached into his waist. He hadn't wanted to show the gun so soon, but some people need a little extra convincing.

"Like I said, I'm going to go in there, and you aren't going to announce me. Do you understand?" Her eyes pasted to the gun, she grew small and weak before him. He had to talk with Veronica before Eliot could act. He wouldn't have shot her if she'd fought him off, but she didn't know that. Maybe she would call the police as soon as he was gone, but by the time they came inside he would have Veronica to vouch for him and Eliot to hand over. If everything went well. She curled up in her chair, hands on her lap. She didn't care enough about this job to risk her safety. Her main goal was just to get through the day so she could get on with her life at five o'clock, and with a man holding a gun in front of her that goal took on a whole new meaning.

Leonard pushed through the double doors and tucked the gun back into his pants. He didn't want to tip off the drones that an armed man had come in among them. They might think a madman had come in to shoot up the place. Or visit vengeance on them. Most of them probably deep down would have been relieved. He turned toward the secretary and put his finger to his lips. Silence. Against the roar of the crowd in their cubicles, she wouldn't have heard him if he had said anything anyway.

He knew where he was going this time, past the streaks of suits, the shouts into cheap plastic phones, and the smacks of frustrated hands into flimsy keyboards. The kids howling in their cubicles could have been in their own universe as Leonard passed them. No one turned his head, so no one saw the crease in the back of Leonard's jacket and the metal it concealed. As he approached the corner, he saw a sealed door at the end of the hallway. That would be where Eliot sat. He turned to Veronica's, opened it, and stepped inside.

Veronica swung her cold green eyes to attention. Her fingers stopped twitching at the keyboard. Leonard closed the door and the noise of the office was nearly totally shut out. Veronica pushed away from her desk.

"What are you doing here?"

"I found something out, Veronica. I found out where they are going next."

"I told you to call me. I told you I could meet you. Do you know what could happen to you in here? Do you know what could happen to me?"

"There isn't time, Veronica. It's happening today. It's happening right now."

She stood up from the computer. She stepped past him and closed the door. Cut off from the floor, the office was small and plain. You can work so hard to make it and what you get are twelve feet by twelve feet and a couple of fancy computer monitors.

"A cop got killed last night, Leonard."

"Like I said, there isn't time."

"The paper said where it was. The building he died in front of. Wasn't that where Davenport lived?"

Leonard looked at her hands. People who are nervous, who are worried, or who are lying show it in their bodies. At DIMAC, when he was interviewing suspects, Leonard would notice the wrists that wavered, the fingers that tapped aimlessly. Nervous extremities would tell him that a building inspector or a bus driver was making it up as he went along. Veronica Dean stood calm and still. She had told him that the cops were working for Eliot. She was in as much danger as he was. He was going to have to trust her.

"He came after me, Veronica. He wanted to kill me. He tried to."

"I understand."

"I was at Davenport's. I found what you were looking for. Then Del Rio showed up and tried to kill me. You didn't see that in the paper."

"No." Her eyes opened, broad and sweet and full of sympathy. "I'm sorry. I told you there was danger."

Leonard nodded. "I know."

She came around the desk, a serious figure in the cold angular office. "You said you found something?"

Leonard reached around and fished out the drive. Best not to let her know about the gun. Just because she said that she understood doesn't mean she couldn't get suspicious. Finding out that he was walking around with Brian Rowson's gun might change her mind. He suddenly wished he hadn't even brought it. It wasn't as though he would use it on anyone. He spread the papers on the desk.

He handed her the drive. She booted it eagerly. Leonard pointed out what she already knew, and showed her what she was just learning too.

"Most of it is the e-mails that we saw before. Instructions. Acknowledgements. Shorts. But there is something more. It had today's date on the front. It's schematics. It shows the structural supports for—"

"The Bank of Bremen building." Veronica had seen it right away. Just from the shape of the footprint on the first page. The sweet sharp angles and the marking of Albany Street. The shiny downtown bauble that was finally nearing completion, the final jewel in the necklace surrounding what had once been the site of the wreckage.

And if they hit the building, it would be all over. The new administration could survive a spike in the crime rate. It could survive a little more dog shit on the streets, a little more grime on the subways. Leonard himself had seen, just the night before, how the city had grown looser and freer as the order that had been imposed upon it over the past twenty years slackened its grip. Sparks was wrong to think that New Yorkers would once again embrace an iron fist just because a couple of cranes snapped or someone found a few hundred rats in a restaurant.

But no one could keep governing the city if a building came down. Especially if it was a new one, a tall one; if it was shiny and glass and it was put up within spitting distance of where they all remembered their long walk starting. Sergeant Sparks was planning to take out the Bank of Bremen building and Eliot was going to make a profit on the whole thing.

"They are going to blow it up, Veronica. As we speak, Eliot is probably selling the bank short, the construction company. He's going to make a mint."

"We have to tell the police."

"The police won't believe us. The police are looking for me. If I call them they aren't going to ask questions. They're going to lock me up and I'll never come out."

"The FBI then."

"Veronica. No one will listen."

"I can call them. They'll listen to me."

"No, they won't."

He waited for it to sink in. She was smart enough that she wouldn't need convincing. Her plan was too simple: Call up the local precinct and ask them to spring into action and solve a plot to destroy a building. Leonard knew well enough that the police would take their time ambling downtown, convinced they were answering the call of an emotionally disturbed fantasist. And if they stumbled upon Leonard, it would be even worse. He was a man suspected of killing a cop. The moment any law enforcement caught up with him would be the moment he went to jail for the rest of his life. As he leaned over the table looking at the map, he could feel the dead cop's gun tucked tight into his waistband. Once they found him with that, the game would be over.

"What then?"

"We have to confront Eliot. He can call Sparks off. And if he can't, we have to go there and stop him ourselves. I've already told the only person who might believe us."

He could sense her watching him. She might have seen the gun. She would have to understand that it was going to be dangerous. That there were risks they were taking. She had warned him of the danger after all, and he had kept at it.

"I'm afraid of him, Leonard. All of these cops are working for him."

"He's just a quiet old man in a quiet old office, Veronica. And if he tries anything, there are two of us. And if all else fails . . ."

He didn't have to say anything more. She was watching the crease in his jacket as it drifted back over the gun. He had been beaten down by one cop and threatened by another. His back and his head bore the evidence of assaults by armed men. Confronting Eliot would be far from the most frightening thing he'd done in the past few days. Still, he was glad that she would be in there with him. She was strong enough, had faced enough danger herself. He stood up. Veronica's steel eyes watched as his jacket straightened out over the weapon.

"Okay. Let's go."

CHAPTER FORTY-THREE
ELIOT

As Leonard followed Veronica into Eliot's inner sanctum, the man hardly paused at his drawing pad. The noise from the cubicles was stymied; the view was nearly impressive. But the man himself sat unhurried, drafting something in longhand at his heavy desk. Leonard stepped forward, suddenly hesitant to interrupt, like a schoolboy waiting to be granted permission to speak. Eliot finished his letter and set his pen back in its cradle before looking up. His eyes flashed a bit at Leonard, as though he almost recognized him. Like when someone you have only spoken to on the phone turns out to look so different than you imagined.

"Mr. Holm-Anderson, my name is Leonard Mitchell. I worked with Christine Davenport."

"Ah, yes. Of course. I read that the police solved that business with your commissioner. A terrible tragedy."

"They didn't solve anything."

Eliot nodded to Veronica. "Ms. Dean. I see that you have met Mr. Mitchell—the government worker? I had the pleasure of working briefly with his supervisor."

It was a soft enough jab, and Leonard could take it. He walked toward the expansive corner of the office, toward what seemed to be a real enough fireplace. The Buildings Department wouldn't let someone actually run a fire in one of these buildings, but the hearth gave every impression of being genuine. Veronica swooped in behind him. With her backing him up, Leonard had the strength to confront the man behind the desk.

"It's over, Eliot. We've found your man in the police department. Sergeant Sparks. We know what he is planning to do today. What he's been doing over the past few years, for your benefit. We have seen the plans for the Bank of Bremen building."

Eliot glanced over Leonard and Veronica. He seemed to be searching the room. Looking for a way out maybe. Then he turned toward the window. "You know, you can almost see the Bank of Bremen out the window, if your angle is right. You have to crane a bit to look around another of these monstrosities we all work in."

"Call him off, Eliot. If he goes through with it, you'll go to jail. We have enough to tie you to him. Tell him to back down. I'm sure you don't care about the people who are going to be killed, the damage you'll do. But call it off for yourself. Just to save your own skin."

Eliot was still looking out the window, still trying perhaps to catch a corner of the building in question by tilting his head just so. He answered Leonard without turning his head around.

"I'm afraid I have no idea what you're talking about."

"The little disasters, Eliot. The money this firm made by betting against the crane company just before the collapse. By shorting the chemical plant in Staten Island before the leak last spring. The water taxi. The restaurant with the rats. Every one of them a boon to your firm. But you know this already. And you already know that we know because Christine Davenport showed you what she had found before she came here. And that's why you had to kill her."

Eliot turned finally from the window. "Your boss did show me that list. She did ask me how it was that this firm had made so many prescient bets about such terrible things. I like to think I have an expert team of analysts, but no one is that good, really. And when she gave me that list, those e-mails, those trades, I started my own investigation. I hadn't seen those trades singled out like that before. I made some very interesting findings."

He was still in his chair, sitting gently and at ease. Leonard could feel Veronica behind him. Both of Eliot's hands were visible. Leonard didn't need the gun. Eliot was just a banker in a suit. *Don't escalate.* Leonard moved his hands away from his waistband. *But stay wary.* Leonard was watching the man closely, waiting for the moment he might have to pounce.

"You see," Eliot went on, "this game is a tough one. Blood can be spilled. But there are rules, and at the end of the day, I prefer to succeed within them. You ask me about trades that I made. Look at my desk, Mr. Mitchell. I don't make trades. I evaluate the work of my staff. I instill confidence in them. I don't look at the price of practically anything from one day to the next. But everything my staff does is recorded. Every trade is accounted for. And so I had an accounting done. Would you like to guess, Mr. Mitchell, who it is that placed every one of the trades that your commissioner asked about?"

"He doesn't have to guess."

Leonard turned at the sound of Veronica's voice. Her severe eyes were staring him down and her posture was suddenly hard, but Leonard didn't notice that. He had been so intent on Eliot that he hadn't even felt what she had done. And now the only thing he saw was that in her right hand she was holding the gun from the back of his waistband.

"Veronica."

"What good does it do to come armed, Leonard, if you can't keep your wits about you." He hadn't even noticed it was gone. She had been standing right behind him while Eliot was speaking and slipped it away.

"You told me that Eliot was in charge of the scheme."

"You wouldn't have gone to Davenport's apartment if I had told you that you were working for me."

"You've been behind the whole thing. You orchestrated the collapse. You're going to blow up the building."

"No, Leonard. Your friend the cop is going to blow up that building. I'm just going to make a fortune off of it."

"Why tell me it was Eliot?"

"Your friend Mulino killed my best source. I have sources all over the world. Feeding advance notice of when they are making attacks. Sleeper cells need start-up funding too. And I had an inside line on the most effective stateside operation."

"Detective Rowson."

"He knew it was risky. He had been in charge of the rats in the restaurant. He had been in charge of the water taxi. He was supposed to be afraid. But once I told him how much money he could make by telling me, he wasn't so afraid anymore."

"So what about the e-mails? What about all the other countries?"

"Rowson told me what was going on in New York. I have a source in Indonesia who tells me when a gas pipeline will be targeted. I have a friend in Yemen who tells me which convoy is at risk. And each of those interests is owned by public companies. And the stock in each of those companies suffers when the attack goes down. And I know how to make money off of suffering. Detective Rowson's operation was local. And it was never going to be found by the police. Because it was being run by the police."

"And when he got found out, he was set up and he was killed."

"Maybe. Or maybe he just got shot by someone who thought he looked suspicious. Or maybe he really was going to take down that ship and Mulino saved the day. I know it cost me plenty when I woke up and the ship was still afloat. I'd ask Rowson what happened, but he's too dead to tell me."

"And once Rowson was dead, Davenport found out."

"She did. And the police have ways of taking care of people who are going to betray them. She wasn't going to tell me anything either. But I knew I could count on you to find out for me. You climbed right up into her home and brought me just what she had been trying to hide."

So Veronica herself was just catching the crumbs of other people's conspiracies. Only in it for the money: she didn't care if the bombs were being set by terrorists abroad or police at home, what mattered was knowing ahead of time and turning it into profit. The information age. But right now, no matter what Leonard knew about her, there was nothing he could do to stop her. For the second time in twenty-four hours, Leonard had the same gun pointed at him. If he had followed her orders and called her, told her to meet him somewhere, then she probably would have just taken the flash drive and killed him. By forcing her to confront Eliot, he had probably saved his life.

Eliot himself was quietly shifting himself up in his chair. With a gun pointed his way, he sat oddly stronger. He crossed his hands in his lap and pointed his chin at Veronica. "So the plan is to kill us both now? Shoot us and then walk to your office and make the trades, then take the elevator to the lobby and saunter over to your apartment? Mr. Mitchell here just showed you the sergeant's plans for the first time, I am led to believe. You haven't even made your bet against the bank yet? As far as you know, this attack is going to happen today. It would be a shame for you to miss it because you were so busy murdering us."

Veronica guided the gun down to hip level, watching both men carefully, calmly. For the first time since she had taken out the gun, Leonard saw a hint of fear in her eyes. He was too cowed now to attack her himself. But Eliot was right: She had let Leonard lure her in here before she had a chance to make any trades. She hadn't been able to take him outside and kill him. She hadn't been able to get on the phone and short Idlewild Construction. He had made her confront Eliot, and now she was as stuck here as they were.

And Leonard wasn't alone anymore. Now he had Eliot. Not the villain after all, Eliot could get a senator or the head of the FBI on the telephone if he deigned to pick up such a device. For a woman holding a gun, Veronica looked peculiarly cornered. She walked backward toward the door out to the trading floor.

"I'm going to go into my office for a few minutes, gentlemen. You can both stay here. When I finish what I'm doing, I'm going to put this gun in my purse and leave the building. I never had any intention of hurting either one of you. Once I leave, neither one of you will ever hear from me again. You can do your best to stop Sparks from doing what he's planning, but I'm not sure you can. In fact, I'm about to go bet against it."

As she backed away, she lifted the gun and waved it before the two men, just to let them know she was serious. She tugged at the door, slipped out through the trading room to her office, and rushed to her desk. Eliot's door slowly drifted shut, cutting out the noise from the crowded hallway.

Eliot burst up from his hardwood chair and dusted his slacks, suddenly bright, brisk, and full of energy. He tugged at the hem of his jacket to smooth out the crease from sitting so long. Leonard saw the trim elegant man in a new light: not the evil mastermind of a plan to profit off of misery, but a sage from another time, scornful of the world he was born into and what you had to do to succeed in it.

"I'm not proud of myself, Mr. Mitchell. I never have thought any more highly of what I do for a living than of what anyone else does. But there are lines I don't cross and there are rules that are in place for a reason. I should have noted what she was up to sooner. It took me a few days of auditing to be sure. Now, we have about five minutes. If you'll come with me."

Leonard stared dumbfounded as Eliot crossed the empty expanse of his office toward the fireplace. Eliot reached around the side of the mantle and twisted an unseen latch, opening a false door to a grim industrial stairwell.

"I am required to have a separate fire stairwell in this office, given its size and its distance from the stairwell on the other side of the floor. I found the proposition ghastly and had my designer cover it with the fireplace, which is also not permitted. My own little inside joke, I suppose. It never occurred to me that it would come in so handy."

The door open, Eliot stepped into the cold concrete atrium, thick metal handrails guiding him toward a narrow set of dark solid stairs. The stairwell exposed the lie of the manicured office; Eliot worked in just another anonymous corporate husk, no matter how many knick-knacks he had collected to warm it.

"Are you coming?"

"Where are we going?"

"Down twenty flights, and then to the Bank of Bremen. There is a disaster to avert yet, young man."

CHAPTER FORTY-FOUR
DOWNSTAIRS

Leonard was trailing as the old man skipped downstairs quickly, nearly giddy. His shoulder had started throbbing again; he could feel the ache in his back from sleeping on the floor of Roshni's office—and for only a few hours at that. But below him, a man more than thirty years older was swinging along, negotiating the sharp turns of the bright descent while singing softly to himself. Leonard couldn't make out the tune. He was nearly two full flights behind when Eliot looked up at him.

"Hop to it, my friend. She's going to find out that we're gone soon enough. She may even be smart enough to simply take the elevator and beat us down."

Eliot had seemed creepily lethargic when he had been glued to his chair. Now, bounding across the steps, it was as though all the energy he had been saving while curled up behind his desk had been let go at once. Leonard lunged forward and skittered down the last few steps of a landing, holding to the iron rail and swinging himself round the corner. His right arm was practically useless, numb from where the bandage had dug in and cut off the blood. He gave it another go and sprang ahead. He was nearly even with Eliot, still singing and clattering to himself. Close enough, at least, that he could ask some questions, even as his breath was giving out on him.

"She told me it was you."

"Well, of course she did. And of course you believed her. I'm a man who sits behind a desk wearing a suit all day. So obviously I am capable of anything. My name is on the door of a Wall Street firm. So you think I'm likely to murder tourists for a few thousand dollars."

Leonard was jogging, huffing along behind Eliot, whose breath was crisp and controlled despite the fact that his feet were shuffling frantically down the stairs.

"I believed her, is all. It's not that I would have suspected you."

"If I had come to you and said I had found out that she was running this very same scheme, would you have believed me?" Eliot stopped on a landing to look back at Leonard, who stood silent. "I didn't think so."

"I think she was telling the truth when she said she had only learned about it. The cops thought they were trying to scare the city. And after all, the only thing she has to bribe them with is money. But the men working on this have been paid in fear."

Eliot smiled, looking brighter and younger. "Well then we have one puzzle left, don't we?" Having a problem to solve seemed to fill him with new energy.

"How long have you known?"

"I knew there was something wrong when your boss gave me the binder. But I didn't know it was Veronica until a few days later. After Ms. Davenport had been killed. And even then, there is something of a distance between knowing and having proof."

Even Eliot was beginning to slow. Leonard couldn't count how many stories they had descended, and he couldn't see how many were left below them. They had started at the eighteenth floor, and it seemed as though they had been going down forever.

"We have proof now."

"We have a woman who has pointed a gun in our faces. We are a long way from proof."

"She has the gun. That gun belonged to a cop who has been killed. We just need to get downstairs and call the police. They will storm the office."

Eliot stopped for a moment on the stairs. "What good will it do, young man, to catch her? She tricked you. She tried to kill you. So I understand that you think she deserves punishment. And she most likely does. But the truth of the matter is that she is a parasite. My industry, unfortunately, breeds parasites. You squash one and another blooms in its place. We should be looking for the source. She used you to find out what Davenport knew. And what Davenport knew is more important than Veronica herself."

Leonard thought on this for a moment. Eliot was right. They could call the police, they could sound the alarm, and when they arrived the only person they would catch would be a woman who had made a little money off of other people's crimes. They would have lost the original wrongdoers. Not to mention that if the police storm the building and are suddenly called to an emergency at the Bank of Bremen, they wouldn't even catch her at all. It would not take long for her to disappear while the city convulses over another skyscraper coming down.

"Okay. We go to the building. I think I know who we are going to find there too."

"Do you?"

Leonard nodded. "At least one. Maybe more. And I know a detective who will listen." And he thought of the call he had made that morning. He had only been able to leave a message. But if that message was heard, there would be more help still.

"How do we call him? Your detective. I don't carry a cell phone. Do you?"

Leonard had left Roshni's phone in the locker when he stole the suit. It had been that or the gun. "No."

"And we are to walk up to a pay phone and dial this detective? You know his number by heart? Or we should call 911 and tell the operator we know that a police sergeant is about to blow up a bank, and see if she puts us straight through to the commissioner?"

"No. We're going to do it ourselves."

Eliot stopped for a moment and smiled at Leonard. As he stared at Leonard, the manicured face and the seamless hair appeared suddenly soft, a little bit undone. A very serious man who had shed his mask and let loose with the fact that he was secretly mischievous.

"Right you are."

Just below them, Leonard could see a bright-red sign. EXIT. Finally. The sweat had flourished across the back of his neck now, but it would only be worse outside. He pressed on. Eliot was right. Their only chance was to get to the building before Sparks. They were two unarmed men planning to take on a uniformed police sergeant carrying a semiautomatic weapon and most likely a load of explosives. It was worth a shot.

"All right, Eliot. Let's go."

"Lovely. And do you have a plan, exactly?"

"I'm sure we'll think of something."

This suited the dapper man just fine. "My thoughts exactly." Eliot turned the corner toward the doorway. Leonard reached him just as he stood touching the matte-gray metal, its fire bar cocked in place.

"Now, the moment I push this open, Leonard, a fire alarm will sound throughout the whole building. They will have to evacuate it. Our friend will be asked to leave with everyone else, whether or not she has made her trades, and whether or not she has the gun with her. But chaos is going to be to our advantage, at least for a little while."

Leonard put his hand on the door. It was cool. It was quiet. There would be no more cool and no more quiet for a while once they slipped out into the trash-covered streets.

"Come on," said Eliot. "This is going to be fun."

CHAPTER FORTY-FIVE

UNDERGROUND

James Sparks had always figured that he was going to have to do the hard work himself. Rowson and Del Rio had been just short of incompetent. He wasn't surprised that either one of them was dead. It's what you get for recruiting dirty cops. Not that the clean ones wouldn't have been on their side: as far as Sergeant Sparks was concerned, every officer in the city should have backed the project. But a dirty cop is easier to control. Someone who owes you something. Someone who knows he is one slip away from explaining to his wife and kid that he's been fired and is losing his pension and will have to live off of Social Security after all. Sparks's ultimate boss had given him the chance to recruit them. Had cleaned the records of Rowson, Del Rio, and the rest of them. All Sparks had to do was instill enough fear in them. But someone who was sloppy enough to get caught once can only take you so far.

He had spent all night convincing himself that Mitchell would get taken care of by morning, then woke up to the cold truth that he was wrong. No word from Intake. Leonard Mitchell was on the loose. No telling what Del Rio had said to him before getting killed. He could have gone to the three-letter agencies by now. And someone just might have believed him. Sergeant Sparks didn't fear getting caught, though, as much as he feared failing. After all he had done over the past year, he wasn't going to fail now.

Which was why he had spent all morning in the basement of the new building. It had been easy enough to get in. No one asks questions when you're in uniform, not even if you're carrying a bulging backpack that was obviously not issued by the department. Without the schematic he had to guess where to put the clay to be most effective. Then again, even if he didn't take the whole building down, even if all he managed to do was make the thing shudder and force the insurance company to spend an extra six months shoring it up, that would be enough. That would make people wonder who was protecting the city. Whether they would be safe.

He'd started in the corners, laying thin strands of the Semtex behind the boiler room, the elevator shaft. He had about a pound left and had bundled it near the center of the building. He hadn't been able to cram as much as he'd hoped into the backpack, but the small load he had brought would be plenty.

After he laid out the explosives, he deftly tucked the wire and detonators into each molding. He had learned to do this part right, to always be careful. The whole thing was going to be set off with a cell phone, and while it had to be sensitive enough to get the signal even below ground, you had to be careful not to set the stuff on too much of a hair trigger. Sergeant Sparks was not interested in dying for his work.

He set in the last detonator and stepped back to admire his craftsmanship. He didn't need the two cops, and he didn't need to wait until nighttime to set up the building. He could sidle away now and watch the whole riot on television. He walked back up the stairs and past the guard. It was just two o'clock.

As he made his way through the lobby he saw a harried man talking to the security desk. The building wasn't officially open for business yet, but plenty of people had stopped in now and again. Something about the man was out of place. Sparks couldn't see his face, just the back of his suit, his slightly ragged hair, his posture crouched as though trying to shield his right shoulder from something. As Sergeant Sparks cocked his head to watch the man, who was gesturing frantically now at the poor schlub behind the desk, he walked face first into another man at the door of the building.

He sprung back, but the other guy had fallen to the floor. Around seventy by the look of him. Frail, in a double-breasted suit on one of the hottest days of the year. Probably had come into the building to take in the air conditioning. He was sprawled now across the great green marble tiles, clutching his right knee with both hands.

"Ahhh. Oh. You hit me, Officer."

The man was curled into a ball, wailing. Sergeant Sparks stepped forward. The building was loaded with explosives and he had to get out of there. But he didn't want to get caught, either, and running over an old man on his way out of the building would have been too suspicious. He reached out a hand.

"I'm sorry. I was just . . . I'm sorry, sir."

When you're a cop, you are supposed to grovel to everyone. Every drug-slinging mope is a sir and every ten-dollar whore is a ma'am. The kids can yell and wail at you, call you every sort of farm animal name that they like, and you're expected to come back with calm and reserve. You curse them out like they deserve and it will end up on YouTube with you as the bad guy. It was one of the reasons Sparks had been doing what he'd been doing. What had seemed so appealing when his boss had brought him the idea. Maybe people would start to speak to the police with dignity again, if they knew what they were being protected from.

The man's grip was firm for someone so old. He tugged down on Sparks and the cop nearly toppled onto him. With a heave, the sergeant pulled the man into a standing position. Suddenly, the old man's arms were all over him. The man had seemed small, but was pressing all around him now; it was everything Sparks could do to keep himself steady. The man's hands were around his waist, and he was groaning.

"My hip. I think you broke my hip, Sergeant."

Sparks was ready to leave him and flee the building, but he couldn't shrug the guy off. The man yanked closer, unsteadying Sparks, until he was nose to nose with him. Sparks stared at the man's sleek chin and his square eyes, wondering how he could have been fooled into thinking that the man was timid and frail. The lips parted gently and the man whispered into his ear, "Surprise."

The man shoved off and Sparks stumbled back. As he did, he banged into another man. Sparks hadn't noticed someone standing behind him while he was in the dance with the old man. Untangled, he reached for his gun. He would just shoot his way out and set off the building. Anyone who could say that they'd seen him do it would be killed in the blast anyway. Except his gun wasn't there. The man he had banged into had lifted it while he had been struggling. He turned and his eyes came in to focus. He saw a skinny young man in a nice suit that didn't quite fit, taunting him with his weapon.

"Good to meet you in person, Sergeant." Sparks recognized the man from the picture in the paper. Leonard Mitchell. The one who had killed Officer Del Rio.

"Stealing an NYPD firearm is a serious crime."

"I'm well aware. I'm familiar with a number of serious crimes. Sabotage. Blackmail. Burglary. Murder. You think maybe we should start counting them up? See who's got the better tally?"

The sergeant stepped toward Leonard slowly. Men who aren't used to carrying guns don't hold them right. The weapon was in Leonard's hand but his grip was loose; he wasn't aiming it. Sergeant Sparks wasn't threatened at all. If the moment was right he would spring for it.

"You can count up whatever you want. I was doing what I was doing for the good of the city."

"Except you and I know that isn't true. You were doing it because someone was telling you."

"No one ever made me do a thing I didn't want to."

"Of course not. But you got transferred to Harbor too. Didn't you? How many complaints did I see? Eleven? Thirteen? Sexual harassment? Inappropriate comments?"

"Nothing happened with any of those women."

"Not for lack of trying. And if you had gone to the trial room on that, you would have hit rock bottom. You only had one way left to get any power."

Sparks stewed. He had been promised that those had been scrubbed from the file. Not just redacted like the screwups by Del Rio or Rowson or the others. But physically swiped from the paper files in the bottom of some cabinet in 1PP. If he hadn't gotten that promise, he wouldn't have been here.

"I have plenty of power as it is."

"No you don't. You can't scrub people's histories. You can't orchestrate a sanitation strike with a handful of cops working for you. You can't send sanitation trucks out to dump trash and make the strike look even worse than it actually is."

"I can do a lot."

Sparks kept his eyes on the man as he spoke. He didn't like to be accused of anything. Least of all if it was true. "You've been working this game for Victor Ells, Sergeant. Just trying to make the mayor look bad so he can swoop in and take over. You weren't just paid off. You were promised something."

"I told you I don't care about the money." Leonard remembered seeing Sparks's name in Roshni's file. He might not care about it. But he was getting plenty of it. And he was likely getting something else too.

"What did he offer you? Chief of Detectives? The Academy? Commissioner? You've been murdering people just to get Victor Ells in charge of the city."

"Maybe Ells deserves to be in charge."

"If that were true, he wouldn't need you to blow things up. He wouldn't have asked you to murder Christine Davenport once he learned she was on to him."

"That woman," Sparks said, "brought all of this on herself. She could have kept quiet and ended up with an awful lot of power."

Leonard nodded, started to look down. Sparks sensed his chance was coming. They always go soft when they start thinking about people they could have saved. The kid whose buddy tried to leap from one building to the next and blames himself. The guy who thought his girlfriend could handle an eight-ball. They feel guilty and that's when you move in and get them to confess.

Or simply take them out. The moment Sparks noticed Leonard's glassy contemplation, he lunged at the gun. Leonard snapped out of his dream and yanked back, but was nowhere near quick enough. As Sparks sent the gun spinning across the field of green marble, he made a quick calculation: Getting out was more important than getting the gun back. He still had his cell phone, wired to the Semtex below, and as soon as he could get far enough away that he wouldn't come down in the blast himself, he could use it. He bolted for the door.

Behind him, he could hear the chaos of the two men, shouting to the doormen and the passersby to get out of the building. They were more intent on wrangling civilians to safety than on catching Sparks. Just as he had figured, they had made a mistake. Because if he could get clear enough of the building himself, it really wouldn't matter if they were inside it or not. They would be caught in the collapse all the same.

He turned left on Albany Street at a full sprint. It would only take him a minute.

CHAPTER FORTY-SIX

THE FALL

As Sparks ran, Leonard took flight. Eliot could handle the evacuation. Someone had to stop the sergeant. He huffed south, toward Rector Street. Leonard's old office stood on the right, and on the left was an above-ground parking garage. Mainly empty, waiting to get torn down, the thing housed a couple of fleets of city vehicles. The ones used by minor agencies where the staffers really never had need for a car. Leonard saw Sparks turn left and run up a narrow stairway. He followed into the darkness.

Leonard climbed to the second floor of the parking garage. He couldn't see a thing. They were only a block and a half away from the bank. If Sparks blew it up now, they would both be choking with soot and dust. He could make out thin dull shadows of worn-out cars rumbling into the darkness, but no sign of the sergeant. At least he knew the cop no longer had his gun.

"Are you out there, Sparks? Don't do anything stupid."

Leonard could sense a figure now, bobbing from behind one of the cars. He walked toward it. Sparks stepped silently through the shadows, his eyes glinting in the dark.

"Oh, I won't. I won't go stalking the deputy mayor in Crown Heights. I won't throw a cop out a sixth-floor window. I won't do any of these things because if I do, I'm likely to get arrested. Or maybe even shot."

Leonard started walking slowly backward. Sparks was coming toward him. Leonard could sense he had a good ten feet before the ledge. He'd already lured one cop too close to the edge of a building. It was worth a try.

"You take out that building now and it could come down right on this garage, Sparks. You could kill us both. You didn't get into this to kill yourself."

The sergeant kept walking. Leonard couldn't help but feel that Sparks had a better feel for space than Del Rio did. That he wasn't likely to tumble off the edge. He was closing in on Leonard.

"That's right, I didn't. But I didn't set out to get caught, either."

"You haven't done so much yet. You could always pin it on Del Rio. On Rowson. They were the ones leading it. You haven't killed anyone." He wasn't about to mention the people on the water taxi, the woman who had been struck by the falling crane. Getting Sparks to believe he wasn't too far gone was part of the plan. If Leonard could talk him down, it would be something. It would at least buy him time. They could always go after him later; it doesn't matter what they said to him. Just like it doesn't matter if a cop lies to you in the interview room. The truth is fair game when the stakes are high. Even if Leonard could slow the sergeant down so that Eliot could get someone in the building who could defuse the bombs. Just yanking at the wires would have been likely to set them off.

Sparks crept closer, and Leonard readied himself for the fight. The sergeant had both hands out, fists clenched. He wasn't going to trigger the bombs just yet. When the sergeant was within five feet, Leonard took his chance and charged, hoping to push him backward toward the edge. But he had misjudged the man's strength—he was rock hard and didn't budge. Leonard nearly bounced off of him. Sparks grabbed Leonard's arm and Leonard tugged him closer. As the two of them tangled together, Leonard looked him square in his small sleek eyes. It was Sparks who spoke.

"You must know how it is. Dealing with people making demands of you. I bet you get pretty sick people coming into your office making complaints all day long. Maybe you wish they were grateful. I just got fed up with them and decided to take matters into my own hands. Ells thought he was using me. But I was using him."

There it was in a nutshell. Sergeant Sparks was as sick of the mopes and the skells as anyone. Kids jacking liquor stores, drunks beating their wives, people calling the cops to ask for protection and then calling to complain about the cops the moment they walked out the door. Who wants to patrol the city and keep the animals safe from each other only to find that you are their common enemy? He was working for Ells, sure. He had been bought off like the rest of them, maybe. But deep down, it didn't matter. He might have done it anyway. Sparks had simply had it with the general public.

And Sparks was right: Leonard did know how he felt. What is the point of fighting to rid the city of corruption when corruption is just the status quo for the powerless and the powerful alike? The average person on the street has no better a soul than the dirtiest cop on the force. He just doesn't have a badge and a gun. Maybe Leonard couldn't blame the guy much for turning. Maybe he had been closer than he thought to turning himself.

Sparks stepped toward Leonard. Leonard took his last step backward, feeling the edge of the platform. Sparks wasn't in danger now. He wasn't going to just slide by and fall. Leonard's heel came down right at the edge. Not secure enough. He began to teeter. Don't look down. His left knee buckled and he waved his right arm. He was slipping backward, thinking of Del Rio, going down the same way. He started to tumble when something grabbed his right wrist. Hard, firm. Secure. Sergeant Sparks pulled him back from the edge and tugged him close, chins almost touching.

"You don't think I'd let you die that easily, do you? Without even getting roughed up a little bit first?"

Leonard winced. The sergeant hoisted and launched him against a cement column. His spine went hot and his head cracked, and he could feel the sticky warmth of blood oozing out the back of his head. The sergeant walked up to him again. Two-a-days in the weight room and carrying eighteen pounds on the gunbelt every day can beef you up. Leonard held up his arms to stop him, but they were feeble in the face of Sparks's assault. The cop grabbed him by the shoulders and threw him to the ground. Leonard could barely reach his hands up to break his fall. His palms scraped hard against the asphalt, and before he could stop himself his cheek cracked open as well. Blood there now too. He pressed himself up onto all fours. One of his wrists didn't seem like it was bending right.

He had made it to his knees when the sergeant confronted him. He couldn't move his right hand. Sergeant Sparks looked down with a broad smile on his face. He planted his left leg and reached back with his right, as though getting ready to kick a field goal. Leonard started to scamper backward but he was in too much pain to move quickly enough. The sergeant's iron foot came screaming at his face, Leonard's left hand offering too little protection.

And then nothing. Leonard's eyes were closed and his hand was clutched and he was braced for the pain when it didn't seem to come. Instead there was a sound. A deep harsh boom. And still nothing. Leonard allowed himself to squint open for a moment, to see what happened. The sergeant was lurching in front of him, his thigh blossoming burgundy and the smile suddenly twisted. The man's eyes were shocked with pain and the right leg was swinging out from under him. Sparks looked down at the wound, gritted his teeth, and planted his foot to steady himself.

Secure, he started toward Leonard again. Then another boom. This one to the head. This one took him out completely. Sparks's arms flew sideways, the last message from the shattered brain telling them to prepare for a fall. But they weren't going to do any good. His body stumbled sideways, already limp, and slid into a heap on the asphalt.

Leonard leaned forward and tried to lift himself. His right hand was useless. With the left one he could brace himself upward. Then to one knee. Then he could hoist himself to standing. He surveyed the ruined body of Sergeant Sparks. Leonard hurt all over. The body bled out into the sea of quiet cars, and Leonard looked out to see where the shot had come from.

Detective Ralph Mulino lowered the nine millimeter in his right hand and smiled at Leonard. Sparks's gun. Fresh from the lobby of the Bank of Bremen.

"Don't get too close to that ledge. You aren't steady, in your condition."

Leonard nodded and stepped back toward the cars. Gaining composure. Breathing deep. Mulino lowered the gun and climbed upstairs. He held a hand to Leonard and smiled.

"Come on down. If you trust me."

Leonard couldn't tell if the back of his head was covered with blood or sweat. His shoulder still ached from the beating and he thought the sergeant had probably broken his wrist. But Detective Mulino wasn't going to hurt him. He held out his left hand and let himself be guided down the stairwell and back to the open air.

At the bottom of the stairs stood a man whose jacket almost matched his trousers. "You look like hell," Tony Licata chirped. "But thanks for the tip anyways."

So Licata had gotten his message that morning after all. Had called up the only cop that would have believed the story. Just as Leonard had asked. Leonard propped himself against a wall and slid to the ground. He hadn't sat on a sidewalk in years. He looked up at the Bank of Bremen building two blocks away. Still standing. Everything in the city looks taller from below. Licata had brought Mulino downtown just in time.

Mulino heaved. "Your friend here kept me from getting sent over to Wall Street to look at a false alarm that someone pulled."

Leonard nodded. Veronica was going to walk right out of the building with the gun in her purse and no one would ever see her again.

"They find her? Veronica?"

"She has a pretty good head start now. But I'm sure they will."

"I wouldn't bet on it this time."

Detective Mulino nodded. Eliot had been right. What does it matter whether you catch the parasite or not. The real criminal was just above them, the second cop that this detective had shot in a week. They wouldn't let Leonard investigate this shooting. Mulino would probably need him as a witness. He laughed to himself thinking about it, how in a month or two he would be testifying at the Firearms Discharge Control Board about the cop who had saved his life by shooting another cop. Licata whipped out his notebook and slipped up the stairs, ready to take notes on the gruesome scene. Another story to be written.

As Leonard turned his neck to watch the reporter go, the pain swooped in hard. He leaned forward and felt maybe that he was going to vomit. He sucked in a deep breath and convinced himself that he was going to be okay. Then he passed out.

CHAPTER FORTY-SEVEN

ONE UNDER

Leonard was sitting on the sidewalk of Albany Street while a paramedic stitched up the back of his head. He was groggy and tired, but he was still alive. Mulino stood as close as the tech would allow. "You know it wouldn't have killed you to tell someone what you had found out, rather than go vigilante on us."

Leonard would have looked up, but the latex hand pressed his head forward. He spoke into the ground. "I wasn't sure who I could trust."

"Sure. I guess I know how that feels."

Eliot Holm-Anderson stood behind Mulino, looking down at Leonard. "That's quite a blow you took."

"You oughta see the other guy." Sparks was already bagged and being packed away for his trip to the morgue.

Eliot was close as well now. Leonard couldn't see any of them, just a half-dozen very interesting pebbles that had spilled out into the sidewalk from somewhere. Eliot was congratulating him, but it sounded maybe as though really he was congratulating himself. "You did well, young man. And the building was secured. It looks as though we pulled it off."

"Veronica got away, didn't she?"

Eliot's tone darkened. Trying to convince himself of something now. Then again, he was a man who had made a fortune convincing people of things. "She won't go far. If she made as big a short on the Bank of Bremen as she said she would, she's almost certainly going to be broke in a day or so. Hiding out from the international authorities is an expensive pastime."

The paramedic finished up and tapped Leonard on the back of his head. He looked up. Eliot in his suit, in the heat and dust, as square-jawed and pristine as ever.

"And Ells?"

It was Mulino's turn to answer. "That's going to be fun. If you've never seen them do a perp walk straight from City Hall to the Tombs, you ought to head over. Bring popcorn."

Leonard shook his head to clear it. His hair was wet; the wound itched. He checked Eliot again; his suit was starting to dampen. It wasn't just the blood. It had started to rain. A light summer shower had begun sometime after he'd hit the ground, and his head had hurt and his eyes had dimmed so much that he couldn't even tell. Small puddles were forming in the dirt. The water was cool, refreshing, washing away the film of a hot city summer. Mulino helped him to his feet.

"You have a long couple of weeks coming up, Len."

"I would have let you know sooner. I wasn't sure you would believe me. There were people trying to kill me. There were cops trying to kill me."

Mulino smiled. "My general policy when the shitstorm hits is just to arrest everyone and let the district attorney sort it out. You want to explain away anything wrong you might have done, you'll have plenty of time. For now I think you are going to take a trip with me."

Eliot stepped in. "You don't have to arrest him. He prevented this. It could have been awful."

"That kind of decision is above my pay grade. We've got a warrant for him. We're going to hand him over. Tag along, you can serve as a character witness for him, back his story up."

Leonard nodded and started toward Mulino's unmarked car. The rain was heavy now, puddling up around his feet, loosening the dirt into mud. They all sank slowly into it. Leonard turned to Mulino.

"Detective."

"Yeah?"

Water was streaming past Mulino's ruddy cheeks. His clothes had darkened and he looked slower, heavier, than he had before.

"Let's get this over with."

Leonard slid into the sedan and Mulino closed the door. He let Leonard ride uncuffed. Leonard snapped the seat belt shut and listened to the pebbling of the rain, waiting for Mulino to get in the car and bring him back to the world.

EPILOGUE
NEW CONSTRUCTION

The coffee was the best part. Locked up, Leonard had missed friendship, he had missed work, he had missed all the little freedoms of his life. But he had missed coffee more than anything. During the six-month program at Moriah Shock, the closest thing to coffee that Leonard had drunk was pale gray and may have been squeezed from the mops. Now, on a bright spring day, he had a rich dark cup from the fancy place by the subway station. The whole neighborhood had changed, it seemed, overnight. Four blocks from Ebbets Field there were artisanal cocktail bars, a store selling clothing for very thin women, and the coffee place. Not even a Starbucks. Local. Fresh. New. The wave of development had swept through Leonard's neighborhood during the winter he had spent in prison.

The program at Moriah Shock had saved him two and a half years. Leonard's lawyer knew his way around the system, and everyone understood that Leonard had been a victim as much as anything. But prosecutors aren't willing to just congratulate you and set you free when there are two dead cops in your wake. It sends the wrong message to everyone else. The lawyer had talked the charges down to trespassing, reckless endangerment, leaving the scene of an accident for what happened with Officer Del Rio. That was the big one. Calling it an accident. The terms of the plea could have capped out at thirty-five months. But if you're under thirty-six months and you didn't actually hurt anyone personally, you can swap your term for the six-month program at Moriah Shock—basically a military boot camp on the site of an old mine in Essex County.

It had all been worked out in advance, really. The lawyer had told him about it. You can't sit down at the mess until there are eight men in order, you have to put your shoes in the same place every night, and you spend most days resurfacing country roads. But it is outdoors mainly and there are no fights. Almost everyone else was in for drugs. A couple of guys who had pled to mail fraud to make sure everyone still knew it was a prison and wasn't rehab. And Leonard. It had been hard work, but it had been a short stint. Plus, there are worse habits to learn than tucking your sheets in hospital corners.

The feds had taken in Ells, and he was suffering through an interminable investigation by his former colleagues. Leonard had been in and out of the Shock program and the federal prosecutors had yet to tell Ells what precisely he was going to be charged with. And despite Eliot's prediction, they never had found Veronica.

So on his first day out, he had picked up the coffee and taken it to the park. Lakeside. They had built a whole complex, ice skating in winter, sprinklers for the kids in summer. Adults milled outside with their coffee and croissants and other delectables that hadn't been on offer in this neighborhood a year ago. On his walk over, Leonard had passed four buildings on their way up. Condos. Fifteen, eighteen, twenty-two stories.

Just past the basin, in the park proper, Leonard saw a heavy man standing by a trash can in a Parks Department uniform. The trash can rattled and clattered; delicate muffin wrappers and other upscale detritus were strewn around the sides. The man was watching something captive inside. Construction stirs up animals underground. Each time a wobbly

SRO was torn down to make a new condo, everyone living there had to go find a new place to squat, the people and the vermin alike.

Standing at the edge of the basin, nursing the coffee, Leonard watched the children swarm through some game of tag, cops and robbers, prisoner. After digging ditches and running the obstacle course for six months, Leonard couldn't settle properly in his suit. It was baggy around the waist and tight in the shoulders.

The man from the Parks Department had found a rake; he held the rake up like a whaler's harpoon and thrust it down. The sharp shock got the attention of the rest of the parents, who momentarily glanced away from the lights of their lives to see what he was up to. The clattering returned to the can. He'd missed it. The parents turned back to Daisy and Clyde and Lillian, unaware maybe of what the man was hunting, or certain that he would take care of it before it sprang out into the world.

Leonard smiled. The rat was just the first wave. The real New York was on its way back. The garbage strike had just been a preview. Sure, the organized sabotage had played its part, but truth be told, nothing could keep the real city from blossoming out from under the prison that had been built for it. The people of brownstone Brooklyn would have to get used to graffiti and petty crimes and the occasional junkie in a doorway. There had been a stabbing in one of the bars on Flatbush just a week before, and people were beginning to clutch their bags a little tighter on their way to the subway.

Leonard recognized a boy in the crowd. Around five, bright eyes and tousled hair. He didn't know many kids. But the face, sharper than most, stuck out. A jaw already. A slightly harder look. A little bit less joy in the eyes than the other boys. Running behind the pack as they tried to tackle some imagined monster.

The man from the Parks Department quickly flipped the can over and started banging on the edge. Inside, the sound of plastic thrashing together, tangling upon itself, tearing and rippling as the prisoner scoured for a way out.

Leonard suddenly remembered where he had seen the boy. At bring-your-child-to-work day at DIMAC. It was Christine Davenport's son. The one whose room he had been through looking for evidence. The one who had fled town at his mother's advice. Just before she was killed. It explained the sad look behind the bright eyes. Leonard scoured the parents across the basin's edge. A lithe, frumpy man, holding his own cup of expensive coffee, was staring hard at the boy. Protecting with his gaze, worried that he would lose anything more, after having lost so much already. Davenport's husband. A professor of something. They had moved out from Manhattan to Brooklyn. A fresh start probably. A new place to live. A little peace and quiet.

Leonard was staring at the father when the man from the Parks Department lifted the trash can, holding a broom and a dustpan as though he would scoop the vermin up. Instead, the thing sprang over his arm and scurried lithely atop the concrete basin and among the children, determined to get back somewhere dark and wet and comfortable. The children parted, screeching, looking for mommy or daddy or the nanny. Only the Davenport boy didn't leave. The rat too, stopped, just a foot in front of him. The boy stared down silent as the little beast looked up at him, sniffing. The boy lowered his eyes and swatted at the rodent, proving that he wasn't intimidated and would not be afraid. The animal cowered and turned, fleeing toward a drain or corner or some safe haven from these broad-shouldered beasts.

Leonard looked up from the standoff at the father. He had been watching too. His eyes were wet now, but it was impossible to tell if he was crying with the pain of loss or with pride for his boy. Sensing he was being watched, the man snapped up and met Leonard's stare. He nodded. The two men watched each other as the scene returned to its ritualized chaos. They both knew that this was only the beginning.

ACKNOWLEDGMENTS

I decided to write this book over the course of two lunches at the Mexican restaurant where the Vinyl Diner used to be on Ninth Avenue: the first with Claire Lundberg and the other with Loren Noveck. Claire and Loren both encouraged me to take the leap from writing plays to writing a book, even though I would bet that at some point over the past four years, listening to me pull my hair out and ask if they would look at just one more draft, each of them wished she hadn't. They gave sharp notes and strategic counsel and never once complained. I cannot thank them enough.

So many friends read drafts of this book and helped make it better. I am deeply in debt to Tennessee Jones, Jeremiah Grünblatt, Robin Hessman, Jonah Goger, Wade Carper, Alexander Boldizar, Maura Teitelbaum, Amy Wagner, and Andrea Stolowitz, all of whom improved this manuscript immensely. Some of the themes in this book were hashed out more than a decade ago in late-night sessions with Joel Arberman, and I'm in debt to his creative brand of paranoia.

I have also benefited from strategic advice and insight from authors who have been down this path before. Jane Cleland, Joan Sullivan, Jenny McPhee, and Justin Peacock all helped guide me through a new and unfamiliar world. I am additionally grateful to Christian Parker, Nancy Dalin, and Wendy Blum for their helpful comments and support along the way.

None of this would have happened without the efforts of Kim Witherspoon and Monika Woods at InkWell Management, who not only helped guide the book through three more drafts after I thought I was done, but who gave their all for an untested novelist. I am especially grateful to Alison Dasho at Thomas & Mercer for her faith in the book, to Kjersti Egerdahl for shepherding as it continued to grow and change, and to Alan Turkus for his guidance and leadership. Thomas & Mercer has built an extraordinary team: I benefited enormously from Charlotte Herscher's terrific insights, Jennifer Blanksteen's attentive eye, and the precision brought by Nicole Pomeroy, Evan Edmisten, and Daniel Born. Mark Ecob designed a cover that beautifully evokes the book. I'm greatly indebted to Jacque Ben-Zekry, Dennelle Catlett, and Sarah Burningham for their work promoting the book, and to Sarah Shaw and Tiffany Pokorny for their support along the way.

Special gratitude goes to those I worked with at New York's Civilian Complaint Review Board: my experience working with Franklin Stone, Florence Finkle, Shari Hyman, Eric Dorsch, and many others formed the backbone of this book. My parents, Susan and Claude Case, encouraged my creative work but more importantly taught me to look carefully and critically at the world. Most importantly, I want to thank my wife, Claudia Case, for leaping forth with me on this and so many other adventures. Without her love, support, and friendship, I would be nothing.